"I thought you were asleep..."

Ella stood there, hands raised as though she didn't know what to do with them.

Touch him?

God help him, Brett had been reliving the touch of her fingers on his skin since they'd arrived at the cabin last night.

Who was he kidding? He'd never stopped having fantasies about the woman.

He'd known he couldn't be married to her. Had no doubts about that one. Even now his resolve didn't waver.

But making love had never even come close to bringing out violence in him.

"I'll just get us going again and head to shore," she said. She turned and the light of the moon gave him a bounteous gift. A clear view of two things. Ella's lips. And her nipples where her sweater had dropped open.

She was chewing on her lower lip. All the sign he really needed. But the hard points of her nipples were added fuel for his raging fire.

Both were indications that Ella was as hungry for him as he was for her...

Dear Reader,

Welcome back to The Lemonade Stand. *The Good Father* is a very special book in the Where Secrets are Safe series. It's the story of a man who created his own safety net without knowing it.

If you've read any of the other books, you've heard about the mysterious founder of The Lemonade Stand, a unique women's shelter set on the coast of California. We hear of him, of his generosity and his decisions. We just never meet him. We have no idea who he is. Nor do any of the people who work at or are associated with the stand.

Brett Ackerman is a man with secrets. A man with an atrocious past who limits his future rather than risk any more atrocities in his life. He is also that founder. He created something he'd wished had existed when he was growing up a victim of domestic violence. Stepping outside the story, I created The Lemonade Stand because I wished something like it had existed when I was a young newlywed unable to tell anyone what was going on behind closed doors.

I'm not Brett. But he and I have something in common. We both hid from our pasts, tucking things away, thinking we'd dealt with them, only to find that they'd been there all along. I hope you'll give Brett a chance. Follow on his journey as he struggles to help a friend and finds himself in the process. I promise you warmth and happiness at the end.

All the best,

Tara

PS As always, I love to hear from my readers! You can reach me at staff@tarataylorquinn.com.

TARA
TAYLOR
QUINN

The Good Father

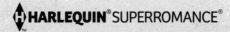

HARLEQUIN®SUPERROMANCE®

Recycling programs
for this product may
not exist in your area.

ISBN-13: 978-0-373-60915-4

The Good Father

Copyright © 2015 by Tara Taylor Quinn

Printed in U.S.A.

The author of more than seventy novels, **Tara Taylor Quinn** is a *USA TODAY* bestselling author with over seven million copies sold. She is known for delivering emotional and psychologically astute novels of suspense and romance. Tara is the past president of Romance Writers of America and served eight years on that board of directors. She has appeared on national and local TV across the country, including CBS *Sunday Morning*, and is a frequent guest speaker. In her spare time Tara likes to travel and enjoys crafting and in-line skating. She is a supporter of the National Domestic Violence Hotline. If you or someone you know might be a victim of domestic violence in the United States, please contact 1-800-799-7233.

Books by Tara Taylor Quinn

HARLEQUIN SUPERROMANCE

Where Secrets are Safe

Wife by Design
Once a Family
Husband by Choice
Child by Chance
Mother by Fate

Shelter Valley Stories

Sophie's Secret
Full Contact
It's Never Too Late
Second Time's the Charm
The Moment of Truth

It Happened in Comfort Cove

A Son's Tale
A Daughter's Story
The Truth About Comfort Cove

MIRA BOOKS

Where the Road Ends
Street Smart
Hidden
In Plain Sight
Behind Closed Doors
At Close Range
The Second Lie
The Third Secret
The Fourth Victim

The Friendship Pact

Visit the author profile page
at Harlequin.com for more titles.

For all those who have been hurt and want
to believe in love and happiness anyway.
It's out there!

CHAPTER ONE

H<small>E STOOD NAKED</small> and felt the water splash over him. Eyes closed, arms raised with his hands splayed above him on the porcelain tile, Brett Ackerman dropped his chin to his chest. Water pressure that was fine for cleansing wasn't strong enough to wash away the tension knotting the muscles along the back of his neck.

He stood there, anyway. Planned to let the hot water run out and then to remain in the cold for as long as he could take it. His pain was his own fault. He'd been out too late after several grueling days of work, flying back and forth across the country twice.

He'd been celebrating. Ten years since he'd sold the dot-com he'd started his junior year in college. A decade of his life had passed, and here he was. Standing alone in the walk-in shower in his elegant, historical, two-story walk-up across a quiet street from a flowered lot that led to the ocean beyond.

He owned the house. The lovely two acres across the street. And another house down the street, too, that was split up into bed-and-breakfast-type rooms that were all rented on an extended-stay basis.

He owned them both, and lived in this one, alone.

Just as he'd walked home alone from the quaint neighborhood pub on the corner in the wee hours of that Tuesday morning in September. Where he'd celebrated by nursing two cocktails over a period of several hours and playing video trivia games with anonymous opponents.

His life was on track. Exactly as he'd planned.

And that fact was worth celebrating.

His cell phone peeled, an urgent sound partially muted by the shower. It was only seven. He wasn't due at the Americans Against Prejudice board meeting in LA until nine. His unscheduled tour of the home office facilities would follow immediately after. While the other board members were at lunch.

His phone continued to ring. Brett continued to stand under the shower—remaining strong against the temptation to pick up—stubbornly determined to relax.

As a nonprofit regulator—a self-made position that in ten years had grown into something approximating a national Better Business Seal of Approval designed to assure nonprofit donors that their monies were not being misappropriated—he was currently sitting on more than fifty boards around the country.

The phone fell blessedly silent, and Brett lifted

his face to the soothing heat sluicing over him. Enjoying the moment.

Then his phone started to ring again. *Shit.* He'd made it through the first summons, but there was no way he could ignore a second, right on the heels of the first. At seven in the morning.

So much for a little naked relaxation.

ELLA WALES ACKERMAN, RN, the brand-new charge nurse in the Neonatal Intensive Care Unit at Santa Raquel Children's Hospital—a newly completed facility just outside Santa Raquel—was in the unit's nursing office early on that Tuesday morning, going over charts and checking her email before her shift began. The thousand-bed facility had only been open a few weeks, and already they had thirty patients in their fifty-bed unit.

Thirty babies fighting for their lives.

She read chart notes from the night before. Saw that the little "ostomy" guy had coded again, but was stabilized. His liver was shutting down due to the nutrition they were forced to give him intravenously until they could do the surgery that would put his stomach back together. If they couldn't keep him stable, get him well enough to tolerate the surgery…

He was stable. They'd do all they could for him.

"Ella?" She glanced up as Brianna Wood, one of her nurses, a twenty-eight-year-old transfer from San Francisco, stopped in the office doorway. "I know you aren't on the floor yet, but I just wanted to let you know, we got word an hour ago that a new patient's coming up from Burbank sometime this morning. A two-pound, six-week-old girl. I don't know the particulars yet, just that she's in a warming bed and breathing on her own."

"Let's put her in D-4," Ella said. The pod was their least crowded and also one that, so far, had no patients with ventilators. They talked about the attending physician and waiting for orders, and then Ella asked, "So, did you talk to him?"

Brianna had been planning to ask her boyfriend to move in with her. Which meant leaving his job as a nuclear medicine technician in San Francisco to relocate to Santa Raquel. The long-distance relationship wasn't working out well.

"Yeah."

"And?"

"He said he'd see..."

The woman wasn't crying, but Ella could almost feel the effort it took Brianna to keep her emotions in check.

"You thinking about going home, then?" She'd hate to lose her. Not only were they still staffing, Brianna was a damn good nurse, too. But if she would be happier...

"Absolutely not. I love this job. And if he's not sure now, my moving back isn't going to make him any more so."

There was a lot Ella could say about the importance of having a life beyond the man you loved, but she was the woman's boss. And admittedly jaded where men were concerned. "He could change his mind."

Brianna shrugged. "Maybe." She looked hopeful for a moment. "Do you think I should? Go back?"

"I can't answer that."

"Would you?"

She shouldn't answer that, either. "No."

Brianna's nod gave her pause. "But...if you want to go home, I'll give you a glowing reference," Ella added with a small smile. She'd never been a boss before. Was used to being just one of the nurses—someone who could offer personal advice and opinions without undue professional consequence.

"You don't wear a ring..."

The question on Brianna's pretty face called out to Ella. She was new in town, too. And other than her sister-in-law, Chloe, who was living with her temporarily, had no one to confide in. Or even catch a movie with.

"I'm not married."

"Have you ever been?"

Closing the charting program on her computer, Ella stood up. "Yes, I have been. Now, let's go get D-4 ready before shift change. If you want to grab a cup of coffee after you get off, I'll see what I can arrange…"

So she shouldn't fraternize. A cup of coffee with a valuable employee who was hurting was just good business.

As it turned out, Ella didn't make it to D-4 or coffee with Brianna. Before she'd even clocked in, the three-month-old in C-2 coded, and it took a couple hours to get him stabilized. By the time Ella finally made it to the break room for a cup of coffee, Brianna was long gone. And she sat by herself, sipping her dark roast, and thinking about things that weren't productive.

Like Brett. And the baby they'd spent three years and ungodly amounts of money trying to conceive. The baby he'd never wanted. The baby who'd been born too soon to save, leaving his mama with little hope of ever having another child of her own. And here she was, four years later, saving other people's preemies.

When she'd graduated from college, Ella hadn't planned to work with seriously ill babies. She'd focused on pediatric nursing. And a job on a PIC unit at a large hospital in LA had been available. Whenever babies had been in for procedures, she'd been the one doctors had requested to assist them. They said she was good with the babies. That she seemed to have a natural ability to calm sick infants.

Funny, a woman who wasn't capable of conceiving naturally or of carrying a baby to term, having that ability.

No, she wasn't going down that depressing road again. Her twenties were casualties buried on the shoulders of that road. And though her journey had been painful, she'd finally turned the corner.

She was thirty-one now and taking charge of her life. This new job as charge nurse seemed almost symbolic.

She'd moved from LA to Santa Raquel. A move that would force her to face her past, to confront her present and to build a future.

Standing, Ella checked the pockets of her scrubs to make certain that she had her pager, her pen, and the ID card she had to swipe to get on and off the unit, and turned toward the door of the deserted break room. Time to get back to work.

She had her plan, and her life was on track.

Calm settled over her.

Maybe it was the calm before the storm. Or maybe she'd finally put herself on the path to real peace. Either way, there was no going back.

BRETT WAS PULLING into the parking garage in LA, half an hour early for the board meeting, when his phone rang again. As it had been doing all morning. As it normally did. Glancing at the screen, he recognized the number immediately.

And issued a silent curse that his hand was shaking as he pushed the call button to answer.

"It's good to hear from you. Is everything all right?" He spoke quickly, aware that his mother was not going to give him a chance to speak again.

"There's a new member on the High Risk team. A nurse. Ella Ackerman. I thought you should know before you see the email."

Click.

The sound in his ear wasn't a surprise. Although, even after more than fourteen years of this bizarre no-speaking, no-physical-contact relationship he and his mother had, the abrupt hang-up still bothered him.

So did the news he'd just received.

Ella was in town? On the High Risk team? A team comprising professionals—medical personnel, lawyers, social workers, law enforcement—whose jobs brought them in contact with potential domestic-violence victims. The team had been designed to bridge the communication gap between various professional bodies to help prevent victims from falling through the cracks. The idea for the team had come from The Lemonade Stand, a women's shelter in Santa Raquel. He'd been instrumental in getting the team set up. And now Ella was on it?

Could the day get any worse?

ELLA HAD A spare minute in between an assessment of a five-day-old baby who was being readmitted due to failure to thrive and a meeting with the HIPAA committee—a committee comprised of hospital staff to develop and implement programs that would help educate and remind staff of the Health Insurance Portability and Accountability Act guidelines—and slipped into a vacant office just outside the NICU, pulling her cell phone out of her pocket.

"Hey, how's he doing?" she asked as soon as her sister-in-law, Chloe Wales, picked up.

"Fine. His fever's down, and he's watching *Cars*." Cody, Chloe's two-year-old son, had had a reaction to an inoculation and given them a scare the night before. "He's asking for his daddy, though." Chloe's tone changed. Took on a note of doubt that Ella recognized only too well.

"He's two, Chloe. He'll adjust." One way or the other.

"I just…I miss him, too. You know?"

"I do know. And I also know that my brother needs help. And the only way we can help him is to make him want to help himself. To give him a chance to see that he needs to help himself."

"I know."

She and Chloe had been through all of this a handful of times over the past four years. Jeff would act out. Ella and Chloe would talk about it later. Chloe would be strong and determined that if Jeff acted out again she'd leave or call for help.

Jeff would be the perfect husband and father for a week or a month. He'd be remorseful and open and giving. Dedicated to his family. And then he'd slowly focus more and more on the stocks that were his livelihood. He'd become consumed by them. When they were up, he was up. And when they were down, he was down. If they went down too far, so did he.

That's when Chloe ended up bruised. In the beginning, the bruises had all been on the inside. Her emotions and heart had been damaged as he'd blasted her verbally. Then it had been finger marks from a strongly squeezed arm. Then a bruised shoulder from a push into a door.

All things Jeff hadn't meant. Things he'd been deeply contrite for. Sincerely, deeply contrite.

This latest time, seven months after his last bout of uncontrollable anger, he'd grabbed his son by his forearms and slammed him into a chair. While Cody had screamed in terror, he hadn't been physically harmed. Not yet.

"I just…I miss him. And he misses me, too. He's so sorry and…"

"You answered his call." Jeff had been phoning Chloe for more than a week. Ever since Ella had made the four-hour drive to Palm Desert to pick up her sister-in-law and her nephew and bring them back to stay with her in her apartment.

The arrangement was temporary. Just until Jeff got help.

"He's my husband," Chloe said, an edge to her voice. Which faded as she said, "I know I shouldn't have, El, but bills are due, and I'm the one who pays them. I did it online, but I just wanted to let him know. When I picked up, he was choked up and…"

"You didn't tell him where you're staying, did you?"

"No. But I wanted to."

"Next time you want to, you hang up and call me immediately."

"But you're working. Those babies' lives are in the balance and—"

"Yours and Cody's are, too, Chloe. Make no mistake about that." Since she'd first heard about her brother's occasional lashing-outs, she'd been reading up on domestic abuse. Researching how best to help both the abuser and the victim. And then she'd ended up with a job offer in Santa Raquel, exactly where she knew she needed to be to get him help.

"My cell will roll over to my pager if I don't answer it," she said now. "As soon as I see it's you, I'll get back to you as quickly as I can."

"Okay."

"You have to stay strong, Chloe. Remember the sound of Cody's terror. Not his laughter. Remember the ugly words, not the great memories. Just until we can get this all sorted out."

Jeff would come through. Ella had faith in him.

He had to. Because from what she'd read, if he didn't get the help he needed, Chloe and Cody were clearly headed for real danger.

"I know. I can't go back until he gets help or it will just happen again. I can't do that to Cody. But Jeff needs me, too, and it's so hard. I hate that he's there alone…"

"Being alone, losing you and Cody, is the only thing that's going to open his eyes to where he's headed."

"I know."

"So, how about we go to the beach as soon as I get off work today? We can grab some dinner at one of the places on the water."

"Uncle Bob's?" They'd been there over the weekend, and Chloe had really enjoyed herself. "Assuming Cody doesn't relapse."

"He should be fine. A reaction to an immunization is generally over as soon as the symptoms disappear."

Chloe didn't need to create worries where there weren't any. She had enough real demons to fight.

"You called Jeff because Cody was sick, didn't you?" Ella asked quietly now. She'd suspected as much.

"Yeah."

"If I hadn't asked, were you going to tell me?"

"Yes."

"We've got to have complete honesty between us, Chloe, or this isn't going to work."

In the six years since Jeff and Chloe had married, the other woman had quickly become the sister Ella had never had.

"I know. I was already stressing about it, which is why I hadn't called you, and I know that honesty between us is crucial to the support system that's going to see me through this. I'm sorry, El. It won't happen again."

"It might. If this was as easy as making decisions and sticking to them, domestic violence would be much easier to fight. But we'll get through all of this. I promise you. You aren't alone, and you aren't ever going to be alone."

Ella knew how being *alone* felt. After she'd lost the baby and her marriage had fallen apart, she'd been utterly and completely on her own in a world of pain. She'd do whatever it took to make sure Chloe didn't ever have to experience that particular hell.

"Have you called Brett yet?" Her sister-in-law's voice took on a stronger note.

"No."

"I wish you wouldn't do this. You've suffered enough. It's only been in the last couple years that you've seemed to come alive again."

"And that's why I know I can see him," Ella said, glancing at her watch. She had an assessment in ten minutes. "Besides, he's our best hope where Jeff is concerned. And I do have to do this,

Chloe. You and Jeff and Cody—you're my family. I'd do anything for you."

"You know I'm here for you, too, right?" Chloe asked. "More than just helping you find a house, and cooking and doing the laundry."

Chloe was pretty much a gourmet cook and selling her current contributions far short, but, having been vulnerable and alone herself, Ella understood that Chloe desperately needed reassurance of her deeper value.

"Are you kidding? When I finally found out I was pregnant, and Brett started to change… and then losing the baby after all those years of hoping…you're the one who kept me going. You kept telling me that someday I'd wake up and face the day with anticipation again, and you were right. I love my life. And you're going to love yours again, too. I promise."

"I love you, sis."

"I love you, too. Now go hug that boy for both of us and think about what we're going to order for dinner."

They shared meals, she and Chloe, when they went out to eat. Neither one of them ever finished a whole meal. And sharing was a money-saving venture that allowed them to go out more.

It was all in the plan.

And life was finally, firmly, on course.

CHAPTER TWO

IT WASN'T BRETT'S way to put things off. The more unpleasant something was, the sooner he tended to it. A lesson learned from his past. One that defined his present and safeguarded his future.

Someone from Americans Against Prejudice—and Brett was fairly certain he knew who—was misusing a line item in the annual budget. Filtering monies meant for the general operations and sinking them, instead, into a legitimate investment in beachfront property. Brett was fairly certain the filterer had made the investment with the intention of skimming profits off the top for himself.

And that wasn't the worst of it. The beachfront investment was only what had triggered his suspicions. Now he had one hell of a mess on his hands. He was fairly certain that the entire Americans Against Prejudice board, working together, had hired him as a cover for their illegal lining of their own bank accounts with charity funds.

Which meant they were either overly confident or just plain stupid. Didn't they know that he'd started one of the first—and still one of the most reputable—public-record-finding dot-coms in existence? He was an investigator. A person who could find anything there was to be found.

And so, while the ladies and gentleman that he'd been sitting on a board with for three months were enjoying lunch at a nearby French restaurant, Brett, the sole nonvoting board member, was alone in the executive offices rifling through files. Thank God they were mostly computerized, and he could scan them quickly.

Fortunately he found the information he needed within minutes. Not so fortunate was the fact that his suspicions had just been confirmed.

Before the members of the board would have had time to order their gourmet sandwiches and have them delivered to their table, paid for by nonprofit monies, Brett had reported every one of them to the local police.

ELLA'S PLANS TO be home early were interrupted by her cell phone ringing just as she was leaving work that afternoon. Lila McDaniels, managing director of The Lemonade Stand, was on the other end.

"I'd like to meet with you," Lila said after introducing herself. "I've just read the email naming you as the most recent addition to Santa Raquel's Domestic Violence High Risk team. And while those appointments are made by a committee, the idea for this program originated from our facility, and I make it a point to get to know everyone on the team."

Ella had heard about the team in a recent hospital staff meeting and, thinking the opening was a gift from angels, had applied immediately. She'd heard back within the week that she'd received the appointment. Committee work was a required and ongoing part of most professional hospital positions. At least if one had an eye on career advancement.

Ella's motive for seeking this particular committee position was much more personal, however. And if securing the position meant taking a detour on the way home, then she'd do so. She'd agreed to a four o'clock meeting in the director's office. And now, following the instructions Ms. McDaniels had given her, she was looking for the small public parking lot in front of the facility. The question was, did she pretend she'd never heard of The Lemonade Stand before? Or did she tell the woman that she knew the man who'd founded the place?

Had known him intimately?

And had spent years recovering from the pain he'd caused her?

BRETT WAS BACK in Santa Raquel in time to have an early dinner. He ate his peanut-butter-and-bacon sandwich pacing in front of the sliding glass door that led from his kitchen eating area to the deck and the garden and acre of woods beyond. Still in the navy blue suit he'd worn to attend the morning board meeting, he'd loosened the knot of the red tie a bit. His one concession to relaxation. His wing tips were shined. His watch in place.

Brett's life was a mission—and all pieces were accounted for.

Except one.

That phone call he'd had that morning.

His ex-wife was in town. She had to be if she was on the High Risk team.

Facts listed themselves off in his mind as he paced and chewed in rhythm. Peanut butter and bacon. One of the few good things in his life that came from having known his father.

The old man would take credit for Brett's choice of repast. And probably try to draw some major conclusion from the fact that the unhealthy and unrefined meal was still his favorite.

Turning to pace back in the direction he'd come, Brett admonished his father's memory for being in his head at all. Let alone right now.

Ella was in town. No mystery as to why his father was suddenly coming to mind.

She was in town, and she hadn't contacted him.

Not that she had any reason to. They had no connection—nothing in their lives that would necessitate them to be in the same area at the same time. He'd made certain of that. Schmuck that he was.

Even his own mother, while she'd agreed to act as his business assistant, wouldn't be in the same room with him. Or even have a real conversation with him.

She was in his home, in his life, only when he wasn't there.

But Ella seemed to be with him wherever he went. Try as he might, he couldn't shake her.

Which made getting rid of her presence in his physical space, his town, anywhere he might run into her, paramount.

WITH HER PAST and her present, her current career, Ella didn't get ruffled by much these days. Her dream of sharing a passionate, all-in relationship with another person was packed firmly away with the rest of her childhood memorabilia.

And the second she met Lila McDaniels, she felt a bit like a child again. Believing that everything would be okay. Because of the kind look in Lila's gaze as she introduced herself?

The unusual reaction was a warning to her. She wasn't as unaffected by the world around her as she wanted to be. Note taken. To be dealt with as soon as she was alone.

"We can take a tour of the grounds later," the older woman said, whisking Ella through an entrance that reminded her of the heavy, pass-key-admittance-only door that led into the NICU. "For now I thought we'd have some tea."

No question about whether or not Ella liked tea. But she did, and tea sounded good. Still in her pale peach scrubs with little bears all over them, and wearing the black rubber-soled shoes that tended to squeak a bit when she walked, Ella followed the older woman through a large, nicely appointed office into a smaller living space furnished with an elegant, claw-footed chintz couch, matching claw-footed side tables and two rose silk wing-back armchairs. The room was delightful. And took her breath away.

"Did you do your own decorating?" she asked, feeling instantly as though she could spend the next ten days in that room, reading books and feeling…safe.

The thought startled her. She didn't feel unsafe. She'd lived alone for years and was perfectly secure.

"Yes, I did. A little at a time." Lila's gray pants and white blouse, her short, mostly gray nondescript hair, looked out of place in the colorful room. "Here at The Lemonade Stand, we believe that the strongest healing comes from within. We encourage our residents to look inside themselves for their inner beauty, their inner strengths. Their inner worth. We also believe that if one is told she's bad or at fault enough times, or if one is forced to live with violence and ugliness, the beauty within becomes locked away. So we try to surround ourselves and our residents with outer beauty, with elegant and peaceful surroundings, and with kindness, in the hopes that we can help them begin to counteract the violence they've been exposed to and begin to access their inner bounty."

Ella had a feeling she was hearing an oft-given speech. "As soon as I heard that I'd won the committee appointment at the hospital, I read up on all of the other team members," she said, still standing, facing the older woman. "I've got The Lemonade Stand's pamphlet memorized," she continued, wanting Lila to make no mistake about her sincerity or value to the team. "I want to be fully prepared and able to help if I find myself with a victim in need."

Not just for Chloe and Jeff. But for the mothers of any of her babies. Or any of the other children who came into the hospital with "at risk" symptoms.

Lila's gaze changed. Only for a second. The calm, the kindness, covered the subtle glimpse of whatever had been there, but she was fully focused on Ella as she asked, "Have you ever been a victim?"

"Not in the way you mean."

Taking her hand, Lila led Ella to one of the two armchairs and took the other, all the while holding Ella's gaze. "In what way do I mean?" she asked.

"I've never been abused."

"So, in what way have you been a victim?"

Whoa. Ella sat back. Feeling as though she'd been slam-dunked. And as though she wanted to cry on this woman's shoulder.

"I haven't been," she assured Lila McDaniels, racking her brain for a way to explain what she'd meant. "My folks were great parents. I was disciplined by having my reading time taken away. Or by being sent to bed without dessert. They never raised a hand to me. Nor has my father ever been even remotely violent with my mother. They were high school sweethearts and are still happily married."

"There must have been arguments. No two individuals live in complete harmony forever."

"Of course they fought! They still do. I've certainly heard raised voices. But nothing that ever crossed the line into emotional battery. Or personal attacks, either, that I can think of."

Lila's gaze was still intent. "And what about since then?"

"I'm...I've never been in an abusive relationship." Pressure built up beneath Lila's inquisitive stare—as though the woman was certain, in spite of what Ella was telling her, that Ella was a victim.

Ella's gaze didn't waver. Even for a second. She of all people knew that Brett was not an abusive man. Knew, too, that there were other ways to break a heart.

Studying Ella for another few seconds, Lila finally said, "We just need to know, up front, because if you've been a victim, your perspective might be different," she said by way of explanation.

"You're saying that if I was a victim, I wouldn't be welcome on the team?"

"Of course not." Lila's frown, her quick gasp, caught at Ella, putting her strangely at ease. "Oh, my word, of course not. I just…I like to know. So I can help if need be… I'll go get that tea."

Lila was clasping her hands together as she left the room. Ella watched her go, curious about the woman, and wishing that the managing director was a member of the High Risk team so she'd have an opportunity to get to know her better. She wasn't, though. The Lemonade Stand's representative was a woman Ella had yet to meet—Sara Havens, a licensed professional clinical counselor.

And in retrospect, Lila's not being on the team was just as well. At the moment, Ella didn't have time to make a new friend outside of work. She had her hands full with settling into a new town, a new job, finding a house and putting her family back together.

She just had to make a good enough impression to secure the High Risk team position she'd already landed.

Which was just par for her life—having to fight for what she thought she already had. Like Chloe, fighting to keep them sisters when she'd thought they were family for life. And Brett…no…she'd stop that train of thought right there.

Lila called from the kitchen, asking Ella if she wanted milk in her tea. Ella declined.

She wasn't going to think about Brett.

Not yet.

Not until she had to.

And only then until she could get what she needed from him.

CHAPTER THREE

BRETT HAD TO be in Chicago for an eleven o'clock meeting Wednesday morning. He'd be spending the few hours he had in his first-class airline seat studying the agenda for Music Muscles, a non-profit music-therapy organization that was one of his newest clients. One that, so far, gave him no cause for concern. From there he'd head to Detroit, where he was spending the night before an early Thursday-morning meeting, and then it was off to Washington, DC, that afternoon.

Leaving his black BMW in secured parking, he pulled the carry-on out of the trunk, slung his leather garment bag over one shoulder, his matching briefcase satchel over the other and strode straight to the preferred security line in the terminal at LAX.

After he'd checked in, with limited time before they'd be calling him to preboard, Brett reached beneath his suit coat to the holster secured to his leather belt and pulled out his cell phone.

Her number had been on the High Risk team email he'd received the morning before. He'd typed it into contacts only so that her name would come up if she phoned, and he could avoid answering.

He found the name. Hit call. And then waited. Airline staff had opened the Jetway door. He only had a minute or two.

One ring. Two. And then three. He glanced at his watch. It was before seven in the morning. Her shift at the hospital didn't start until eight, and her apartment was a twenty-minute drive away. He was, after all, the king of online investigating. He'd sold the dot-com. Not his abilities.

He still sat on the board of the company he founded—with his percentage of the take being donated to The Lemonade Stand every month.

On the sixth ring a flight employee announced that it was time for him to board. And he was sent to voice mail.

Brett didn't leave a message.

ELLA GOT A new patient on Wednesday. A three-pound, nine-week-old girl who came to them from the Santa Raquel hospital with a peripherally inserted central catheter and a ventilator. The tiny thing was only now at thirty-four weeks gestational age. But if all went well, she'd be running and playing with her siblings soon enough, with no memory of how rough her life had been at the start. She was a lucky one. Her heart was good. Her lungs appeared to be developing normally. And as soon as her organs were mature enough to function on their own, she could hopefully go home.

In the meantime, she'd need a diaper change every three hours, a daily assessment and very careful monitoring.

Ella felt as if she needed monitoring that day, too. She must have checked her voice mail half a dozen times. And looked for text messages twice as often. Maybe she should have picked up Brett's call. But if she was going to do this, she had to be the one in charge.

But she'd wanted him to leave a message so she'd know how much of a problem he was going to be.

She hadn't thought for a second that he'd be glad to hear from her—or to know that she'd invaded his home territory. Maybe she'd even taken a tiny bit of pleasure in having done so—in having a legitimate reason to rock his boat.

A reason he wouldn't be able to refuse.

Because one of the things she was certain of in her life was that she knew Brett Ackerman. He wouldn't turn his back on a friend in need if he felt he could help. Ever.

And most particularly, he wouldn't turn his back on Jeff.

Jeff, Ella's brother, had been Brett's college roommate. They'd met in their freshman year. Right after Brett's little sister had died. And his mother had had a breakdown resulting from the loss and from having withstood years of domestic violence at the hands of Brett's father. She'd lashed out at Brett. And then put herself in self-imposed isolation for having done so. Leaving Brett alone to cope.

Alone except for Jeff. Who'd been a solid rock in Brett's life, refusing to let him suffer in solitude. Brett had credited Jeff with saving his life.

Now it was time for Brett to save theirs.

ELLA WAITED ALL DAY Wednesday for him to call back. To leave a message. Clearly he'd heard that she was there. He had her new cell phone number. And Brett was definitely one who faced his battles head-on.

There'd been a time when she'd admired that about him.

She wanted to be the one to initiate their first conversation. But a hint as to his mind-set first would be good. Was he angry? Curious? Was it possible he'd actually missed her?

She would give him until her last break on Thursday before calling him. She didn't want to speak to him for the first time in four years in front of Chloe. While she knew she was over Brett, she wasn't positive that there wasn't any residual pain lurking inside her. Chloe didn't need more guilt added to her already overflowing plate.

At five minutes after two on Thursday afternoon, just as she was leaving the floor, she got a page. She was needed on Pod B stat. A baby had just been admitted. He was nine months old, had spent the first four months of his life at a NICU in LA, and was being readmitted due to an infection around the area of his G-tube.

"I wanted you to see this," Dr. Claire Worthington said as soon as Ella approached the crib where the baby lay completely still. She saw the finger-shaped marks on the little guy's thighs immediately.

"These look too big to be female," Ella said. It was the first thought that sprang to mind.

"His grandmother brought him in. Said his mother's under the weather."

"His paternal grandmother?" Ella asked, assisting a nurse from the PICU as she taped a newly placed line.

The baby was more than five pounds underweight. "According to his medical records he's lost four pounds since his check two weeks ago," Dr. Worthington said. "The grandmother claims that the mother refused to let anyone use his G-tube. He was being bottle and spoon fed through his mouth." The area around the feeding tube looked as though it hadn't been touched in a couple days, at least. Which could easily have caused the infection.

"Has social services been called?" If not, they'd be the first call on Ella's list when the doctor finished giving her orders and the little guy was settled.

"Not yet," Dr. Worthington said, a grim look on her face. "I'll be filling out a suspected abuse report and know that you're the go-to person."

"You suspect the mother?" But the bruises on the baby's thigh…

"I think if Mom had done this, she'd be here, claiming that something was physically wrong with him. She'd be defending herself. It doesn't fit that she'd let Grandma bring him in. Grandma didn't stay—she just dropped him off and said she had to get back. She appeared nervous. Besides, these bruises, while clearly thumb-shaped, are too big."

"I'll give my High Risk Team contacts a call and get someone out to the house ASAP," Ella said. She should have thought of it first, even before social services. For now, little Henry was in good hands. But his mother…

Filled with adrenaline, Ella forgot all about her break, about her ex-husband, and made her first call as a member of the Santa Raquel High Risk team.

She was needed.

And that was all that mattered.

BRETT WAS IN a hotel room in Washington late Thursday night, sitting at the desk with his laptop, going through the day's email, when he saw the notice about Henry Burbank and his mother, Nora. He wasn't a member of the High Risk team, but due to his relationship with The Lemonade Stand and his seat on the board, he received all emails pertaining to their work.

According to the police report from the day's home visit, Nora showed no visible signs of bruising. The woman exhibited fear as she refused a physical examination. Her husband stood over her the entire time the officer was there and, though a female officer tried to coax her away, she refused to leave his side. The report stated that there were no signs of affection between the two, and Nora spent most of her time looking at the ground. The grandmother had alarming bruises on an arm that she claimed came from the banister when she started to slip going down the stairs. She also adamantly refused a physical examination.

There'd been one previous call to the police regarding the couple, from a neighbor claiming to have heard a loud male voice and something crashing, but when the officers had gone out, they hadn't seen anything amiss, and all three adults in the home insisted that everything was fine. They'd all appeared to be in good health.

Mom, Dad and Grandma, all three, gave the exact same story regarding the bruises on baby Henry's thighs. He'd moved suddenly while being changed, and his father had saved him from a fall off the changing table.

The mom, Nora, was being blamed by Dad and Grandma for the baby's ill health, with claims that she'd force-fed him through his mouth, but the young mother had told police that she'd only ever used the G-tube to feed her son and had kept it cared for exactly as she'd been taught at the hospital. But when they'd asked how often the mother had fed her baby herself, as opposed to someone else feeding him, she'd clammed up.

Child Protective Services would be investigating further before the baby would be released back to his parents' care.

They had nothing concrete at the moment to keep Ted Burbank away from his family. Which meant that the possibly abusive man had visitation rights at the hospital with his son, Henry.

Charge nurse Ella Ackerman, the ex–Mrs. Brett Ackerman, was on full alert.

Brett needed a drink.

ELLA WENT INTO work early Friday morning. She'd had a text from Rhonda, a four-to-twelve charge nurse, telling her that Henry's mom had just called to say she was on her way in and would like them to hold off doing Henry's early morning assessment so that she could be present. Rhonda's text came because of the note Ella had left on Henry's chart, telling everyone to let her know anytime Mom or Dad were present, or expected to be present.

Because there wasn't enough evidence, or a family member willing to testify, the police couldn't do anything for Henry or Nora yet. But Ella could.

That was what the High Risk team was all about. Everyone working together to devise individual plans for the safety of high-risk victims, or potential victims. Henry coming to them with a life-threatening infection, signs of poor G-tube care and bruises made the case high risk.

And the team hoped that if Ella could get Nora alone, maybe the mother would speak more openly. At least Ella hoped so. She'd only spoken to one member of the team, an Officer Sanchez, from the Santa Raquel police department. Her first regular monthly High Risk team meeting, where she'd officially be introduced and meet everyone else, wouldn't be until the following week.

She was being inducted by fire, the middle-aged officer had told her when he'd stopped by her apartment the night before. Thankfully Chloe had been giving Cody a bath, so Ella had had a few minutes to speak privately.

Ella was on the floor with a welcoming smile when Nora Burbank showed up at the exact time Rhonda had said to expect her. The twenty-year-old was in jeans with fancy stitching and jeweled pockets, and a T-shirt, both clean and newer-looking. Her dark, waist-length hair was pulled back in a ponytail. She had rhinestoned flip-flops on her feet. No tattoos. No makeup.

And no visible signs of physical abuse. Just as Juan Sanchez had relayed.

"You're here alone?" she asked after she introduced herself as Henry's nurse and walked the woman through the secure door to Pod B. Sanchez had warned her that Nora wasn't likely to show up alone.

The young woman looked at the floor as she nodded. And otherwise kept her gaze trained in front of them. On the stations they were passing. Not on people. Not on the nurses and orderlies bustling about in the hall, nor on the young patients in cribs and those in need of an Isolette, who were situated in the open unit.

"Ted got called into work. He thinks I'm at home," Nora said softly, chin almost to her chest. Ella had the impression that the soft tone was more the woman's usual demeanor than a reaction to the very sick children around them. "His mom's supposed to be watching me, but I went out the back door when she went to the restroom."

Watching her?

"You drove yourself here?" They were nearing Henry's crib.

"I don't have a car," Nora said. "I took the bus…" Nora's words broke off as she caught sight of her son and hurried forward, tears in her eyes and a smile on her lips. The young woman was obviously comfortable around the various tubes connected to her son. And mindful of every single thing that happened over the next two hours. Nora assisted with bathing and changing the baby. She handled his feeding completely on her own. With the ease of a professional.

She spoke to him. Sang to him. Distracted him when he got a poke. And played age-appropriate games with him, from peekaboo, to track-the-tiger—having him follow a stuffed animal with his eyes, bringing the toy close enough for him to reach for and eventually letting him grab it.

Ella had no proof that Ted Burbank was anything other than, in her opinion, overly protective and too controlling of his family, but she was certain of two things. First, there was no way Henry's mother would ever have willingly fed her son by mouth, willingly allowed anyone else to do so, or allowed any improper handling of the G-tube. Nora watched every member of the medical staff with an educated eye.

And second, little Henry meant the world to her.

Nora began watching the clock shortly before eleven. Ella had purposely been on the pod all morning, but seeing patients other than just Henry. She'd kept an eye on Nora, though, and noticed when the woman started to become more agitated. As soon as she finished administering TPN, intravenous nourishment, to a baby whose stomach couldn't digest food, Ella made her way over to Nora.

"You ready for a break?" she asked the young woman who'd been holding her son for the past hour.

"I have to leave," Nora said with another glance at the clock. "Ted comes home for lunch at twelve-thirty."

And his mother couldn't make his lunch for him?

"Surely he'd understand if you missed lunch just once."

"He can't know I've been away."

"His mother knows."

"She won't say anything to him."

"She's your advocate, then?" There'd been bruises on Grandma's arms. But the older woman had blamed Nora for the baby's ill health. Because her son had been right there?

"No, she thinks I'm the whore who trapped him. But he'll be pissed at her for losing sight of me, so she won't tell."

"Will he hurt her?"

Nora's chin fell to her baby's forehead. "No, of course not."

"You don't have to go back, you know." She wasn't a counselor or experienced with victims of domestic violence. But she knew some things. "You don't have to stay with him."

Nora looked down at her son. Swallowed, and then, with a peculiar strength in her gaze, met Ella's eyes. "I know Ted's a bit aggressive at times, but he takes care of us," she said with utter conviction. "He means well. He tries hard. He works long hours to support us…"

Were these Nora's words? Or Ted's? Repeated over and over to the point that Nora believed the thoughts were her own? Were they true, or had Ted manipulated his young wife to the point that she didn't have a mind of her own? Ella had done a lot of reading.

She knew how these things often worked.

But…

"Aggression isn't okay." She said the only thing she knew to say. "And—"

"I have no one else." Nora's words were a statement. "My family disowned me when I got pregnant." She nodded toward the sleeping baby she still cuddled, in spite of her announcement that she had a bus to catch. "I'd just graduated from high school. I've never even had a job. But even if I had, it's not like I can just leave Henry with a sitter or at a day care and go off to work. He needs full-time trained care…"

Sounded as though Nora felt trapped…

Not once had Nora said she loved her husband. It was something Chloe said all the time about Jeff.

Pulling up a chair, she sat in front of the other woman, sending up a quick mental prayer that she was doing the right thing, and said, "I know of a place you can stay while Henry's here," she said. "It's not far. And someone would see that you got back and forth to the hospital. For that matter, I could pick you up in the morning on my way in

and take you back each afternoon after my shift.
I go right by there."

Or close enough. She went by the exit.

Nora didn't immediately shake her head. The
negative reaction took a good minute to come. "I'd
have no way to care for him when he's released."

"You could bring him to this place with you,"
she said, warming to her subject as she thought
of the conversation she'd had with Lila the other
night. The things the woman had told her about
The Lemonade Stand. The things she'd seen when
Lila had taken her on a tour.

"I'm serious, Nora. One phone call and you can
have a new home. A new life. This place…there's
a nurse on staff so if Henry had a problem, he'd
be safer there than he'd be at home."

And if she was overreacting? If she was interfering in a family life that was none of her business? Causing problems where there weren't any?

Nora wasn't telling her no.

If there weren't any problems, if Ted was a
good, loving husband, he'd understand if his wife
needed a little time away to get herself emotionally stable, wouldn't he? That was all this would
be, then. Nora getting help.

Having a preemie was difficult for anyone, let
alone for a child barely out of high school. But
being disowned by those who should have been
looking out for her?

Whatever the reason, Nora looked like a woman who was running out of hope.

"You can stay at the…place…until you have a job. A home. They help women in your position find jobs. There are full-time counselors on staff. Means to get training. Toys for Henry. Other women for you to be friends with. You'd have your own suite with Henry. A crib. Clothes. The cottages all have self-contained kitchens…"

"I…" Nora was crying now. Looking from Henry back to Ella.

"There's a pool. And a day care. It's a very unique shelter for battered women, Nora, and you're one of them, aren't you?"

A sob escaped Nora, though Ella mostly noticed it from the way the other woman's chest shook. They were in a busy pod with patients and hospital professionals moving around them—and they were all alone, too. Emotional scenes with parents in the NICU were, unfortunately, not uncommon.

"Ted… He wouldn't let me… He said his boy has a mouth and he could learn to eat…"

Henry had had so many tubes in his mouth during the first weeks of his life that he'd developed an oral aversion. The hope was that as he got a little older, and with proper care and developmental therapy, he'd be able to chew and swallow without activating his gag reflex.

"He'd force food down his throat and then when Henry threw it back up, he'd refuse to give him more until the next mealtime. He said when he got hungry enough, he'd eat."

"There's red tape we'll have to go through," Ella said, scared and determined and wishing she knew far more than she did. "But the people at the shelter will help you with that. There's a lawyer who donates her services to the residents who can't afford to pay for them…"

Ted Burbank had the right to full access to his son. Something would have to be done to revoke that.

If…

"Tell me, Nora…has Ted ever hit you? Or threatened you in any way?" Had the man threatened to kill her? From what she'd read for her High Risk team training, death threats were taken very seriously by law enforcement and the courts.

But she couldn't lead Nora to such a confession.

Nora stood, carefully and capably settling her son back in his crib without disturbing the monitors on him. Without disturbing him.

Ella stood, too, ready to block the woman's way long enough to try to convince her one more time to take advantage of the help being offered to her.

Instead, Nora turned, faced the wall and lifted her shirt. The bright red welts were clearly new. Ella could see the imprint of a belt buckle there. And Nora had been sitting back, rocking her son all morning.

Clearly the woman was used to pain.

"You need to get her looked at," a resident who'd been at the crib next door leaned in to say to Ella as he passed. She nodded.

"Let me make the call," Ella said to Nora as the woman pulled her shirt down and turned around.

"He'll come here…"

"I'm going to call the police officer who visited you last night. There are professionals used to dealing with these situations, Nora. They'll help you. And make certain that you and Henry never have to go back to Ted again."

She believed what she was saying. And hoped to God that those trained professionals upon whom she was relying would come through.

Thinking of Lila McDaniels, she experienced a moment of calm as she left Nora with her son, giving word that if Ted Burbank showed up he was not to be allowed in the NICU and alerting security to the situation. Then she went into her office, closed the door and made a call to The Lemonade Stand.

CHAPTER FOUR

BRETT'S PHONE SIGNALED five new voice mails when he took it out of airplane mode upon landing at LAX Friday afternoon. From his first-class seat, Brett pressed 1 to retrieve his messages. He'd be first to deplane, but the Jetway wasn't even connected to the plane yet.

The first two messages were from members of the board of directors of Americans Against Prejudice. He'd been fielding calls from various AAP board members for two days. Some had been cajoling, others angry. All of them attempting either to manipulate or intimidate him. In two days, only one member of that board had called him out of shame. Probably fear-induced.

That had been the only call Brett had returned.

The Jetway moved toward the plane. He could see it through the window and stood, phone still to his ear, and with his free hand, retrieved his bags from the overhead bin and put them on the seat beside him.

Message three was from Detroit. A call he'd been expecting. A follow-up with a nonprofit museum he'd toured the morning before, confirming their desire to acquire his services and give him a seat on their board.

He didn't really have time in his schedule, but the museum was a hands-on science, music and technology facility that could make a real difference with the next generation of Detroit leaders. And their meeting schedule mostly coincided with the Washington, DC, group so he could make both with one trip.

The fourth message came up as, with his one free hand, he slung his bags over his shoulders, and picked up his briefcase. A confirmation of a haircut appointment he had the next morning. He nodded at the captain and the flight attendant standing in the open doorway of the cockpit as he disembarked, and was almost to the gate and that much closer to his car when he heard the fifth message.

"A front-yard sprinkler head sprung. George fixed it."

He didn't wait for the click he knew would follow. His mother took good care of him. He'd come up with the plan shortly after he'd sold the dot-com and finalized details for The Lemonade Stand. His mother liked to take care of people. And he'd banked on the fact that if she thought he really needed her, she wouldn't be able to say no. He couldn't travel as much as he did, and focus on the job as he needed to do, without having someone to take care of his private business matters for him—including his charity work. And he valued his privacy—as she valued hers. She'd understand that he didn't want a stranger managing his affairs.

His plan had worked. She'd agreed almost without hesitation. Through email. And the setup had backfired, too.

She took care of him. She just wouldn't see him. Or have a back-and-forth, two-way conversation with him. She knew his schedule and tended to his home when he wasn't there. And if she needed his input, or to relay information, she texted him. Or emailed. Or left the occasional voice message.

The one concession she'd made a few years ago, when he'd threatened to hire someone else to care for him, was to give him access to her home so that he could help her, too. But even then, she'd extracted a promise from him that if her car was there, he wasn't to enter.

She didn't trust herself to see him. To get caught up in a relationship with him. And then turn on him again. Her fears were likely groundless. And the walls they built around her sky high.

After more than thirteen years of her personal silence, Brett was beginning to accept that some things were never going to change.

As it turned out, Ella drove Nora to The Lemonade Stand as soon as she got off work that afternoon. The vulnerable young mother had asked if she could stay with her son until then. She hadn't wanted to go with a stranger—a member of the Stand staff who'd been planning to come get her—and because hospital security had already had to call the police on Ted, who was in custody, there was no harm in Ella leaving the hospital alone with Nora.

No risk of them being waylaid or followed by an irate husband. Not that night. As soon as Ted was arraigned, or had hired an attorney, he'd be out of jail. He hadn't hurt anyone—this time. He'd just refused to leave the hospital without his wife and had been arrested for trespassing.

And after that night, Ella could come and go as she pleased. Ted had never met her. Had no idea a member of the hospital staff, or anyone else for that matter, was helping his wife pull off her rebellion, and he was no longer allowed access to the NICU. At least not for the next week. The restraining order Nora and her infant son had been granted was only temporary.

Ella had no doubt it would become permanent the next week when Nora appeared before a judge.

Lila had met her at the outside door of the Stand, ushering them inside with the warmth Ella had known Nora would find, and five minutes later, Ella was climbing back behind the wheel of her Mazda CX-5. The small, four-door sportutility vehicle she'd purchased just before quitting her job to move to Santa Raquel still smelled new and added to the overall euphoria she felt.

Nora was going to be fine. Baby Henry was going to be fine. And her new life was turning out far better than she'd even hoped.

So, of course, it was time to get on with it. Right now. While she was filled with such an acute sense of energy and purpose.

Sitting in her car in the parking lot, Ella dialed a number she knew by heart, but refused to program into her speed dial or add to her contacts. She couldn't let it get that personal.

If Brett didn't pick up, she'd leave a message. As busy as she was, he was busier. Working all over the country in various time zones. And flying across them when he wasn't working. Maybe they could talk through messages. He was good at that. Had been communicating that way with his mother for the entire time Ella had known him.

Running over the words she'd leave on his recording as she listened to the phone ring, Ella started her car. Maybe she wouldn't have to—

"Can you meet me at Donovan's in half an hour?"

What the…?

The first contact they'd had in years, and he didn't even say hello?

"Yes." She didn't know where the hell Donovan's was, but it must be in town, which meant her GPS would find it. And Santa Raquel wasn't big enough to require more than thirty minutes to get from one end to the other.

"Tell the hostess to show you to my table." Click.

Ella's first reaction, after she'd picked her jaw up off the floor, was to call him back and tell him to go to hell.

She might have, if not for two things. First, Brett was emulating his mother. Which meant he was emotionally vulnerable. He wasn't immune to her.

And second, she needed him.

Far more than he had the ability to hurt her.

Still sitting in the running car, she did a quick internet search for the restaurant. Typed in the address to her GPS.

Ten minutes. That was the drive time between where she was and where he'd be waiting for her.

At his table.

Holding court.

Unless she got there first. And asked the hostess to bring him to her table. Car in gear, Ella pulled out, driving just past the speed limit. Not fast enough to get a ticket. Just as fast as she could safely get to where she was going.

Would have been nice if she'd had a chance to change out of her puppy dog–plastered beige scrubs and into a pair of tight jeans and an equally tight black sweater. He'd always liked her in black. And tight would show him she hadn't gained a pound since their college days when he'd hardly been able to keep his hands off her.

A toss of her hair and bit of fresh makeup wouldn't be remiss, either. But none of that was going to happen.

His Highness had given her no time to prepare.

And that was just as well. There was no need to impress him with her womanly wiles. The woman lurking inside Ella was off-limits to him.

"WHAT DO YOU mean she's already here?" Brett was not in a good mood when he walked into the beachfront Italian eatery before the dinner rush that Friday afternoon. He hadn't even had time to stop home and drop off his bags, wanting to just get this last meeting done with and then go home, take a swim in his heated pool and crash on his couch with a beer and some mindless television.

"She arrived ten minutes ago, Mr. Ackerman. She said she'd rather be seated than wait…"

Cheryl—he knew because he read her name tag—was a familiar face at Donovan's. And he was a nice guy. So he smiled, said something inane like "good" and indicated that she could lead the way.

The place was moderately busy, but empty enough that he could have chosen a table where he could have his back to the wall, able to see the entire room when his lovely ex-wife sashayed into the room, and steel himself against the effect her sexiness always had on him.

He'd had a solid plan.

And she had a table with a view. Along a wall of windows in the cliff-top eatery that looked over the ocean. If there was a bottle of wine sitting at the table, he was leaving.

"Over this way…" Cheryl rounded a large table, heading across the room. He didn't need her guidance. He'd noticed the back of Ella's head the second he'd entered the room. The way she held herself, back straight, that unruly dark hair up in a ponytail…

As if she was still a damned college student, not a charge nurse who should have short hair that was easy to care for and stayed out of the way.

A guy couldn't get lost in short hair…

"I'll take it from here," he said when they were still a good six feet away. He was about to see Ella again.

And was suddenly struck with the knowledge that he couldn't have witnesses. He almost turned to leave.

Would have if he knew how in the hell to turn his back on unpleasantness. But he didn't. No, Brett was the type who saw a divorce attorney *before* the separation.

"Ella." Taking a perverse pleasure as she jumped when he came up beside her table, Brett pulled out a chair.

A glass of water sat in front of her.

Not wine.

Good.

"Have you ordered?" he asked.

God, she looked good. Great. Better than ever. How long had it been since he'd seen her? A year? Two?

Four years, three months, one week and two days. Give or take a week, his mind, its usual relentless self, reminded him. He hadn't kept count. Not even he was that anal. No, he'd lain in bed the other night—wide awake when he'd needed to be well rested for his meeting the following morning—and completely relived that last time. She'd been clearing her things out of the home they'd bought in Santa Barbara after he'd sold the dot-com.

He'd lain in bed and counted how long ago that had been.

And marveled at how far he'd come since then…

"You look good, Brett." Her smile, oh, God, that smile. He had no idea if she'd ever answered his question about ordering.

And a waitress was approaching.

"We'll have a bottle of wine," he blurted. Just a small bottle. He named the one. It went well with…

What the hell. He liked it. And knew she did, too.

"I don't…" Ella was shaking her head.

He pretended not to see. "And bring us the

bread-and-cheese plate," he continued, naming a popular Donovan's appetizer.

Bread, wine…and time. Just enough to deal with this situation. And not a second more.

"Would you like two glasses with that?" the waitress, someone he didn't recognize, asked.

"Yes."

Ella didn't argue. Brett relaxed just a tad.

And the woman left.

CHLOE WASN'T EXPECTING her anytime soon. Ella had called her sister-in-law before leaving the hospital to let her know she was working late and had no idea when she'd be home. Chloe had said she'd fix Cody fish sticks for dinner. She'd taken him to the complex park that afternoon. Had met another mother there with her toddler. A little girl.

She'd sounded more relaxed than Ella had heard her since she'd brought Chloe to Santa Raquel to stay with her.

"I didn't need any wine," she said now. But she lied. She did need it. If she was going to get through this meeting without throwing herself at her ex-husband's chest and begging him to hold her.

The temptation was made worse by the fact that she knew he'd do it if she asked. And then he'd let her go.

Because that was Brett's way.

And she'd fall apart again.

Because that was what being with him did to her.

"Just one glass," he said.

She nodded. Saving her strength, her arguments, for what mattered.

"The view is lovely." She stared at the ocean. *Awkward.* But he was the one who'd chosen their meeting place. And the one who'd ordered—requiring any serious conversation to wait until they'd been served.

"When they first built this place it was a warehouse."

"With a view?"

He shook his head. "No, this wall of windows was put in when it was converted to a restaurant."

Who cared? Who cared? Who cared? She glanced to the side. Looking out into the room.

Where was that wine?

More important, the waitress who needed to deliver it so that they could be left alone.

"You're wearing the same cologne." She'd picked it out. After he'd sold the dot-com and they'd had their first taste of money. They'd gone into an expensive department store and smelled what had seemed like a million different scents. She'd chosen one for him. He'd chosen one for her. They'd bought the home in Santa Barbara. He'd put plans for The Lemonade Stand in motion. And started his nonprofit policing business...

"You're not."

Not what? Oh. Wearing the same cologne...

It had been one of the last things to go after the divorce was final. She hadn't been able to bear giving it up. And then later, hadn't been able to stand the scent. It reminded her too much of him.

Another sideways glance. Still no waitress… Wait, yes, there she was, at a table across the way, taking an order.

"Your hair is shorter." His legs were as long and perfect, his suit fit him to perfection and that dimple just above his jawline still turned her on.

"Yours isn't." Did his voice have a bit of an edge? She stared at him. Wishing, as she had so many times in the past, that she could get through to him.

Their hearts had always been connected, but he closed his mind to her when it came to his most inner sanctum.

No waitress yet. No wine or bread.

She couldn't wait anymore. "I've moved to Santa Raquel."

"I know." Kind of hard to pick curtness out of two words. But she needed it to be there. Needed to know that he was emotionally affected by her choice to invade his home territory…

Ella pulled herself up straighter. No. She needed Brett to be…Brett. Self-sufficient and capable. If he had any needs, if she was privy to them, she'd be compelled to try to meet them. And end up heartbroken when she failed.

"Here you go." The voice startled her. As did

the arm that reached between Ella and Brett, putting first one then the other wineglass down in
front of them. All that time waiting, and Ella
hadn't even seen the waitress coming.

An unopened wine bottle was all that remained
on the tray the woman held and, taking it, she set
the tray down on a vacant table behind them, held
out the bottle for Brett to examine, and at his nod,
pulled a corkscrew out of her pocket and turned
it into the bottle.

Ella watched every move. Cataloged them all.
Putting every ounce of energy she had into col-
lecting her thoughts, which would help enforce
her emotional barriers against this man, and get
on with the life she was currently living.

Brett was given a sip of wine to taste. He approved it. And Ella's glass was filled to the halfway mark. Without waiting for him, waiting for
the toast that had been a tradition with them, she
took an unladylike gulp. Stopping short of chug-
ging the remaining liquid in her glass.

Another staff person arrived with a variety of
house-made breads and gourmet cheeses arranged
on a silver platter. He moved the salt and pepper,
and an unlit candle on the white tablecloth, and
set the platter down. A small white china plate
appeared in front of her.

Then another in front of Brett. Her Brett. Sitting right across from her again. As he had for
several precious years.

And it was all too much for her. The romantic restaurant. The wine. The town and new job and new life. A woman sitting in a shelter because the man she loved had beaten her...

Feeling the sting of tears behind her eyes, Ella clasped her hands in her lap, stared out at a ship on the ocean and told herself to breathe.

CHAPTER FIVE

RATHER THAN HELPING, the glass of wine only made things worse. So Brett helped himself to a little more. Two was his limit whether he was driving or not, so the second was going to have to do the trick.

Deaden the parts of him that had once been in love with this woman. At least long enough to get rid of her.

Before she settled in.

She was going to have to move back to wherever she'd come from. Or somewhere else. He'd pay whatever it took.

There was no way the two of them could live in the same town without her getting hurt. He cared about her. She'd feel that. Start to expect things. Or, at the very least, want them. And he wouldn't give them to her. Their pattern was clear.

She wanted happily-ever-after.

He wanted to be left alone.

Because alone was better than doing to others as his father had done to their family. Brett wasn't going to make the mistake his parents had made. They'd both grown up in abusive homes. They'd promised each other they wouldn't carry the pattern with them. That promise had destroyed lives.

He wasn't going to pretend to himself, or to Ella, that he wasn't damaged goods.

Thoughts sped through his mind as he watched Ella pick up a piece of white Italian bread, dab a bit of grape jelly on it and top it with a piece of cheese. She liked jelly on crackers with apples, too.

"How's your mother?" Her gaze met his directly for the first time.

And the impact nearly killed him. His heart slammed against his chest, and his mind went blank.

"Same." The one word was all he could give her.

"She's still handling all of your personal business? Including the house?"

"Yes."

"And you still haven't seen her?"

"No." He had a phantom personal assistant. She handled his mail, his charity work and the various individuals who helped take care of his home. Landscaper, cleaning service, pool service. She even had access to his personal calendar via Google. She left curt messages or sent two- and three-word emails.

"Do you at least talk? Actually converse, I mean."

"No."

She glanced away.

"She left a key to her place on my desk a couple years ago. I go in once a week to take care of anything that needs to be done." She let him get her Christmas decorations out of the small attic in her garage. And he'd changed some lightbulbs in the cathedral ceiling once. Mostly he just visited with her phantom ghost. Sat on her couch and felt her presence.

Ella's shocked glance in his direction pierced him. "That's great, Brett." Her smile burned into him. "She's softening!"

"Not really. I threatened to hire someone to take her place."

He sipped his wine, frowning at his ex-wife. He didn't blame Ella for scrambling for conversation. He blamed her for moving to Santa Raquel.

And filled his mouth with bread before he actually blurted out his frustration.

"I need your help, Brett."

"Why did you move here?" His gaze was piercing. It had to be.

"I'm a pediatric nurse, and Santa Raquel Children's Hospital is slated to be the best in the state. With all of the new positions to fill, I was offered the chance to be a charge nurse…"

In another lifetime that would have been reason enough to move.

He held her captive with a look and didn't relent.

"I have to prove to myself that I'm completely over you. That living near you doesn't matter to me. Personally."

He sat back. Took another sip of wine. Thought about the hard alcohol he refused to touch. About how his father had used it to numb his pain. And then brought pain to his loved ones.

"I'm happy, Brett," she said. "I've built a good life for myself, and I like where I am."

Brett nodded, wanting to tell her how glad he was to hear those words. But he wasn't sure he believed them.

"But Chloe, you remember her?"

As if he'd forget being the best man in her brother's wedding. Or forget the woman who'd once been like a sister to him. Clenching his fingers around the stem of his wineglass, he acknowledged her remark with a small nod.

"Well, Chloe has been getting on me to start dating again. I keep telling her I'm happy being single, but she keeps trying to hook me up."

Was she trying to make him jealous? Because it wasn't working. He would have loved nothing more than to see Ella happily married.

Safely obliterating any temptation he might ever have to attempt to avail himself of her sweetness in the future.

Ella took a sip of her wine. He watched the glass touch her lips. Imagined how they'd feel to that glass if it could only have a second of humanity. Felt sorry for it that it could not...

"Then one day about a year ago she suggested to me that I wasn't as over you as I thought I was.

She claims that I'm a victim of our broken marriage and that until I face that fact, until I can see you and know for certain that I'm over you, I'll never have a completely joyful life of my own."

Chloe needed to mind her own damned business.

"A move's a little drastic, don't you think? You could have just called. I'd have stopped by so you could see for yourself that it's done."

Done. It had to be done. He'd known that. Acted on it. Still believed. Without even a smidgeon of doubt.

"My therapist told me that I can hide and pretend forever, but to really take charge of my life, I'd need to come out into the open, take the air into my lungs and start moving forward."

"Your therapist told you to move to Santa Raquel?"

Ella's smile gave him an ache in the groin. "No, I came up with the idea all on my own. And only after my supervisor suggested to me that I apply for the position in the Santa Raquel NICU."

Her work with seriously ill babies interested him. Immensely. In terms of how she was handling it. How she felt when she got home at night.

He had questions he'd never ask. Needed answers he wouldn't seek.

Because they'd open a box, let out topics they were never going to discuss. Not ever again.

After years of fertility treatments, of humiliating procedures, Ella had finally been able to get pregnant. And Brett had killed her dream.

He'd thought he could handle being a father. Had been sure he'd be different from his own father. Until he'd found out Ella was really pregnant.

And had to accept the fact that there was no going back.

He'd grown more and more withdrawn. Irritable. Terse. Until one night, when terrors had driven him from their bed, she'd come to find him. She'd known something was wrong. She'd pushed him to be honest with her. And he'd turned on her. Raising his voice. Telling her he didn't want to be a father. That he didn't want their baby.

When she'd asked him, with a horrified expression he would never forget, what he wanted to do about it, he'd told her he'd seen a divorce lawyer. That she didn't ever have to worry. She and the baby would be well taken care of.

It was only then he'd realized that she'd been thinking more in terms of counseling. Maybe feared he wanted an abortion.

She'd never considered that he'd leave her.

And he hadn't been seriously thinking about it, really. He'd just been gathering information. In case.

But the damage had been done. He'd split her heart in two.

And when, the next week, she'd lost the baby, she'd turned to Chloe, not him, for support.

He'd wanted to stay with her. And he'd seen his father in himself then most of all. Brett's dad, once he'd known he had a problem, had been too weak to leave his family in peace. He'd needed them too much. And so he'd continued to hurt them.

Brett was not going to be that man.

So he and Ella weren't going to talk about any of it. Not now. Not ever.

Ella took another sip of wine. Leaning forward, he topped up her glass. The sun had set, and the ocean was darkening. Soon there would be nothing but blackness beyond the window.

"I didn't mean to bring up the past," Ella said with a grin that made him sad. "I just need you to know that I have absolutely no interest in you personally, Brett."

Was this the part where one doth protest too much?

"I don't want you to think I'm here out of some pathetic hope that you might change your mind about me. Or to think that I'm stalking you or something."

Protesting too much yet?

"The job is a big part of my decision to move here. And I always loved Santa Raquel. You know that."

They'd visited his hometown. More than once. Each time she'd said she wanted them to settle there. To raise their children there.

Looking back, he saw that even then, he hadn't

ever really believed her fairy tale could happen. He'd just wanted it so badly he'd been a selfish ass, just like his old man, grasping at her hope and hanging on.

Until he couldn't anymore.

Brett sat forward. Set his glass on the table and folded his hands in front of him.

"It's a great job, a great place to live, but there are other great opportunities. I know you, Ella. There has to be more going on."

"I made the final decision to accept the job offer because of The Lemonade Stand."

He frowned, honestly confused. "I offered you a position on the board. You didn't have to join the High Risk team to be involved." She'd supported the idea of the Stand from the very first time he'd mentioned that if he ever won the lottery he'd open such a place. She'd been a sophomore in college at the time. He'd been a junior. They hadn't even talked about marriage yet.

Her fingers, blunt tipped and slender, able to handle crises on a daily basis, climbed up and down the stem of her glass. She traced a pile of crumbs around the white linen tablecloth. *I moved here because of The Lemonade Stand.*

His throat dried out like burned timber.

"Ella?" He needed her to quit studying the damned table and look at him.

Had someone hurt her? On one of those blind

dates Chloe had arranged? Or someone else? Were the police involved?

Why hadn't he known? Jeff had sworn to him that if Ella were ever in trouble, if she ever needed anything, he'd let Brett know...

He couldn't just sit there...couldn't stand the thought of his Ella being...

Sweet God, that was why he'd left her. To save her from loving a man who had the pattern of abuse lurking inside him. He knew the statistics. More than half of abusers had grown up with abuse. It was a pattern that repeated itself. And he'd faced the beast of his father inside himself when he'd lain in bed after finding out Ella was pregnant, when he'd closed his eyes and slept. Night after night. He'd seen his father. The raised hand. Heard the anger. And then his own face had been there...

I moved here because of The Lemonade Stand.

His palm settled on the back of her hand, holding it still against the table. "Talk to me, El."

She looked at their hands. Then up at him. A sheen of tears glistened in her eyes. Panic surged inside him.

"Did someone hurt you?" The words forced themselves out.

She shook her head. But didn't speak.

Every nerve in his body was tense. He couldn't get them to release their grip on him. It was a feeling he knew well.

Bracing for a blow.

Only this one wouldn't be as simple as a fist in the face. Or a belt to the back.

"It's not me, it's Chloe." He heard her, but the words only confused him more. What did her sister-in-law, living in Palm Desert with Jeff, have to do with The Lemonade Stand?

Oh, God. The idea hit him, accompanied by a maelstrom of rejection.

Ella's gaze was steady now. Steady and needy.

"Chloe's hitting Cody?" The godson he knew only through pictures. He'd told Jeff, when his friend had called to tell him about the boy's birth, that, with him being divorced from Ella, he couldn't possibly be anything to the boy, but Jeff had insisted. It didn't mean anything. It was just a title.

The shake of Ella's head caused a new wave of foreboding.

"Chloe's with me," Ella said. "Her and Cody."

"Visiting?"

Another small shake of Ella's head. Brett realized he was still covering her hand with his own, but he didn't let go.

"They're living with me."

"Where's Jeff?"

"Palm Desert."

He sat back, letting his hands fall into his lap. Then reached for his wineglass. "They're divorced?"

He'd never, in a million years, have figured that

one. If anyone was the perfect couple it was Jeff and Chloe. They were crazy about each other. In a way that couldn't be faked. Even Brett, who'd never personally witnessed a healthy relationship in his life, could feel the bond between Ella's brother and his wife.

"No!" Ella's shock righted a world that was quickly spinning out into space. "Of course not."

Until he considered that she'd just told him that Jeff's wife and son were living with her, not him.

Not him.

Ella watched him.

Jeff. Jeff?

If she wanted him to think that Jeff Wales had done something that would make his wife need a women's shelter then she was just plain—

"It's Jeff, Brett," she was saying. "He has… bouts. They've escalated over the past few years. This last time…Chloe asked me to come get her, and I did. Jeff doesn't know. That she's with me, I mean. He has no idea where she's staying. They communicate by cell phone, and she has a pay-as-you-go one so he won't be able to get any details from their bill."

She'd thrown him for a loop. "Have you talked to him? Does he know you know she's gone?"

"He called me, I think trying to figure out if she was with me, but I went on and on about the new job and how I was in the middle of moving into my new apartment and it was only at the end, when I asked him why he'd called, that he told me she'd left."

Brett felt as though he had rocks in his gut. He could just imagine how Jeff must be feeling.

"Your brother is the kindest man I've ever known." The only person who'd ever seen Brett cry.

Ella's older brother had held an eighteen-year-old college-freshman Brett as he'd sobbed out his anguish over his parents. Helped him treat the raw strap marks on his back, left by his father's belt, so that he didn't have to report them to anyone. He'd spent many a night sitting with him that first year they were roommates, listening to him talk, or more often, allowing him complete silence without the aloneness that usually accompanied it, and had never told another soul about any of it.

"I know he is." She was blinking back tears.

"He puts bugs outside rather than killing them."

"I know."

Memories glided through his mind like a picture show. One after another. "And…what about Missy's little sister?" They'd all been juniors in college the year a friend of theirs had brought her three-year-old sister to school for a family weekend visit. The little girl had been afraid of all the guys in their crowd, throwing a tantrum that threatened to ruin the entire weekend, until Jeff had knelt down and very seriously explained something to her, a secret, she'd said. She'd been his adoring fan the rest of the visit. To the point that years later, at Jeff's wedding, one of the guys had given a toast to the guy they'd all deemed the world's greatest future dad.

"Jeff slammed Cody into a chair, Brett."

"Slammed, as in set him down strongly, or as in breaking something?"

"He didn't break anything."

"Has he ever broken anything? Or left bruises?"

"Not on Cody."

"What about Chloe?"

Chin jutting forward, Ella nodded.

And, emotionally, Brett shut down.

His ex-wife wouldn't lie to him. He didn't doubt her word for a second. But neither could he believe Jeff Wales would raise a hand to his wife.

"I need your help, Brett. Jeff needs your help."

He nodded. His buddy sure as hell did need him if someone was trying to pin a DV rap on him. Someone who'd been persuasive enough to convince Ella.

Brett cared about Chloe. A lot.

If he thought for one second anyone was hurting her, he'd hunt whoever it was down himself and have him prosecuted to the fullest extent of the law.

But he wasn't going to stand by and see Jeff hurt.

"Has Chloe had medical treatment?" Records were a way to establish truth. Maybe Jeff's wife had met someone. Had a lover on the side who'd hurt her.

Maybe Chloe had asked to leave Palm Desert to get away from the guy. Maybe she cared enough about her marriage to Jeff to try to salvage it.

People made mistakes.

And deserved second chances.

"No, she's never had medical treatment due to Jeff's anger issues."

Anger issues. Sure, Jeff got mad—who didn't? But he'd never known a more easygoing, laid-back man in his life. Jeff took it on the chin when most guys, Brett included, would have been swinging.

"Have you ever seen Jeff be abusive to her?"

"No."

"You've never seen any of Jeff's outbursts first-hand?"

"No. But I've seen the bruises, Brett."

Okay. So, something was going on with his friends. Something bad. Maybe Chloe was sick or something. Or suspected Jeff of having an affair and was trying to get back at him.

Brett knew full well that no one knew what went on behind closed doors. That a man could appear one way in public or in small gatherings with friends, and another way entirely at home with his family. His father had taught him that, too, before he'd learned it in counseling. And with the research he'd done before opening The Lemonade Stand.

But he'd lived with Jeff. For four years. He'd seen him at his best and at his worst. He couldn't see the man raising a hand to his wife.

The very real concern, the fear, he read in Ella's expression brought him up short. There was a problem.

She'd come to him for help.

"I'll talk to him."

"He's going to deny it, Brett."

He nodded. Was pretty much counting on Jeff's innocence. And then maybe the two of them would be able to figure out what was really going on.

CHAPTER SIX

CHLOE WAS WATCHING a British arts show on cable when Ella got home just after eight on Friday night. It had been a long day and since she had to work in the morning, she excused herself to bed before her sister-in-law got close enough to smell the wine on her breath.

To ask any questions about where she'd been.

She wouldn't keep her having seen Brett a secret from Chloe. Chloe knew that Ella's contacting her ex-husband, Jeff's best friend, was part of the plan to help save her marriage. The main part, since nothing was going to change if Jeff didn't get help and, so far, Jeff was still unable to admit that he needed it. Which was where Brett came in.

If anyone could help Jeff see the truth, it would be Brett.

And he'd agreed to speak with Jeff.

Their plan was on track.

The future looked hopeful.

All of which she'd share with Chloe in the morning.

Tonight Ella needed the privacy of her locked bedroom door and pillows to muffle her sobs as she lay herself down to sleep. She was weepy from the wine. From the emotional roller coaster that day had been—first the situation with Nora and then seeing Brett for the first time in more than four years.

In the morning she'd be her usual cheery self. Or so she told herself as ten o'clock rolled around and she was still lying there, mind racing with memories, a nuance in a voice, a look in the eye, the warmth of a hand.

She told herself again at one. And around two she dozed. To dream of Brett. And jerk herself awake before she could fall into a deep sleep that would only leave her disoriented when she woke. She dozed on and off for the rest of the night. And was up twenty minutes before her alarm was due to go off.

Up, focused and fully in control.

An uncomfortable night filled with distressing images, useless longings and long-forgotten feelings was to be expected after a first meeting in four years. Nothing more than a throwback to what had been. It wasn't permanent. Or even part of present-day reality.

She'd let it go. And Brett's hold on her would let go, too.

Each step she took forward took her further away from him. From a pain she'd never escape if she tried to hold on to even a small vestige of what she'd thought they had.

She was wearing cartoon-character scrubs with

a matching scrunchie around her ponytail, volley clogs, and a shield of calm when she walked into the kitchen to the smell of broccoli quiche at half past six.

"Is Cody up this early?"

Chloe's schedule had been mirroring her son's since they'd moved in with Ella.

"No, and if we're quiet, he won't be until after you're gone. You looked beat last night, and I wanted you to have a good breakfast and a little peace before you have to get back at it this morning."

That shield Ella had erected slipped. People who lived alone weren't used to being noticed. Or spoiled.

But she was glad she had a minute with Chloe.

"Sit with me?" she asked as her sister-in-law dished up a divine-smelling egg-and-vegetable mixture that stimulated an appetite that had been nonexistent when Ella had left her room seconds before.

Pouring two cups of coffee, Chloe placed one in front of Ella and sat with the other still in her hand, taking a sip.

She had to tell Chloe about Brett. But first, "I was at The Lemonade Stand again yesterday."

"With a patient?"

She couldn't say much. And didn't. Telling Chloe only that her visit had to do with the High Risk team, she said, "I talked to Lila while I was there. Lila McDaniels. She's the managing director."

"I remember. You read me her résumé when Brett first started interviewing for positions…"

She'd been in on the beginning stages—the dreaming. Then the dream coming true. The search for a site. The legalities and architectural plans. Even the initial weeding through of potential applicants.

And then her world had fallen apart. Brett had filed for divorce. He'd moved out before they broke ground.

"You remember that?"

"Yeah. Because she had such high credentials, work history that sounded like she was an incredibly well-rounded person and no personal background at all. She had no family or anything that would interfere with the long hours, she didn't mind spending nights at the Stand when needed, and she had the same last name as my best friend from grade school." Chloe grinned.

Ella had had reservations about the woman. About her lack of a three-dimensional life. She'd expressed her apprehensions to Brett. He'd obviously found her suitable in spite of Ella's fears, and his decision to hire her had clearly turned out to be the right one.

"Anyway, I was thinking…you know the core belief at the Stand is that women who've known abuse suffer from a lack of self-confidence, which

makes them self-destructive, and that, if you counteract those negative influences with positive
ones—actions they can feel, not just words that
oftentimes go in one ear and out the other—then
they'll be better equipped to know what it feels
like to value themselves."

Chloe put her cup down. "I value myself, El.
You know that."

"I do." Ella was eating while she spoke. Because she had to go soon. And because she'd
had nothing for dinner but a piece of bread with
cheese. "I value you, too," she added with a grin.
"This is delicious!"

Life had a way of turning you on your end if
you let it get too serious.

Chloe shrugged. "It's a simple recipe. But I
knew you had to leave early, and I didn't have a
lot of time."

In her short time in Santa Raquel, Chloe had
made braised pork chops that melted in your
mouth, a vegetable, rice and tilapia dish that
they'd finished off the night she'd prepared it, and
a chicken salad that Ella wanted in her freezer at
all times. Just in case.

And this morning she had things to discuss. "So
the grounds at the Stand are resort style, the pool,
the bungalows—all elegant. But the cooking—
it's typical cafeteria stuff. You know, feeding-the-
masses type of fare."

Chloe nodded. "Feeding so many people at

once, it can be difficult sometimes to make dishes that everyone will like."

"But you could do it, couldn't you? Plan menus and give them recipes that would appeal to the masses, but still be that step above ordinary?"

Chloe's eyes narrowed as she looked at Ella. "You trying to get me to move to the shelter? Surely you don't think I'm in need of full-time care…"

The question threw Ella. Mostly because it hadn't even crossed her mind. Jeff was the one who needed help in their situation. They'd gotten Chloe and Cody out in time. Chloe had been strong enough to pack her bags and get in the car.

"The women at the Stand—in large part—are there because they aren't safe on the outside yet, or because they don't have any place else to go while they rearrange their lives. You don't fit either category. They're starting over. You're not."

The look of relief that crossed Chloe's face startled Ella. Didn't Chloe trust her to get her back home? Did she think Ella wanted her to leave Jeff permanently?

Or was there more going on?

Filing the questions away, in the interest of time, she said, "I heard Lila say something yesterday to the…woman…I was there with, something about the cooking, and it made me think of you. I thought maybe you'd be glad for a somewhat professional pastime while you're here, and it would be good for Cody, too, because while you're working, he could play with the kids in the private day care at the Stand."

She wanted to give Chloe a sense of herself apart from her family. The woman could own her own restaurant, or run a kitchen in an already established high-end eatery. Maybe, if Chloe were independent, she wouldn't be as vulnerable to Jeff's outbursts.

Maybe if she stood up to Jeff, he'd get himself well sooner...

The thought stopped her short. Where in the hell had that come from?

"You really think I could help?" Chloe was saying, and Ella felt ten times sicker, thinking that Jeff's behavior was in any way Chloe's doing.

She knew better.

"I already spoke to Lila," she said now, taking her plate to the sink and rinsing the remainder of her breakfast down the drain. The disposal would have a gourmet breakfast. Something it wouldn't appreciate at all.

Like Brett hadn't appreciated having a partner in his corner, loving him above all else, willing to watch his back, to protect his heart...

Pulling a card out of the front flap of her purse, she slung the bag over her shoulder and tossed the card on the table. "Lila's at the Stand all day today. She said if you're interested, give her a call."

With a smile, a hug and a quick goodbye, she

was out the door before she made any other stupid mistakes.

Like telling Chloe that seeing Brett again had gotten to her just like her sister-in-law had feared it would. Which was why she hadn't mentioned the meeting at all.

She was tired.

Out of sorts.

Damn Brett.

BRETT CANCELED HIS golf game Saturday morning. He wasn't a huge fan of the sport, but preferred the course to boardrooms when the same business could be accomplished either place.

Instead, he pulled on jeans, a long-sleeved denim shirt, and got his Harley out of the garage. He didn't ride much anymore. But he always kept the thing serviced. There were just some times a guy had to be a guy.

This was one of them.

The three-and-a-half-hour trip to Palm Desert was a godsend. Even with the damned helmet clamped to his head. He was wired for sound and played old Eagles tunes as he sped across the desert. The rumble of the machine between his thighs was like a shot of pure adrenaline. It was the first long ride he'd taken since the divorce.

Clearly time to rectify that lapse.

He didn't call first. Wasn't sure why; he just didn't. Still, Jeff was at home, mowing the grass, when Brett roared up the quiet street where his best friend's five-bedroom house stood on more than an acre of crisply manicured lawn.

"Brett? By God, man, what the hell are you doing here?" Hopping off his zero-turn mower, Jeff jaunted toward Brett, his hand extended.

They shook hands, and then, still gripping Brett's hand, Jeff pulled him in for a hug. "It's good to see you," he said. "Man, you look great!"

"So do you." Feeling a bit choked up, when he rarely felt any emotion at all, Brett stepped back. But he couldn't do anything about the grin that was spreading across his face. "It's been too long, man," he said.

Jeff might be married to a great cook, but he was still in shape.

"I can't believe you're here!" Jeff was grinning, too. Giving Brett the up and down. "And on your bike. I figured you sold that. Ella said you offered it to her in the divorce."

Because he'd offered her everything.

She'd refused to take any of it. His money. His help. His prized possessions.

"Nope."

"You still ride much?" Jeff was circling the bike now. They'd taken a few trips together. A long time ago.

"No, but I'm thinking about changing that. You got a bike?"

Jeff sold his bike when Cody was born. He'd

put the money toward a backyard pool and hot tub and insisted on showing Brett that and then the rest of the house he'd bought when he'd made his first big stock deal, telling Brett that Chloe and Cody were gone that afternoon.

Pulling a couple beers from the fridge, he handed one to Brett and led the way back outside, to the table and chairs on the paver patio by a built-in fireplace and rock water feature.

The things, the beauty of Jeff's home, weren't anything Brett couldn't have himself. The swing set, playhouse and sandbox—all made with matching wood—caught his attention. He didn't realize he was staring until Jeff said, "Cody and Chloe…they aren't just gone for the afternoon."

Brett had already decided how he was going to play this. At least until he knew more. "I know," he said, meeting his friend's gaze head-on. "I ran into Ella in town. You knew she moved to Santa Raquel, right?"

"To take that job, yes, I did, and I can't tell you how sorry I am, Brett. The way she just moved right in on you. I swear, I didn't even know about it until she was already moving in to her place. I'd have advised her against accepting the position if I'd known in time."

Brett would have found it odd that Ella hadn't asked Jeff's opinion if it wasn't for what he already knew about Ella's decision-making process regarding her move.

"Anyway, she told me that you'd called and told her that Chloe had left. She asked me to look in on you, Jeff. She's worried about you."

"She's called a couple times since then. I didn't pick up. She and Chloe…they're close…and I don't want to put her in the middle of this."

Brett couldn't tell if Jeff had any idea where Chloe was or not. But he'd get back to that.

"So what is…*this*? Why'd she leave you, man? Chloe's nuts about you." Or she had been the last time Brett had seen them together. Which would have been before the divorce. More than four years ago. Only a couple years after Jeff and Chloe had married.

Jeff waved a hand in the air, shaking his head. "We can talk about my problems later. For now, tell me why you're here. I mean, I thought you weren't coming around anymore because of Ella, but you say you ran into her. Dare I hope that this visit means what I think it means?"

Brett's foot fell off his knee with a thud. He'd been so fired up to help his friend, coming up with the words he'd say to protect Ella's secret, while proving to her that she was wrong about Jeff, that he'd missed the other side of this story.

"You and Ella getting back together?" Jeff asked, lifting his beer can in a toast before sipping. How a guy could drink through a grin plastered from one side of his face to the other, Brett didn't know, but Jeff managed it.

"No!" Brett's response was emphatic. Strong. Because it had to be. "No way, man. Don't even go there. She just asked me to look in on you. She's worried. Like I said."

Jeff nodded. Still grinning. "Well, whatever, I'm sure as hell glad you're here. I've missed you, man."

Brett had missed Jeff, too. Far more than he'd allowed himself to realize.

So when Jeff asked if he could stick around, grill some steaks, maybe shoot some pool later, offering him the bed in the guest room, Brett agreed to stay.

Not for Ella. Or Chloe.

But because, for the first time in years, he felt as if he'd come home.

CHAPTER SEVEN

ELLA WAITED ALL day to hear from Brett.

He didn't call, text or email.

On her way home from work, she drove by his house. If she saw his black BMW in the driveway, or saw him outside, she might stop. If it felt right.

There were no vehicles in his driveway. And no one in his yard, either. The shades were drawn. Used to be something he did only when he was going to be gone until after dark. And then there would be lights programmed to turn on before he got home.

It wasn't that he was afraid of the dark. No, that would be more like her.

Brett just hadn't liked walking into gloom.

Most particularly not in his home.

Funny, the things you remembered.

He'd said, when she'd left him in the parking lot the night before, that he was going to be home all weekend. She'd been left with the impression that speaking with Jeff was going to be his first priority. He'd said something about wanting to make contact before going back to work on Monday. He had a crazy week coming up.

But then, when didn't he?

Brett had always worked harder than anyone she'd ever known.

He'd said he'd contact Jeff. So he would.

Now she would move on. There was no way she was going to let Brett linger in her mind during the two days off she had ahead of her. She and Chloe were going to shop, swim in the complex's heated pool, watch a movie they'd both missed in the theater and look at some houses. They were going to take Cody to the park, to get chicken nuggets and to pick out his first, toddler-approved learning computer.

All without any thoughts of Brett Ackerman.

IT HAD BEEN a long time since Brett had shot pool. Since before he'd married Ella. Jeff cleared the table on him the first game.

But by the third, Brett was holding his own again. They were playing best of ten for the fifty-dollar bill sitting on one corner of the table. Eight ball. His call on the game. Next ten would be Jeff's preference.

Taking a sip of beer from one of the two bottles sitting open on the bar, Brett assessed the fourteen balls remaining on the table.

"So what's with Chloe?" he asked, bending to take a shot that, if properly executed, would leave his cue ball perfectly positioned to put the twelve ball in the corner pocket.

He made the shot. Exactly as planned. And was

rounding the table to get set for the next hit as Jeff said, "I pray to God it's just more of the postpartum depression she went through after Cody was born."

He shot. Well. Then, cue stick suspended, he glanced over at his friend. "I didn't know Chloe suffered from depression. Is she on medication?"

"Not anymore. And she was only depressed after Cody was born. The doctor said it just happens sometimes, part of the hormonal changes after a woman gives birth."

"So, like, what did she do? Cry all the time?" It was important that he knew the facts. Proper assessments relied on them. And he was there to help.

"That, yeah, but for the first week or two she wouldn't even hold the baby. She said he didn't like her. That if she touched him, she'd make him cry."

Brett listened as Jeff talked about the debilitating, though generally temporary, after-effect of birth that wasn't commonly spoken about. At least not enough that he'd personally known of anyone who'd experienced it.

Had Ella struggled that way? Could it happen if the woman didn't carry a baby full term?

Resting the bottom of his stick on the ground, he used it as a hand rest. "So you think, maybe, this…time away…is some sort of the same thing, except you're the one she can't make happy?"

Leaning back against one of the half dozen or so tan leather bar stools situated around the room, Jeff shook his head. But continued to meet Brett's gaze head-on. "I don't know, man." His chin jutted. Trembled. "I truly don't know. I've gone over every second, every hour, every day in my head. Again and again. Was there something I forgot? Not a birthday or anything major like that, for sure, but maybe some little remembrance, like the anniversary of our first kiss or something? Something I said that she took wrong? Something she found in my pocket that she might have misinterpreted…"

Senses honed even more than normal, Brett said, "Did you give her cause to misinterpret something?"

"Hell, no! Wait." Jeff crossed his arms, trapping his pool cue against his body. "Are you asking me if I've been unfaithful to my wife?"

"You wouldn't be the first guy…"

"No!" Taking hold of his cue stick, he stood. "I don't even flirt with other women, just to make certain I don't find myself in something I don't mean to be in. I love my wife, Brett. I thought you of all people knew that."

"I do." Feeling a tug on emotions that were better off staying dormant, Brett stood toe-to-toe with his friend. "I do, Jeff. I'm just asking because the last I knew, Chloe felt the same way about you. You two…you're that couple that makes it till you're ninety and then dies within a day of each other because one can't live without the other."

Jeff's chin dropped to his chest. And then he stood straight. "I have to believe she still feels the same way," Jeff said. "That's what keeps me going."

He thought about what he wanted to ask. Speaking slowly as he chose his words carefully. "Have…you… Do you…have any reason…to think… Could there be…someone else? For her?"

Shaking his head, Jeff headed to his beer waiting on the bar. Helped himself to a big swig. And Brett, tense and feeling a little angry, missed his next shot.

"I'm going to be honest," Jeff said, remaining by the bar, in spite of the fact that it was his turn. "Not that she ever gave me reason to doubt her, but after she left I went through everything. Searched her computer, her drawers. Her social-media accounts. I felt like a damned creep, but I just had to know, you know?"

"And?"

"Nothing. My wife is as sweet and loyal and honest as we both know her to be. Hell, she hadn't even made a purchase she hadn't told me about."

"So why up and leave? You having financial problems? Something that just overwhelmed her?"

"Stocks are up and down. You know the business. But no. Our personal portfolio has enough safe investments to keep us secure."

"What about work? Anything life-altering happening there?"

"Like, are any of the traders into something they shouldn't be, you mean?"

It happened far more than Brett would have figured before he'd gotten into the watchdog business. "Something like that."

"We're clean," he said. "We run audits with an independent company, just to make sure."

One by one, Jeff was shooting holes in the theories Brett had come up with to explain Chloe's leaving her husband and moving in with Ella.

And not telling Jeff where she was.

"Where is she, by the way?" he asked now, justifying the duplicity implicit in asking a question to which he knew the answer with the idea that all he wanted was to help Jeff.

Jeff took a shot. And then another. He sank four balls in a row, leaving only Brett's striped balls on the table, and motioned to a side pocket as his call for the eight ball.

He sank that, too. Leaned his pool cue against the table, pulled the rack off its hook on the wall, reached under the table for the balls and began placing them inside.

When the fully racked balls were ready for Jeff to break for the next game, he faced Brett.

"I don't know where she is."

Brett could not doubt the sincerity of the response.

And knew an odd second of relief that Ella's secret was safe.

Because he was still protective of his ex-wife? And because the secret meant a lot to her?

Ella—and her secrets—were no longer in his control, or of his concern.

"She just up and left and didn't tell you where she was going?"

"Yes." Jeff, at six-two and two hundred pounds was a big man, but lean. Almost to the point of skinny. With his sandy-blond hair and freckles, his glasses, he looked like the stereotypical guy next door.

"What about her mother? Isn't Chloe's mother in Florida?"

"Yes, and Chloe said she isn't there and begged me not to call her mother and get her all upset. I've agreed not to look for her, and in exchange, she's agreed to answer her cell phone each and every time I call. Or, at the very least, call me right back. I need to know that she's safe."

Ella hadn't told him that Chloe and Jeff were in constant contact. Brett was glad to hear it.

"She hasn't told her mother she left you?"

"Nope." Pulling back, Jeff shoved his cue stick forward, making perfect contact with the cue ball, slamming it into the freshly racked triangle of balls, spreading them all over the table. Two fell. A solid and a stripe.

"I'll take the stripes," Jeff said, proceeding to sink another three balls.

Brett studied the solids. He was likely only going to get one shot at the game. Not that he cared about the fifty dollars balanced there to taunt them, but because he was a guy, and guys didn't like to lose. Not even to good friends.

Jeff missed a nearly impossible shot. Reached for his beer.

"I'd say it's a good sign, then." Brett stood, watching Jeff rather than the pool balls. "If she was looking to do anything permanent, she'd let people know."

"That's what I thought."

Jeff's expression relaxed.

And Brett cleared the table.

CHLOE WAS DUSTING the living room when Ella let herself into the apartment. Cody sat on the floor with a line of little cars around him, watching Nick Jr. reruns.

"El! El!" The little boy jumped up when he heard her, running over to hug her knees and then to grab her finger. "Sit," he said, pointing to his cars.

"In a minute, buddy," she told him. "Auntie El needs to get out of her work clothes, 'kay?"

He was already staring at the television again as he nodded his little blond head. The boy's constant need for technical stimulation bothered her, but raising Cody wasn't her business. Loving him was.

Chloe asked how her day was.

And didn't meet her gaze.

Motioning down the hall, Ella headed back to her bedroom and waited for Chloe to follow her. "Did you go to the Stand?" she asked.

Chloe nodded. And started to dust her dresser. Ella did her cleaning on her days off. Which started tomorrow. "Cody cried when I told him it was time to go. He didn't want to leave."

"But you didn't like it?" she asked, pulling her stained scrub top over her head and tossing it in the hamper in her en-suite bathroom.

Swinging around, Chloe met her gaze. "I loved it, El," she said. But the moisture in her eyes didn't seem to carry the same message. The woman turned back to the furniture.

"But?"

"No but. I have so many ideas, and Lila gave me a budget and told me I can have carte blanche. There are at least three cooks for every meal and other women who do all of the dishes. It's a dream opportunity. She even offered to put in for a small salary for me since I've never been a resident, but I don't need the money."

Ella was glad to see Chloe enthused. If Chloe

could make a life for herself here, the rest wouldn't be as difficult.

She just wished she'd quit dusting and tell her what was wrong.

"Did you have a problem with one of the residents?"

"No! They were wonderful." Chloe looked up again. "Everyone was so eager to help. Almost too eager."

"They've all been through a lot," Ella said, her pants following her top, and then her bra landed last. Pulling on a robe, she stepped out of her panties, too. "And everyone handles turmoil differently. Some are friendly and kind. Others lash out or withdraw…"

She'd done her homework.

"They were fine, El, really."

Chloe was on to the nightstand. Carefully lifting. Dusting. Returning things to their proper positions.

"So what's the problem?"

The smaller dresser got the rag. Then her rocker. And Ella stood there. Waiting.

Afraid Chloe might just dust her, too, she remained still as the other woman approached her. Stood eye to eye with her. "I'm one of them, aren't I?"

"You've been through some of the same things they have."

Chloe nodded. "The first step to recovery is

admittance," she said. Something they'd talked about before, but Chloe's tone was different. As if she had learned something new.

"This isn't just about my husband having trouble at work. I'm a victim of domestic violence."

The Lemonade Stand must have brought the truth of Chloe's situation more intensely into focus.

"You're preventing yourself from becoming more of a victim. And helping your husband before he does something neither of you will be able to recover from."

The high-risk statistics weren't drama. They were frighteningly real and fresh in her mind.

"Seeing myself there, like them, I panicked."

"Did you call Jeff?" It's what Chloe always did when she needed reassurance. Because Jeff always gave it to her.

Because she loved him with all her heart.

And because he was, at his core, a great man. A wonderful father and a loyal and loving husband.

"No." Chloe looked toward the living room, as Cody started to sing along with the television set. "And that kind of scared me, you know?" she said. "I didn't call him."

Hallelujah!

Chloe had just taken one more step on the road to health. And Jeff had more hope than ever of following in her footsteps. If Chloe stood her ground, he'd have to get help to get her back.

Telling her sister-in-law that they were going out to dinner to celebrate, anywhere she wanted, Ella turned on the water and stepped out of her robe.

A shower. Dinner. A good night's sleep; that was all she needed. Life was good.

CHAPTER EIGHT

BRETT DIDN'T DRINK any more than his two-beer limit. Instead, he watched his friend polish off most of a twelve-pack of beer. And still win a hundred bucks off him.

But you wouldn't know Jeff had overindulged the night before when Brett walked into the kitchen, thinking to make himself a cup of coffee just after dawn the next morning. He had a full day ahead of him in Santa Raquel, preparing for Monday morning's meetings, and the afternoon's, too, since he was going to be using his lunch hour to get the haircut he'd rescheduled the day before.

"Thought you'd like some breakfast before you hit the road," Jeff said, standing at the stove over a pan of eggs. "The coffee's fresh, dark roast," he said. Brett took coffee just about any way he could find it, but preferred it dark and strong. As his college roommate knew well.

In jeans and a polo shirt, Jeff looked ready for a good day. And Brett couldn't help but wonder how he'd fill the next fourteen or so hours. His lawn was immaculate. The house appeared clean—Jeff and Chloe probably hired a service—and the refrigerator had been stocked when Brett had helped himself to a bottle of water the night before.

"You got work to do today?" he asked as he poured a cup of coffee and pulled out a chair at the table in the window nook of the eat-in kitchen.

"This evening. I'm going to church later this morning and then to play nine holes of golf."

He didn't remember Jeff being a church-goer. But was glad to know that the hours ahead wouldn't be as empty for Jeff as his house felt.

Putting plates filled with eggs and bacon, potatoes and toast on the table, Jeff brought over his own coffee cup and sat.

"What about you? You got a game in for today?"

"Yeah. At noon." Yesterday's business rescheduled. The food was good. Done well. And the kitchen wasn't a disaster area, either.

Obviously Jeff wasn't new to cooking. Or picking up after himself. He'd been a bit of a slob in college. But then, Brett hadn't cared all that much if his own dirty shorts filled a corner of their room, either.

"So…church… What are you telling them about why you're there alone?" Not Brett's best syntax, but this was…odd. Him helping Jeff instead of the other way around.

"Chloe's helping a sick friend."

"Went to stay with her, you mean?"

Jeff glanced up. "It's church, man. I'm not going to lie to them. I just said she's helping a sick friend and left it at that. And she is. She's helping herself, and we are our own best friends, right?"

Brett would have felt better if Jeff had chuckled. Or been grinning. But genuine loneliness lurked in the other man's gaze. Almost as though he thought himself his only friend.

Driving over there had been the right move.

"So you really think this is a hormonal thing on her part?"

"I hope it is."

Both of them were eating as though they hadn't seen food in days.

"What does she tell you?"

"That we need help. She wanted to go to counseling. I told her I didn't think we needed it. I mean…our marriage…from what I hear at the office, Chloe and I are tighter than most. We have our ups and downs, but we're friends. We like each other, you know?"

"Maybe she needs the counseling and wanted you to go with her. Maybe if you say you'll go, she'll come home."

"Been there, done that. The day she left, I came home from work and she wasn't here. I called her. She told me she has to go away for a while. Just like that. Packed some bags, took our son and cleared out. I told her then, and several times since she left, that I'd go to counseling with her. She says maybe that would be good. In the future."

"Did she take much with her?"

"As much as when we went to the mountains for a month last summer."

"She intends to be gone for a while."

"God, I hope not."

"How long's it been?" Another question he knew the answer to. But one that might stand out in its absence if he didn't ask.

"A week and two days."

"Has she given any indication as to when she might return?"

"None." There was no anger, no bitterness in Jeff's tone. Only confusion. As if he was lost.

And still in love with the wife who'd left him.

Brett was hard-pressed not to get a little angry at Chloe himself. What was she thinking? Jeff was one of the good ones.

"Did you have a fight that morning? Or the night before?"

Finishing up his breakfast, Jeff gathered Brett's empty plate and carried their dishes to the sink. "Yeah. And I've apologized for it. Several times."

Turning, Brett studied his friend. "Apologized for what?"

"My bad temper," Jeff said. "She told me about something Cody did at the park that day, and I snapped at her. Told her I needed a few minutes of peace when I get home before she starts bombarding me with her crap." He turned from the sink. "I didn't mean it, Brett. She knows that. But I just keep hearing those words over and over. Wishing like hell I could take them back. To the point of choking myself on them. I'd had a call on the way home, a stock we'd all expected to go public didn't. I had several portfolios all set to move, had taken money from other markets, which meant a hell of a lot of scrambling, praying and luck or I was going to be calling some important clients with bad news."

There was no doubting Jeff's sincerity.

"That was all there was to the fight? Those words?"

"I wanted to take them back the second I said them. The look in her eye…you'd think I'd killed her puppy or something."

"And that was it?"

"That was it. She was standing in the doorway." He motioned to a door that led out to a hallway and into another branch of the rambling ranch home. "I pushed past her, went to our room and showered, and when I came back out she'd left a note telling me there were leftovers in the fridge and that she'd taken Cody out for ice cream. She brought some back for me, with my favorite mix-ins, and we watched television until bed.

"I told her I was sorry when I got in bed. Tried to kiss her good-night, and she just rolled over. The next day she was gone."

"What did you do when she rolled over?"

"Nothing. I lay there in the dark until I could tell she was asleep, and then I went to sleep. I figured, hell, she was in the bed with me, it couldn't be all that bad. I figured it would blow over by morning."

Brett was standing now, too. In the kitchen with his helmet under his arm.

"Couples fight," Jeff said. "It's not right. It's not okay. But it's…normal."

Nodding, Brett remembered a particular fight he'd had with Ella. He'd told her that he'd never wanted a child of his own. That he'd only agreed to try because of her. He'd rejected his own baby while it was still in her womb.

Because once that child had been a reality, it had hit him that he'd never be able to guarantee that he wasn't his father. Ella was a strong woman. She could get out if he ever developed violent tendencies. But a child…someone who was forever biologically bound to him…a vulnerable, needy human being who couldn't make that choice…

But this wasn't about him. This was about Jeff. A man who was the definition of gentle.

"You want me to call her?" he asked now. He was going to talk to Chloe. No matter what Jeff wanted.

His friends were in trouble.

And unlike Jeff, Brett knew exactly where Jeff's wife was staying.

"She always liked you," Jeff said now. "Would you mind talking to her? If that doesn't put you in a bad position with Ella. The two of them, they're more like sisters than sisters-in-law, you know."

"Ella's the one who asked me to see you, to get involved in this. I hardly think she'd object to me trying to see if I can help."

"Okay, then." Arms crossed, Jeff walked with him out the door. They looked over his bike. Talked again about a time or two they'd hit the open road. Talked about doing so again.

If Jeff ever got a hold of another bike.

And then Brett mounted his machine, determined, as he left his friend standing alone on his long, winding drive, surrounded by his meticulous yard and a home that spoke of success, that for as long as he was needed, Jeff was a priority.

For all that the other man had done for him, it was the least Brett could do.

ELLA'S TEXT NOTIFIER sounded while she was scrubbing her toilet, part of her Sunday-morning cleaning routine. Chloe, who already had the rest of the apartment looking spotless, had taken Cody to the playground a few units down from them. In addition to their shopping and movie plans, they were going to be trying out a couple recipes that evening. Chloe wanted her opinion on their mass likability and was planning to invite the single mother she'd met earlier in the week to join them for dinner.

Thinking the text was from work—her nurses

had been instructed to text her if they lost any patients when she was off shift—and dreading what she would read but knowing there was nothing for her to do about the heartbreaking news, she finished what she was doing before she looked at her phone.

The number wasn't work. It wasn't in her contacts. But she recognized it.

Damn him. How was she supposed to succeed in keeping him completely out of her day if he was going to text her like this?

Knowing she was being irrational, Ella opened the message she'd been waiting all day yesterday to see. The same two questions in her mind now that had occupied a good part of her Saturday. Had he contacted Jeff, and how had it gone?

Going to call Chloe today.

She'd asked him to speak with Jeff. Thinking he'd take care of her brother, while she dealt with Chloe.

Like maybe between the two of them, they could do this good thing. Save a man. A marriage. A life.

I'll talk to her.

Her fingers moved quickly across the small keyboard.

I have her number.

More speed texting.

I didn't tell her yet that I've been in touch with you.

He had to understand that Chloe was vulnerable at the moment. Ella was having a hard enough time keeping her sister-in-law emotionally strong without Brett coming at her.

Let me know when she knows.

She'd asked for his help. Needed his help.
Okay, she wanted his help. This was Chloe and Jeff they were dealing with. They'd been family. Close.
The happiest years of her life…

Will do.

She typed. And then she went to find Chloe.

CHAPTER NINE

"YOU'RE SURE ABOUT THIS?" Chloe, in pressed navy linen slacks and a white contoured three-quarter-sleeved blouse, smiled at her son in his car seat as Ella stopped at a red light and then continued, "You don't have to come with me, Ella. I can meet Brett on my own."

Even knowing Brett, she'd been surprised by the speed with which he'd arranged this in-person meeting with Chloe. She'd spoken with Chloe, texted him as agreed, and within an hour they'd had dinner plans with him.

They were on their way to Uncle Bob's. Chloe's choice. Because Cody liked sitting in his high chair and looking out the window at the beach. He also liked the chicken fingers and French fries, and the place was loaded with families with small children so that if there was an outburst, other diners' experiences wouldn't be immediately ruined.

"If you'd rather do this alone, I'm happy to drop you off. Or you can take me home and you take the car. I've told you repeatedly, you're welcome to the car anytime you want it. It's not like I need it when I'm at work."

They'd left Chloe's car in Palm Desert. Because

they'd been in a hurry to get her packed up and out of there before Jeff came home. And Chloe had been too upset to drive. The plan was to go back and get it.

In the meantime, Chloe was taking cabs or a bus anytime she had to go anywhere.

As soon as things calmed down and Jeff agreed to get help. Which was where Brett came in.

Chloe's silence drew Ella's gaze. "It's okay, Chlo. If you want to go alone, it's not going to hurt my feelings. I want to help in any way I can. Not take over your life."

The puppy-dog look in the brown eyes that turned on her softened Ella's heart and it was already mush where Chloe was concerned. The Chloe she knew had always emanated confidence. Strength.

"This is where it gets tough, you know?" Chloe said as a horn honked behind Ella and she drove on through the now-green light. "Am I selfish for wanting you with me? Knowing how hard you had to fight to get Brett out of your system? Knowing how much he hurt you? Or is this my chance to help you take the final step in getting over him? And do I help you help me by relying on you? Or am I being weak and dependent if I lean on you?"

Flashing her sister-in-law a grin, Ella said, "I think the fact that you're asking those questions means you're right on track."

"Then I want you with me."

The next time Ella glanced over, Chloe smiled at her.

They were going to be just fine, the two of them.

PREPARED FOR ELLA'S propensity to be early—based on their previous meeting, not on the years they'd spent together—Brett pulled into Uncle Bob's fifteen minutes before the scheduled time. Ella wouldn't have known that the place had been his favorite restaurant as a kid.

Because he hadn't told her.

He didn't spend much time thinking about the first ten or so years of his life. Because they only made the next eight years seem that much worse.

There were already kids digging around in the outdoor sandbox just off the dining room—a play area of sorts before such things became popular in modern-day fast-food restaurants.

Ella and Chloe weren't there yet. He was offered a table while he waited for them, but declined. He was standing outside when he saw her car pull into the lot.

He hadn't seen Chloe in more than four years.

And he was about to meet his godson for the first time. Jeff's son.

Ella's nephew. Who was two years younger than her own child would have been.

Standing there in tan pants, a dark polo shirt and loafers, Brett wasn't nervous. He was just ready to get on with it. He'd played nine holes of golf followed by a business cocktail and was ready to spend a few hours at his desk at home before he started a new work week.

Plus, he wanted to touch base with Jeff. Living alone didn't suit the other man as well as it did Brett.

The car parked. He walked toward it, intending to get the first awkward moment over with in the parking lot, rather than in front of curious restaurant staff and patrons.

The passenger door opened, and a woman got out. Dark-haired. Slender and long legged. She wrapped her arms around his neck and hung on.

Brett's arms went around her. He thought to disentangle himself. Felt her lips brush his neck, and then she stood back, tears glistening in her eyes. "It's good to see you again, Brett. Thank you for doing this."

Her words made him uncomfortable. Clearly, Ella had spoken to her. She probably thought he was helping Jeff come to terms with his perceived issues.

Problem was, Brett wasn't yet convinced that Chloe wasn't the one with issues. Even more so after her effusive display of affection.

Four years ago a hug and kiss greeting would have been somewhat normal, but…

His thoughts were cut short as he heard Ella say, "Cody, this is your uncle Brett…"

Turning, he saw his ex-wife standing there with a sandy-haired toddler, dressed in blue pants and a white shirt just like his mama, on her hip.

"Unca?" Cody, with both hands at his chest, turned to stare up at Ella.

"Uncle Brett," she said.

He wasn't. Not anymore. Technically, never had been, since the divorce happened before Cody was even conceived.

But he wasn't going to split hairs.

"Hey, young man," he said. He touched the boy's cheek. Ran his hand over the toddler's head. With those freckles, that hair, he looked like Jeff.

"Uh-uh. I boy." Cody shook his head. But he was gazing at Brett now with open curiosity.

"Uncle Brett knows Daddy," Chloe said. "They were friends in school."

Another curious stare and then Cody glanced between Ella and his mother. "Eat?"

And that was that.

Awkward moment over.

Brett had survived.

ELLA ENDED UP sitting next to Brett. She'd planned it differently. But Chloe chose the chair across from him, which made sense. And she suggested to the hostess that Cody's high chair be placed next to her—across from Ella—which also made sense since she'd want to tend to her son.

And Ella could still entertain him while the other two were talking.

Which put her next to Brett. Close enough that she had to inhale that delicious aftershave with every breath she took. So close she could feel the heat of his leg, the brush of his arm...

Too close to not react to him. Physically. And when that happened her mind got confused.

She heard Chloe order for them. A shared salad. She asked for iced tea. She put her napkin in her lap.

And tried to focus on her nephew.

The man at her side might have taken permanent residence in her heart, but she did not want him in her life.

Not anymore.

He couldn't give her what she needed. Didn't want the kind of relationship she wanted.

He'd hurt her too badly, and she'd never trust him not to do so again.

SUCCESS IN LIFE was all about the plan. Whatever the goal, it started with the plan.

Brett ordered a burger, his standard order as a kid, and tried not to stare at the little guy across the table—imagining Jeff with him, the gentleness with which his friend would explain exactly why he couldn't get down out of his high chair. And why he couldn't drink all of his milk before his dinner.

Chloe did a fine job in Jeff's absence.

But Cody's dad was missing out on key time in his son's life. Which gave Brett a sense of urgency he hadn't had that morning.

And he'd already been damned motivated.

"So…how's Jeff?" Chloe asked as soon as their food was delivered, and she had Cody settled with his chicken fingers, fries and ketchup.

"Good." The burger tasted just as good as he'd remembered. He hadn't expected it to.

"Of course, it's hard to tell over the phone," she said, fork in hand, though she had yet to take her first bite.

"I spent last night with him."

"Here?" Used to reading people, Brett was a bit disconcerted by the mixture of fear and delight in Chloe's expression. "Jeff's in town?"

"No. Ella told me that he doesn't know where you are. I wouldn't bring him here and risk the possibility of him seeing you."

Santa Raquel wasn't that small, but fate had a way of playing its own hand in spite of the cards you thought you held.

"You spent the night at our house?" Another mixture of emotions that complicated things. Or added weight to Jeff's assumption that his wife was suffering from some latent hormonal imbalance.

He was going to have to approach that possibility. As soon as he figured out how to do so without alienating either of the women.

"I did," he said, taking another bite of burger and chasing it with a fry. It wasn't peanut butter and bacon, but it was as good. "He took me for a hundred bucks at the pool table, we had a couple beers and we talked."

"What did he say about me?"

"That he misses you."

"That's all? Nothing else? Where did he say I was?" Without breaking her gaze from Brett, she reached over to scoot a chicken finger away from the edge of the table where Cody had left it.

"He told me the truth. That he doesn't know. And that he's respecting your wishes not to look for you, or alert anyone that you've left him."

"I haven't!"

A look passed between Chloe and Ella, and then Chloe said, "I'm not leaving Jeff for good. I love him. I just have to stay away until he can admit that he has a problem and gets some help. It's the only way I can help him. I've tried talking to him. I've accepted his apologies and tried to make his home exactly as he needs it to be, but it's not enough, Brett. As I'm sure you understand."

Because he'd grown up in an abusive environment, she meant. Or maybe she was referring to the fact that he'd founded a shelter for victims of domestic violence.

Which reminded him. "I heard that you're going to be helping them out at the Stand," he said. A great idea as far as he was concerned. Chloe had not only majored in home economics in college, but she was a culinary-arts-school graduate, as well.

Besides, Brett had tasted her cooking.

"Yeah." She took her first bite of salad. "I met Lila yesterday. She's a great find, Brett. You chose well."

The compliment rolled past him. He wasn't the one who'd conducted interviews. He'd just read reports. His one condition on founding the shelter, his one completely selfish mandate, was that he remain anonymous. He did not feel fit to be a spokesperson for the cause. Or in any way trained to help victims.

He didn't want their gratitude.

Because he didn't feel worthy of it.

He had his strengths. The things he was good at. And those were the things to which he dedicated his life.

"I'm just glad that you're willing to help out while you're here," he said. "They're very lucky to have you." And Chloe knew, as did Ella, that no one at the Stand knew that Brett was their benefactor.

He'd had a text that morning, informing him of the personnel addition. His mother kept herself fully abreast of every aspect of her responsibilities where he was concerned. And kept him well informed.

He couldn't fault her for that.

Or for much else, either, truth be told. Through years of nursing her terminally ill daughter, while also bearing her husband's mood swings, the drinking, the lost income and then the beatings, the woman had endured far more than any human being should ever have to.

If he got frustrated with her silence, that was on him.

Cody started talking about the sandbox again, and Ella, who'd only eaten a quarter of her meal, offered to take him outside to play for a few minutes.

The air felt chilled as she left his side, but Brett was glad for her to go. He'd been so busy trying to keep himself immune to her that her presence was interfering with his ability to form a plan.

Chloe put down her fork the second her son was out of earshot. "Did you talk to Jeff about…his issue?" Her long, dark hair fell over her shoulder as she leaned toward him, and she pushed it back.

"I asked him what he thought the issue was." Brett wasn't going to lie. But aside from that, he'd do what it took to make this right.

"And? Did he admit to getting angry?"

"He told me that he's said some things that he

regrets. He takes full accountability for coming home tensed up from work and taking it out on you."

"He said that?" Her eyes opened wide. "Or did you put the words in his mouth?"

"I didn't know them to put them there. He just told me what happened the night before you left. Alluded to the fact that it wasn't the first time he'd brought his work home with him in a negative way."

But who didn't have a bad mood now and then? When people lived together there were bound to be times when one or the other was irritable. Short-tempered. Angry. None of that added up to abuse. Not even close.

"He told you about me standing in the doorway and him pushing through it?"

"Yes."

Tears still glistening through the hope he read in her gaze, Chloe sat there watching him. As though she was waiting for something.

It was time for his plan.

And he didn't have one.

CHAPTER TEN

NEVER IN A million years would Ella have seen herself waving goodbye to Chloe, who was driving off in her car, while she stood in the parking lot of Uncle Bob's with Brett. But here she was.

Never in a million years would she have expected him to ask her to stay behind for a few minutes, or to offer to take her home afterward. But he had.

The grin on Chloe's face made it only too obvious that her sister-in-law thought Brett's interest in Ella was personal.

Ella knew better.

"Take a walk?" He motioned to the sidewalk that bordered the beach, stretching for more than a mile in either direction.

The area wasn't deserted. The beach, the sidewalk, weren't teeming with tourists the way they might have been on a hot summer Sunday night, but many locals, dressed in pants and shirts, some with sweaters on instead of swimsuits and shorts, populated the area.

"Sure," she said, glad that she'd worn flat sandals with her jeans. It wasn't like old times, she reminded herself. While she and Brett had walked along the beach every single time they'd come to town, they'd never been on this particular stretch of sidewalk together.

And they weren't holding hands.

"It was a great idea, having Chloe work at the Stand," he said as they started out, side by side, with enough space between them that there was no chance of brushing hands.

"It's a two-way street, you know? She helps them, and they help her. I'm hoping that she'll get help for her situation through the residents as she works side by side with them."

She had no way of knowing whether or not Brett agreed with her. He didn't reply. In the old days, the good days, she'd have known exactly what he was thinking. Because he'd have told her. In the latter days of their marriage, the ones during which their relationship had started to fade right before her eyes, he might have nodded.

Today's response was completely expected. Normal. For present day.

But he'd asked for this time. This walk. Not talking wasn't fair to her.

"So what's up?" she asked when, in the past, she'd have remained silent in an effort to give him whatever it was he needed.

"The plan."

"What plan?" She knew the ocean was there, off to her left. Was aware that there were people around them. But Brett, his steps, his breathing, his scent, was her only focus.

Just like always.

"You asked for my help."

"I know. And I'm incredibly grateful that you're being so good about it. Thank you, Brett. I was... nervous about asking you..."

"Nervous? Why?"

She shrugged, instantly uncomfortable. A simple thank-you. That was all that had been called for. It hadn't been meant to turn personal.

But she wasn't going to subjugate herself to his needs anymore. They weren't a couple, and she had no reason to hide.

"I was afraid you'd be angry."

"Angry at you? For asking for my help?"

His surprise astounded her. "Pretty much everything I did in the last months of our marriage pissed you off," she reminded him with a half chuckle. They said that when you got to the point that you could laugh about things, they no longer had the power to hurt you.

They were wrong.

"You almost never pissed me off, Ella." His tone was stern. As though if he spoke firmly enough, he could make what he said true.

His memory was skewed, but correcting him wasn't worth dredging up old pains.

"I was tense with you, I know that. But it wasn't because of anything you did. It was all me. I should never have let myself believe that I could live a normal life as though my childhood hadn't happened."

She felt the blood drain from her face. Afraid.

"Why?" she asked, understanding neither his sudden openness, nor her fear.

"Because I knew I couldn't be the husband you needed me to be. The husband you deserved. And then, when the baby was there, a part of you, but coming from me…I realized what I was doing to him. Or risking doing to him…"

"Maybe you should have spent less time judging yourself and trusting me to be the judge of what I needed." She didn't mention the baby.

His rejection of their child, after all those years of trying, had been her breaking point.

"You deny that you were hurt by my…reticence?"

She supposed, if they were going to work together to help Jeff and Chloe, they had to do this. Now that enough time had passed and they could discuss things rationally. Without letting emotion get in the way. Because the heat between them was long gone.

"I don't deny that."

They walked. Passed people along the way. She couldn't have identified a single one of them.

"You needed something from me emotionally that I don't have in me to give."

"You had it when we met in college. And during

the first few years of our marriage. Through all of the disappointments…"

Those first few times they'd tried to get pregnant and hadn't been able to.

"I was a kid. I grew up."

"You walled yourself off." She'd thought, at first, that it had been his way of dealing with the constant disappointment. She'd had to steel herself from the worst of the pain, too, in order to be able to try again. It wasn't until later, when she'd found out she was finally going to have a baby, that she'd realized how far apart they'd grown. When she realized they hadn't really talked in far too long.

In some ways, he'd become someone she didn't know at all.

Darkness wasn't far off. She should be chilled. And wasn't.

"I am a man who knows his limitations. Who accepts them and is accountable to them. I'm only sorry that I realized it too late. I should never have married you."

If there'd been any emotion in his voice, any sign that he missed what they'd had in the beginning, she might have found more to say.

And she might have been a fool and started to hope that they could have something together again. Because the only limitations Brett had were the ones he put on himself. She'd lived with him long enough to know that.

And since she was never again going to go

through the painful fertility treatments only to have a better-than-average chance of losing her baby, he wouldn't have to worry about being a father.

But there was no emotion because Brett was Brett. He was the man his life had shaped him into being. Reticent. Closed off. Capable of seeing a divorce lawyer before he'd even told his pregnant wife he wanted time apart.

Capable of looking her in the eye and telling her he didn't want anything to do with the child they'd taken years to conceive…

She no longer loved him. The road she was traveling down led nowhere…

Still, just because she was over him didn't mean that it wouldn't be nice to know that he had regrets. That she'd meant as much to him as she'd thought she had. Once.

"If we're going to help with Jeff and Chloe, we need a plan." His voice, the practicality of his words, put an end to her wayward thoughts.

"Okay." Plans were good. Solid. But how did you make one when people's lives and hearts were at stake? How did you plan to get someone out of denial?

Other than change his life so drastically he'd have no choice but to acknowledge he needed help?

Which was what they'd already done. The drastic life change—Chloe living with her—was in effect.

And from what she'd gleaned during the little bit she'd heard between Chloe and Brett when she'd returned from the sandbox with Cody, Jeff was still firmly in denial.

He'd admitted to the fights. Admitted that he'd started them. Because of tension from work. But he had no real idea why Chloe had left.

"A good plan starts with a goal, and I need to make certain that we're on the same page here before we go on."

That was why he'd wanted her to stay back and talk to him? She was relieved.

And disappointed, too.

Which only went to prove that hope died last.

"Am I to understand that your goal, like mine, is to see Chloe and Jeff back together in a healthy relationship?"

He sounded like a counselor in a classroom.

"Yes. Definitely. They love each other. I'll do anything I can to help them save their marriage. But my primary goal, first and foremost, is to see that both of them get and/or stay healthy."

"Agreed."

So…good. They shared a common goal. There was something in that.

"Do you know if Chloe's had a checkup lately?" he asked.

"Medical, you mean?"

"Yes."

She frowned. Glanced over at him for the first

time since they'd set out, but couldn't make out his expression in the darkening evening. She'd already told him there was no documentation of Jeff's abuse.

"Why?"

Jeff had admitted that the fights were his fault. They were just one step away from him admitting to the escalating physical violence that was accompanying those fights.

Before it was too late and he did something that would require outside attention. Medical, as well as legal.

"I just wondered about her overall...stability."

"It's not great, based on everything that's going on, but Chloe's not the one we need to worry about. She's in a position to get help. It's Jeff who scares me. It's like, over the years, he's stretched himself so tightly that now, when something pulls on him, he breaks. And then as soon as it's over, he goes back to his old self again. And hates himself for breaking."

"This is based on what Chloe's told you."

"Yes." And the bruises she'd seen the day after the last fight when she'd taken her sister-in-law's phone call and hightailed it to Palm Desert to get her and Cody out of there.

"You've never witnessed this...change in him."

"No."

Ella wished she had. She might know better

how to help her brother if she could see him in action.

They walked in silence for a minute or two.

"You didn't answer my question regarding her medical care."

"Why? Did Jeff say something about her being unstable?"

"Just that she suffered some depression after Cody was born."

"Postpartum. Yeah, she did. She took medication for about six weeks and has been fine ever since. Why? What does that have to do with anything? Is Jeff putting this on Chloe? Saying she's depressed?"

"He's looking for explanations," Brett said.

"And you? Do you believe him? Is this why you wanted to see Chloe? To judge for yourself if she's emotionally stable? In one dinner?"

"I'm not taking sides here, El. I just want a full picture so that I can be of assistance. Come up with a clear plan."

Of course. She'd forgotten who she was talking to. The modern Brett, not the emotionally vulnerable man she'd fallen head over heels in love with the day she'd met him. The robot, not the man.

"Chloe gets regular medical care. I know this because she'd had an appointment the week before she came here to get her birth-control prescription renewed. On top of that, I'm an RN. I live with her. I'd notice if there was anything amiss."

"It's getting late. We'd better turn around."

They'd come about half a mile, and darkness had fallen. The sidewalk, however, was lighter than it had been due to the old-fashioned lamp poles that lined it. They turned on automatically at seven o'clock every night, and they'd just come on, bathing them in a kind of boardwalk glow.

Ella didn't argue, though. She and Chloe had a movie to watch. And another day off tomorrow to fill with fun things.

"Our goal, then, is to see Jeff and Chloe in a happy marriage again."

She wanted to shake him up. To see if he was shakable. But she avoided the temptation. Jeff respected Brett. He'd listen to him.

He was the only person she believed could reach her brother, help him see the truth before it was too late.

Because Chloe was going to go back.

Ella didn't kid herself on that one. She was married to Jeff for better or worse. In sickness and in health. She adored the man.

She needed him.

Ella just prayed, every day, that she could keep her sister-in-law in Santa Raquel long enough for her brother to get healthy.

"Yes," she said. Yes, their goal was to see her brother and his wife in a happy, healthy marriage.

"Obviously I'm the Jeff part of the plan, and you are the Chloe side. Seeing that Jeff won't put you in the middle, and he and I are good. And Chloe's staying with you."

"Which Jeff doesn't know." She couldn't have Brett going all solitary man on her and disrespecting Chloe's choices.

"I'm not going to tell him, Ella. Not without discussing it with you and Chloe first."

She relaxed. One thing anyone could count on with Brett Ackerman was that he kept his word. The value of the Ackerman watermark on any nonprofit organization spoke to the power of Brett's word.

He was a good man to the core.

Remembering that was okay.

"I intend to keep in close contact with Jeff."

To "work" on him, of course. Ella read between the lines of what Brett was saying, because with the Brett of today, that was the only way to understand his true meaning.

"I think it's also important that you and I stay in regular contact," he said.

"I agree." Her answer was instantaneous.

"I also think it would be good if the four of us, you and me and Cody and Chloe, met up another time or two. I stand to gain more with Jeff if I can tell him I know for certain that Chloe is fine, and I can only do that if I know firsthand that what I say is true."

"How do we tell him that, let him know that

you've seen her, without him figuring out where she is?"

"She has friends in LA. I'm there on business every week. I travel frequently. For all he knows, I saw her in Palm Desert over the weekend. I could arrange to meet up with her anywhere."

"What if he asks you where she is?"

"He won't. Just like he's not asking her. He's respecting her wishes. Again, this is your brother we're talking about. You know him."

He'd shoved his wife into a doorjamb so hard it left a bruise all the way down her back. "And if he does ask?"

"I'll tell him the truth. That I agreed not to share that information."

Brett had an answer for everything.

She would do well to remember that.

CHAPTER ELEVEN

BRETT HAD ONE more stop to make before he went home for the night. He called Jeff on his way. Assured himself that Jeff was fine, for now. Jeff had had a good day out on the course and was buzzing about some stock that had just taken a larger upswing than he'd predicted, meaning that he was going to have a busy but good week. He was at his computer, working already, when Brett called.

The conversation was brief. But healthy. Work was the panacea. Brett knew that firsthand. And felt confident that his friend would be perfectly capable of giving his wife some more time to figure out what was going on with her life.

He was at his mother's gated community moments later, used his access card to get in through the security gate and made quick work of checking over her place, reading the note she'd left for him—telling him that she didn't need anything.

To satisfy himself, he opened the cupboard under the sink. Her trash was all emptied—she wouldn't even leave him some garbage to dump—and she had a fresh case of water in the refrigerator. Couldn't leave it for him to carry in from the garage. Not that she wasn't perfectly capable of lifting a case of water, but it would be nice to be able to do something for her.

He checked the water-softener salt. The level was good.

Scribbling a note to her, telling her he loved her—as he did every single week—he was back out again.

She wouldn't come home if his car was out front, and he didn't want to risk finding out what would happen if he broke their agreement to always park out front when he visited so she'd know he was there.

He'd been tempted, though. He'd actually parked his car on the next block and walked over once, with the intention of waiting inside to confront her, but had turned around and gone back without entering. Her home was a safe place. But it hadn't always been. His job, as someone who loved her, was to ensure that it remained a place where she felt safe.

Which meant that it was a place where she didn't have to worry about losing control and beating on her son's chest a second time.

Work kept him occupied until ten, at which time he stripped down and took a swim in the heated pool in his backyard. Then it was inside to shower.

That was the part he should have skipped. A little chlorine left on his skin, or in the bed, wouldn't have been as damaging as standing beneath the warm spray, his naked skin invigorated and chilled, basking in the purely physical pleasure until the sensation reminded him of other times. Other showers. Ones he hadn't taken alone.

A vision of Ella, her long legs naked and wet, came to mind. Waylaying his well-trained thoughts. Steering them off course.

It was as if he could still smell her from earlier that evening. Knew every nuance of her voice. Felt her heat beside him and heard the click of her sandals on the sidewalk. His penis grew, and he closed his eyes, trying to bring himself back under control.

He was going to help her. Help Jeff. He really had no other choice. Ella believed Chloe. Because Chloe was the only one talking to her. Jeff didn't want to put her in the middle.

Brett had talked to Chloe and to Jeff. He had both sides.

And he believed Jeff. He also agreed with Ella's assessment that Chloe could probably benefit from time spent at The Lemonade Stand. The counselors there were superb. And since they all ate, it stood to reason that they'd all run into Chloe some time or other.

The immediate plan was to help keep Jeff patient any way he could. To give Chloe time to figure out her emotions.

The success of the plan hinged on three things. He had to help.

He was going to do so without hurting Ella any more.

And the only way to do that was to make damned certain that they didn't let this get at all personal.

NORA WAS AT the hospital shortly after Ella arrived on Tuesday. They'd found a bus route that she could take from outside the Stand straight to the hospital, and she'd been doing so every day since.

The young woman looked rested. She smiled. And if baby Henry remained stable, he'd be released to her care early that week.

There was already a crib waiting for him in Nora's room at The Lemonade Stand.

Ella made a note on the chart she was keeping on Nora and Henry for her report to the High Risk team when she attended their first meeting on Wednesday. She was keeping a chart on another patient, as well. A twelve-year-old boy had come in over the weekend with what appeared to be a cigarette burn on his arm. He said that he'd been playing at the family bonfire and sent up some ashes, one of which landed on his skin. The doctor on call had been certain the burn came from something pressed against the skin and held there.

Mom and Dad had both been present at the hospital. Police were notified. There'd been a previous domestic disturbance call to the home the year before. Called in by a neighbor.

In separate interviews, both parents verified the boy's story.

A ten-year-old sister did, as well.

There was nothing anyone could do but keep a watch on the family. Ella's report to the team would ensure that elementary school and junior high counselors and a social services staff member would keep both kids on their radar. Officers from the Santa Raquel Police Department would make well checks in the neighborhood.

Notes had been made to the boy's hospital chart, a flag added to the family's address, so that if anyone came in again, the doctor on call would be alerted to the situation.

When Ella looked at the domestic-violence statistics she'd been given, she was overwhelmed by the size of the demon they were fighting, but on Wednesday afternoon, as she sat at a conference table at the local police precinct, looking around at the other people who sat there—different races and levels of education, different genders and ages—with one common desire to eradicate the disease of domestic destruction, she knew that they'd win. Have an impact, at least.

Having traded her scrubs for black dress pants and a white blouse, she tried to blend in as she sat quietly and took notes. When she was called on, she made her report. And throughout the meeting wrote down three names she'd been given—one from child services, and two from Officer

Sanchez—to check against hospital charts for recent injuries.

At the table she finally had the opportunity to meet Sara Havens, a counselor at The Lemonade Stand and the Stand's representative on the team.

With her shoulder-length dark blond hair and blue eyes, Sara looked like a stereotypical California beach beauty with nothing more on her mind than getting the perfect tan. Until she was asked to give an overview of the team's core approach, as well as a profile of their victims, as a reminder for the seasoned members and to educate the newcomers. There were two other new members in addition to Ella.

Soft-spoken and unassuming, Sara captured Ella's full attention and respect as soon as she opened her mouth.

"You can't just tell people what they have to do and expect them to do it," she told the table at large. "We're dealing with individuals who feel pushed into a corner—a lot of them literally as well as figuratively. So while, yes, we're fighting a dragon and have to be willing to use every effort to slay it, we have to tread softly. To approach with an outstretched hand, not a raised fist. If we threaten, we risk doing more harm than good. We're trying to prevent crime here. In most cases, the next choice isn't ours—it's theirs. We're just here to try to shape that choice."

She had more to say. Then, and later in the meeting, as well. Every person around the table had a chance to speak. To give a report or a simple introduction if there was no report to give.

Sara reported on a case she and her fiancé, a bounty hunter, had just worked on with the team. The victim was at The Lemonade Stand; all warrants against her had been expunged. The gunshot wound she had incurred from her husband was healing, and her parents had temporary custody of her infant son until she and child services— Sara gave a nod to Lacey Hamilton, the team's child services representative—determined that she was mentally and emotionally well enough to give him a stable home.

Ella added baby Toby and his mother, Nicole Harris, the victim Sara had just mentioned, to her watch list. Just in case.

The meeting ended shortly afterward. Feeling overwhelmed, awed and ready to do her part, she put her folder in her bag, slung her satchel over her shoulder and was on her way out the door when she felt a tap on her other shoulder.

Sara Havens stood there, a welcoming light in her eye. "I'm Sara. Lila told me to make sure we meet."

"I've been looking forward to meeting you," Ella told the counselor in return. "I've heard a lot about you."

"You'll need to meet Lynn Bishop, too. She's our resident nurse and chief medical officer. Lila told her about you at our last staff meeting."

Ella had heard about Lynn—she and her husband lived at the Stand along with his brother and sister-in-law, who were both mentally challenged. The number of people she knew in town—and wanted to know—was growing.

In a very short time, Santa Raquel was becoming home.

Sara told Ella about a couple other staff members as they walked together out of the police station to their cars. As Ella said goodbye and turned toward her own vehicle, Sara touched her arm again.

"Can we chat a minute?" She motioned toward a bench on the edge of the sidewalk.

Curious, Ella followed her. Clearly Sara had a favor to ask. Ella hoped it was one she could grant.

"It's about your sister-in-law," Sara said as soon as they were seated. "She's not my client, and I haven't spoken with her, but Lila told me about her situation and asked that I keep an eye on her for you."

Ella hadn't known. But… "I can't thank you enough for that," she told Sara. "She's so vulnerable right now, and I'm holding my breath every day that she doesn't go back to Jeff before he gets help. He's never hit her, so she doesn't think she's as at-risk as the other women were…"

"I understand that he bruised her pretty badly, though."

A vision of Chloe's injuries two weeks ago sprang to mind. "Yes." Ella swallowed, looked away and then back. "My brother's not the stereotypical abuser," she said. "He's so easygoing…I can hardly remember him ever being angry when we were growing up. I don't know what's gotten into him…"

Sara said nothing as Ella paused. But her gaze showed that she was completely focused on Ella and Chloe's situation. "I think that's part of what makes it so hard for Chloe. Jeff's normal demeanor…he's like that dog that lets you hang off his ear. He's gentle. Soft-spoken. Kind."

Sara was nodding, and Ella stopped, worried that she wasn't painting an accurate picture, that she was protesting too much, or not enough.

"It's easier to wall your heart off to a mean person" was all Sara said. "Or one who has a hair trigger and keeps you constantly alert to potential danger."

The sun was setting in the late-afternoon sky, practically blinding Ella if she glanced to her left. Feeling her eyes grow moist, she looked away from its brilliance.

"My ex-husband…he was a victim of domestic violence," Ella heard herself saying, though this wasn't about her. They were talking about Chloe.

About helping Chloe…

But she continued, anyway. "He described his home as a minefield. He said he never knew—whether he was getting up in the middle of the night to go to the bathroom, or coming down to dinner when he was called—if he'd tip off an explosion."

"Was it his mother or his father?"

People came and went several yards away from them. One or two at a time.

"His father. The way he tells it, for the first ten years of his life, his dad was a great guy. The best. But then they found out his sister had leukemia, and his dad lost his job. I don't know which came first, the drinking or the beatings, but they both came. And for the next eight years, my ex was on alert every day, setting himself up as his mother's protector. He intervened whenever he could. And bore the brunt of his father's outbursts when his mother wasn't around."

Ella stopped short of giving Brett's name. And then wished she hadn't mentioned him at all. His anonymity at The Lemonade Stand had been the one sticking point for him. He'd been unwilling to compromise on that. Period. He'd felt, erroneously in Ella's opinion, that if people knew the founder was a victim, they'd be less likely to take The Lemonade Stand seriously. He'd also once told her that he couldn't stand the idea of being scrutinized as a victim everywhere he went. But that had been long ago.

And Ella had been protecting his secrets for so long…

"In cases like that, fear, either of retribution or of an inability to make it alone, is often what keeps someone there. And while it's a horrible, criminal situation, it's also sometimes easier to treat. Assuming you can get the victim safely away."

Which was the purpose of their team.

Sara waited, as though allowing Ella time to continue. She'd already said too much.

"Cases like Chloe's, in some ways, can be a lot tougher to help," Sara continued after many seconds of silence had passed. "The bond of trust between your brother and his wife is still intact. Her sense of safety, while somewhat breached, has not been broken."

Two sentences, and Ella's perspective crystallized in a way she could grasp. Work with. "She's not afraid of him."

"She hasn't built walls against him. More likely, at this stage, she's trying to understand, to empathize, in an effort to be able to help him herself."

"She makes excuses for him."

"That's her way of trying to make sense out of something she doesn't understand. She's trying to find a way to justify actions that are out of character without accepting that maybe the man she fell in love with has changed."

"Is that what you think? That the Jeff we all know and love has suddenly become a monster?" She blurted out the words without stopping to consider how she sounded.

"No." Sara's quick covering of Ella's hand brought her back to the current situation. They were there to help Chloe.

"I'm only saying that Chloe is probably too confused to be able to act rationally at the moment. Her head tells her one thing while her heart is telling her another."

"I do agree with that." Which was why Ella was living second to second, always worrying that she'd get a call at work telling her that Chloe was on a bus back to Palm Desert.

"Good, because you need to understand her struggle to be able to deal well with what else I have to tell you."

Her chin fell. "What?" Was Chloe gone already? Was that why Sara asked for this chat? Had Chloe said something at lunch that day? Or not shown up at the Stand at all?

"Our residents' cell phones are taken away when they arrive at the Stand," she said. "They're kept at the local precinct…"

Just in case, Ella surmised, based on what she'd read, but also on what she'd heard that day. The police would need to be able to listen to messages. And wouldn't want them traced to the Stand, either.

"Every resident is given the option of having a prepaid cell while she's with us. They aren't prisoners, and if they have other loved ones who can help them once they resume their lives, we find that it helps for them to be in contact during the recovery process…"

Ella hadn't known that. It made sense. But what did it have to do with Chloe?

"Our residents are made aware of the danger of being in touch with their abusers during their recovery process. If he continues to control her mind, she'll never heal. If he reminds her of who she was, fills her head with 'abuse talk,'—you know, telling her it's her fault, or reminding her that if she leaves him she'll have nothing, she'll lose everything…"

Ella nodded, familiar with the material.

"Because of their heightened awareness, a couple of the women who work with Chloe in the kitchen came to me this morning. They said that Chloe's husband has been calling her."

"I know they're in touch. But only occasionally. They still have bills to pay and responsibilities to tend to. For now no one else knows that Chloe's left him."

"He called her four times in two hours yesterday. I made it a point to be busy in the kitchen this morning and witnessed three calls myself."

Ella and Chloe had played cards last night after Cody went to bed. Her sister-in-law hadn't said a word about speaking to Jeff.

"You're sure it was Jeff?"

"Positive. She called him by name the first time. And ended all three conversations with 'I love you, too, babe.'"

Babe. Chloe had always called Jeff that. A term of endearment Ella had always liked.

She didn't now.

Chloe was lying to her. Not uncommon in domestic-violence situations, but still, Ella was hurt.

"Did she seem upset?"

"From what one of the other girls said, he seemed to be trying to find out where she was. Which was why their alarm bells first went off."

Brett had said he'd talk to Jeff. Tell him that he'd seen Chloe and that she was fine. Hadn't he done so?

She'd assumed he had. He always did what he said he was going to do. But it wasn't as though he reported in to her. Brett Ackerman hadn't been all that great about sharing even during the last couple years they'd been married. She knew better than to expect it of him now.

"Did she tell him?"

"No." Sara's glance was warm and filled with compassion. "I made certain of that much. And the last time he called, I heard her chuckle before she hung up."

Jeff was charming her. Or was he keeping her mentally enslaved?

Ella hated that she could even think such things about her brother.

But it was for his own good. She was trying desperately to save Jeff from himself. From a future that could kill him. If it didn't kill someone else first.

"I have no idea what to do."

"You don't have to do anything," Sara said, taking her keys in hand. "Chloe's an adult. She's taken the first step—coming to stay with you. Feeling her way. Finding out who she is with Jeff, and apart from him. If you push too hard, you might just push her away."

"So you aren't worried about the calls?"

"I'm concerned. I'm planning to try to engage her in a serious conversation, get her into counseling if she's ready to go that far. And I wanted you to know so you could be aware."

Standing as Sara did, Ella thanked the other woman. Agreed to stay in close contact. And felt as though she'd gained a hundred pounds in an hour as she walked slowly to her car.

CHAPTER TWELVE

ELLA HAD INTENDED to go straight home after the meeting. Chloe was spending the entire day at the Stand to oversee the dinner hour, which meant Ella would have a little time to herself in her apartment.

As much as she loved Chloe and Cody, as adamant as she was about wanting them with her, she'd been living alone for a long time and had been looking forward to having some space for a few hours. To be able to talk out loud to herself if she wanted to. Or sing off tune.

But home spoke of Chloe, too. Chloe's and Cody's things were scattered around the apartment. Reminders everywhere of the problems they faced.

Ella had a potential new house to drive by. A for-sale option Chloe had found on the internet the afternoon before and suggested she look at. She'd taken the address with her when she'd left the house that morning.

And didn't get it out of her purse.

Just as she didn't think about where she was going when she turned on her car. Didn't consider options, or ask herself what she should do. Didn't give herself a chance to object.

Putting her car in Drive, she pulled out of the police-station parking lot and headed straight to Brett's place.

To share the burden of Jeff and Chloe's situation with him.

Because she wasn't like him. She asked for help when she needed it.

His bag was packed, by the door, and he was ready to catch a flight later that night. With a pool towel in hand, Brett was walking naked through his living room when he heard the front bell ring.

It wasn't a common occurrence. His place was set back from the road, and labeled with no-trespassing signs, so he didn't get door-to-door salespeople, or religious advocates knocking on his door. He hardly knew his neighbors. And the rest of his life was run by someone who refused to see him.

Wrapping the towel around his waist, he went to investigate. He saw her car first. And then, through the peephole, Ella, in street clothes, her dark hair curling around her shoulders, looking… good.

Too good.

He considered pretending he was already out back in his enclosed backyard, under water in the pool. Considered turning his back, walking outside and diving in. She'd have no way of getting his attention.

And even as he considered doing so, he pulled open the door. If he thought he had to avoid her, they had a problem.

"Oh!"

Whatever words had been on her lips, ready to be delivered, didn't make it past her open mouth as she stared at him.

"I…I'm sorry…" She was backing away, one step at a time. "I didn't realize…"

Intrigued, a bit turned on and not unhappy to see her, Brett switched gears when it occurred to him how the situation might look, from out on the porch, looking in.

Not yet dinnertime. Him clearly naked beneath his towel…

She could easily assume he had a woman inside.

"It's not what you think…" He spoke quickly, before she turned tail and ran. When he and Ella had lived together, they'd made love before dinner on a regular basis. They'd been apart all day. And were hungry.

"I should have called," she said, awkwardly looking around—everywhere but at him.

"Probably," he allowed. "But more because your chances of catching me at home are slim."

Yet she had.

"I was just going for a swim. You want to join me?"

The question was uncharacteristic. As was the fact that he'd uttered it without forethought. Uncharacteristic to the man he'd become.

Not uncharacteristic to the much younger man who'd once been married to this woman. She'd always had a strong effect on him. And instead of dissipating, it had only grown stronger the longer they were together. Most particularly as he watched her put herself through procedure after procedure because she'd so badly wanted to bring their child into the world, and then try to comfort him after every disappointment. He'd been strangely detached himself, to the news of no baby, but each time, he'd grown more and more invested in her disappointment. He couldn't make her happy. The conception challenges were hers. They'd had tests. She suffered from a hormonal imbalance that rid her body of fertilized eggs before they could implant. He didn't have to feel guilty about not being able to give her a child. No, his unease was much more selfish, much more like something his father would have felt. He'd hated that she'd had to have a baby to be happy.

He'd hated the fact that he wasn't enough for her.

He'd fought the intensity. Keeping himself in check as he'd learned to do. Preventing any chance that he'd do something unforgivable.

And he'd seen the hurt in her eyes. Day after day after day. Because of the baby they couldn't conceive, he'd told himself. But he'd known that his distance was hurting her, too. He just hadn't been able to do anything about it.

"I don't have a suit."

She hadn't said no. She'd made an excuse. Wasn't going to swim with him. But she hadn't said no.

The distinction counted.

It shouldn't.

"Although a swim sounds good." The words came slowly. Hesitantly. As though she reserved the right to take each one back as she uttered it.

She was looking at him now. At his chest. He could almost feel her reaching out to him, running her fingers through his chest hair, pausing to tease his nipples, as she'd done so many times in the past.

"I need to speak with you, Brett." Her frown held a question as she watched him. And for a second he wondered if he'd imagined her words. About swimming with him.

Or maybe it had just been the intonation he'd mistaken. She'd been making a casual comment, and he'd heard innuendo.

"It's important." Arms crossed now, she stood on his front porch, slender and tall with her dark hair tumbling around her shoulders, looking sexy and serious. Professional. Turning him on…

He spun around abruptly, before his body betrayed him. "I'll just go get dressed," he said. "Come on in." Leaving the door wide, he strode back to his master suite, concerned about where this project was leading him.

ELLA WASN'T GOING to be affected by him. Or by his home. She'd never seen the inside before, of course. They'd only visited Santa Raquel during their marriage, not lived there. They hadn't owned a home there. And he wasn't hers anymore. Not her lover. Not her husband or partner or spouse.

But he had been once.

There was something in that.

As much as she told herself there wasn't. As much as she tried for there not to be, there was.

So. Fine.

She knew. She was on top of it.

The danger was in not knowing what was behind you, catching up to you, preparing to take you unaware.

Meaning to stay in the foyer by the front door, her gaze focused off in space, Ella caught a glimpse of something in the room off to her right. A sunken room with lush beige carpet. And brocade furniture. An antique armoire.

The frame she'd seen drew her closer, and she saw that she'd been right. He had the photo they'd always kept in their living room on the mantel above the fireplace. It was a landscape, a small patch of beach with the ocean in the distance. Not anything that would stand out to anyone. Except the two people who'd made love for the first time there and then taken a cell phone photo of the beach as a promise to each other to never forget their first time.

She'd given him the framed photo on their wedding night.

And had wondered, after the divorce, what had happened to it.

Footsteps sounded behind her, and Ella turned, intending to say something to him about the photo—about the fact that he'd kept it, but all she saw was his back. As though he'd seen her standing there and had turned away.

"Come on out, and I'll get us some tea," he called from several feet down the hall, as though she knew her way around his home.

She followed the sound, wishing she could have just stayed in the foyer by the front door. Years of work, of healing, suddenly felt at risk.

She couldn't help looking around her as she came into the large kitchen with the bay window alcove that held a butcher-block table with fall leaf quilted placemats. A gourd acting as a bowl to smaller gourds painted like fruit sat in the middle of the table.

And beyond the window was the loveliest backyard she'd ever seen. Bougainvillea climbed six-foot stucco walls off in the distance, cornering a rock waterfall. Behind the wall were some woods. She could see the tops of the trees. The pool took up half the yard and was flanked by a built-in fireplace and grill.

"Are those orange trees?" They were off to the side of the pool.

"One navel, and one ruby-red grapefruit. There's a lemon tree on the side of the house."

Lost in the beauty of his home, she didn't think about the past. Or the future. She wanted to sit down. And stay a while.

"Here's your tea," he said, handing her a glass.

She took a sip to soothe her newly parched throat—unsweetened, with just a hint of lemon, exactly as she liked it.

He'd remembered. "These are lovely," she said, pointing to the place mats. Their home had been nice, too, but they'd both been students when they'd first married, living paycheck to paycheck. "My mother's doing," he said, standing there with his tea, watching her.

She wanted to see the rest of the place.

And knew she didn't dare. She was strong. Happy. And intended to remain that way.

She'd lost too much of herself to this man the first time around. Giving him everything, trusting that he was as invested in her as she was in him, only to find that he'd seen a divorce lawyer without even telling her that he wanted out.

Trusting that he wanted a baby as badly as she did only to find that he didn't want one at all.

She wasn't going to be drawn in again. Even if that meant they stood there, awkwardly holding glasses of tea while they talked.

Opening the sliding glass door off to one side of the alcove, Brett stepped outside. "Let's sit out here," he said and because she needed to get out of his house, she followed him.

He'd put on black pants and a striped business shirt.

"You have a meeting tonight?" Setting her glass on the table, she sat in one of the four padded chairs around it.

"A plane to catch. I have an eight o'clock board meeting in Oregon in the morning."

A busy man. An important one. But he evidently had time for a glass of tea. In lieu of the swim he'd been about to take?

The pool was kidney shaped. Had a basketball hoop at one end, a hot tub off to the side and was surrounded by landscaped flower beds.

If they hadn't divorced, this could have been her home...

"Did you talk to Jeff?" The question was a little more baldly stated than she'd intended.

"Of course. I said I would." Sitting across from her, he raised an ankle to his knee and gazed out toward his yard.

"You told him you'd seen Chloe and that she was fine?" She glanced at him and then away.

"Yes."

"How did he react?"

Brett's gaze landed on her, and Ella lost her breath. "He was grateful that I'd checked up on her for him."

"Did he ask how you found her?"

"I didn't give him a chance. Before I told him I saw her, I told him I contacted you and asked you to arrange a meeting for me. After all, he knew I showed up because you contacted me saying you were worried about him."

It had happened exactly as he said.

"And?"

"He was glad to hear that she agreed to see me. He sees that as a good sign."

"Good sign?"

"Jeff wants his wife home. He wants to save his marriage. But he's unsure of Chloe right now."

That was what they needed. For Jeff to understand that if he didn't get help, he risked losing his family forever, not just for now.

"Did he say anything about how he thought to go about saving the marriage? Like getting help for his anger issues?"

"He already told Chloe he'd go to counseling with her."

"He needs to go to counseling himself, Brett. To figure out how to handle himself in stressful situations. Then he can talk about possible marriage counseling."

"Is that what Chloe wants? For him to go to counseling? Is that what she's waiting for?"

"He needs to figure out why he's suddenly getting physically aggressive with his family when he's angry. And do something about it. She's waiting for him to realize he has to take accountability and make changes before she can safely return home."

"There's no way she's afraid of Jeff. I talked to her. She didn't exhibit any sign of fear. On the contrary, she misses him."

"She's not afraid of him. She's afraid of what might happen in the future if he doesn't get help." Ella hadn't forced Chloe to leave. Chloe had asked for help.

And not because of one incident, but because of two years of escalating ones.

Brett didn't say anything. Ella let the subject of counseling go for the moment, afraid that he'd have to leave before they talked about her most prominent concern.

"Did you know that he's calling her?"

Brett didn't respond well to drama. To sensationalism. The most efficient way to deal with him was to take all the alarm out of her tone. She knew that. And tried her best.

But damn, sitting there with him in his backyard, such a romantic setting…or maybe it was the caffeine in the tea…she could feel her heart racing.

"They agreed that he wouldn't look for her as long as she answered her cell when he called, or at least called him right back. Just so that he knows she's okay."

"He called her three times in an hour today. And all day yesterday, too."

His pause gave her a moment's comfort. He was taking her seriously.

"Perhaps she didn't answer. He must have been worried."

"The only way I know he called is because she did answer. These are just the calls that happened at the Stand and were witnessed. There could be more. Sara Havens is concerned, Brett. She's the one who told me about them."

Brett might not have met Sara personally, but she knew he'd be fully aware of every member of the staff at The Lemonade Stand.

"Did Sara witness them?"

"Today she did. Some residents overheard her conversations yesterday and were worried enough that they told Sara about them. Sara purposely made herself busy in the kitchen today to get to know Chloe and get a feel for what was going on."

"And after she witnessed the calls she was concerned."

"Yes."

"I'll talk to him again."

He looked sad now, as he gazed out at his yard. She knew how much this had to be hurting him. As far as Brett was concerned, Jeff had saved his life.

He used to say twice. The first time when he'd pulled Brett from the hell of having lost his family—his little sister to leukemia and his relationship with his parents due to the domestic violence in their home.

And the second when Jeff had introduced Brett to Ella.

"If we figure out what's going on, what's brought about the change in him, we can stop this, help him, before it's too late." For Jeff, of all people, to be suddenly aggressive at home—to be physically harming his family—it had to be heartbreaking for Brett, too. "He's my brother, Brett. You know how much I love him…"

Her voice broke, and Brett's glance landed on her. He nodded. Looked like he was going to say more and then stood.

"I've got to get going if I'm going to catch that plane," he said, gathering up their glasses. Neither of them had been emptied.

She stood, too. Told him she'd let herself out; and when he turned to the kitchen sink, she moved in the opposite direction. At the front door, she paused—hoping that he'd come after her?—and said, "Have a safe trip" very softly before exiting his home alone.

CHAPTER THIRTEEN

BOTHERED MORE THAN he wanted to acknowledge by Jeff's frequent calls to Chloe, Brett changed his flight plan for Thursday, stopping off for a layover at the Palm Springs International Airport before heading on to LA. He had an eight-thirty meeting in LA Friday morning with the district attorney regarding Americans Against Prejudice. He was a key witness in the charges being brought against board members, and this meeting could turn out to be the first of many informal depositions before the case really got off the ground.

He'd been planning to get home for the night first, but would now be staying over at an airport hotel he frequented in LA when he had early-morning flights out. He'd made a habit of always having an extra shirt and tie packed in case he was away longer than he'd planned.

He was relieved to see Jeff waiting for him at the Celebrity Bistro, a bar and eatery adjacent to the security checkpoint and accessible to all airport visitors, just as he'd requested.

Better yet, his friend had already ordered their beers. Still in business clothes, with his tie loosened, Jeff stood as Brett came in.

"What's up, man?" Jeff asked, his face lined with concern. "Your message sounded serious."

He'd tried to keep things casual, but he'd only had a short break that day, and Jeff hadn't picked up when he called. He'd left a message meant to get his friend to the airport without causing alarm. Apparently he'd put too much emphasis on the getting-him-to-the-airport part, and not enough on the no-cause-for-alarm part.

Not like him at all.

"Ella stopped by last night," he said, sliding onto a bar stool as Jeff took his seat again and passed over a beer. Brett sipped slowly. Drinking was a double-edged sword with him. One of which he was always aware.

It helped him relax. Was a social tool that put others at ease. And he was absolutely not going to become his father—getting lost in the blessed fog of painlessness.

He wanted to talk about the phone calls. To let Jeff know that he had to be careful as people were watching his moves, judging him, based on Chloe's interpretation of their latest argument. Chloe could very well be making a big deal out of a marital spat that wasn't anything extraordinary, but if Jeff wasn't careful, he could find himself under real scrutiny.

Sara Havens's involvement took this out of the family.

But he couldn't tell Jeff any of that or he'd be breaking his word to Ella. And Chloe, too.

"No kidding," Jeff said, leaning back to assess Brett, a grin forming on his face. "So that's what this is about? My sister? How'd it go?"

"How'd what go?"

"You and Ella. Last night."

Brett shook his head. "There is no me and Ella," he said, taking a long swig from the mug of beer. He was definitely going to want another one.

"You want me to talk to her?" Jeff asked, drinking much more slowly than Brett was. "I know she was pretty broken up by your divorce, but I'd also bet my life on the fact that she still loves you. You take it slow and you'll have her back…"

"Stop," Brett said. How in the hell had this become about him and Ella?

"I'm serious, man. She hasn't dated anyone seriously since you. That's pretty telling, if you know what I mean."

Ella hadn't had a single relationship in four years? What a waste.

And the selfish part of him, the part he'd inherited from his father, was secretly glad. He'd mattered to her. As she'd mattered to him.

Even though it didn't change anything—to the contrary, it confirmed his choice to set her free before their relationship deteriorated as his parents' had—there was comfort in knowing that he'd mattered.

"I'm serious, Jeff," he said, pulling his mind back from the other space. "There is nothing between Ella and me, and I don't want there to be. Period. That's why I divorced her."

"And seeing her again hasn't changed your mind?"

"No." He didn't waver on that one. Not even in the darkest recesses of his mind. Seeing his ex-wife again had only made his path more difficult. Which was why he had to get this thing with Jeff and Chloe resolved and get out of their lives again.

Back where he belonged.

Alone.

He sipped.

He wasn't one of them anymore.

"So what's this about, then? You want me to tell her to leave you alone? I'd hate to do that. She's been hurt enough, you know."

Brett had never told Jeff why he and Ella had divorced. He'd never even attempted to justify his actions. Nor had he ever tried to get Jeff to take his side against Ella. There was no side to take.

Ella had been a great wife. The best. She'd deserved the best husband in return.

Ironic, really, that Ella had never put any stock in the potential for violence within him—thinking his fears groundless to the point that he'd ceased speaking to her about them long before their marriage ended. And yet here she was thinking that her brother, who was the least likely candidate for domestic violence, posed a threat to his wife and son.

"Chloe said something yesterday about you two," Jeff said. "That's what got me thinking in that direction."

"Chloe did? What would she know about me and Ella?"

"Just what you know. That Ella called you about checking up on me. And then she put you in touch with Chloe so you could go see her. I guess Chloe was hoping that once you two saw each other again...I don't know. You know how women are."

He and Ella were not going to get back together. Ever. And if Ella had given Chloe any reason to suspect differently...

For a second, Brett felt a tiny flutter of the unfamiliar inside him.

And then...nothing. Just like him and Ella. He was going to have to make certain that she understood that. Unequivocally.

Though, after the way he'd reacted to her miraculous pregnancy—with no sign of positive emotion at all—he found it hard to believe Ella would ever want a relationship with him again.

Still, to be safe, no more backhanded swim invitations. Or visits to his house.

"I'm here about Chloe," Brett said when he finally got the bartender's attention and had his last beer on the way. He had another hour before he had to board his flight.

Jeff's frown, his stiffening, was instantaneous.

"What's wrong? How was she when you saw her? How was Cody?"

"Chloe's fine. She looked good. A bit tired, maybe, but good. I was glad to see her. Four years is a long time. And Cody, you did good there, my friend. That boy's his daddy all over again."

Brett stopped himself before talking about a future golfer or anything else Cody might be or do when he realized that going on about the kid would only make it harder for Jeff to be apart from him.

"So what's up? Chloe seemed fine the last time I talked to her," Jeff said. "She was in pretty good spirits. Said she'd been cooking for some people and that she'd enjoyed it. Must have had some kind of gathering wherever she's staying."

"When I called to tell you I'd seen her, it was so that you'd know she was fine and leave her alone for a bit so she can get herself figured out and get back to you."

"I know." He bowed his head and then looked back up at Brett. "And I'm grateful. I wasn't sure how much longer I could hold on, and then you show up and go see her for me... It made all the difference...I can't tell you how much... Anyway, thanks."

Brett's instincts for weeding out fakers was honed to the hilt. And there was no doubting the sincerity in Jeff's words.

"How many times have you two talked in the past couple days?"

With both hands on his glass, Jeff looked down into his beer. "I don't know. Too many, I'm sure. I mean, you're right. Her being gone isn't going to do whatever it's supposed to do if we talk like we always do. I get that. But I miss her and…"

He looked over at Brett. "What if she decides that she likes her new life better than the one we shared? I want her to know that I'm willing to make changes if need be. I can work anywhere. If she wants to leave Palm Desert, or…you know, I'm open. I need her to know that."

Brett had made his assessment. Jeff was a love-sick man who needed his wife by his side. Not some stalker putting pressure on the woman who'd dared think she could leave him. He showed no signs of being angry with Chloe.

On the contrary, he was a husband who was willing to do whatever it took to keep his wife happy.

The type of husband Brett had planned to be.

"I just wish I could see her," Jeff said. "If she needs her time away, then she does, and I'm not going to ask her to come home before she's ready. That wouldn't be good for either of us. But not seeing her at all, and having our last memory together being with angry words between us— words I can't get out of my head…"

Ella hadn't spoken with Jeff. Because Jeff

wouldn't put her in the middle. She had only Chloe's side to go on. She couldn't see what Brett was seeing.

"Have you asked her for a meeting?"

"Of course. She said no. Based on the fact that she doesn't want us to be alone together again until she's sure that things will be better for her when she comes back because it would be too hard for her to leave again."

"Makes sense. And also sounds like she's missing you as much as you're missing her."

"Yeah." Jeff grinned. "I read it the same way," he said.

"So maybe it would be in your best interest to quit calling, just leave her alone and give her a chance to really miss you."

Jeff frowned. "I don't like the feel of that. I don't even know where she is. At least when we talk there's some connection. We aren't separated, Brett. We're married. Husband and wife. Besides, Cody's birthday is coming up. He's only two. I don't want him forgetting his daddy, or thinking I don't care enough to wish him happy birthday."

But if, just if, a woman needed to break the mental manipulation she was experiencing from an abusive spouse…if she needed time to free her mind from his influence…

He might not visit The Lemonade Stand, but he knew the rhetoric. He'd been through enough counseling in his lifetime to be fully versed.

Not that he was changing his mind about Jeff and Chloe, starting to think that there could be some truth to the assertions of abuse. There wasn't. It was impossible.

But if Chloe felt as though she was losing herself to him, finding herself too dependent on him—it could happen with Jeff in his high-powered job and her being a stay-at-home mom—then she could very well need some time completely separate from his influence in order to find her own strengths.

It could be that the only way to help Jeff, to get his friend's wife and son back home with him, was to help Chloe have time away from him.

Ella's plan, but with a different spin. The separation wasn't because Jeff had to get well, but because Chloe did.

But Cody's birthday…Jeff had a good point there. If he wanted to, he could press things with Chloe and force her to let him have equal access to their son.

He'd done nothing wrong. Didn't deserve not to see his own son.

Used to sitting at board tables where quick thinking was paramount, used to making important decisions on his own, Brett said, "I've got an idea. How about if Ella and I chaperone a meeting between you and Chloe and Cody someplace neutral for a birthday celebration? And then, afterward, after you've had time to make a good memory to replace the bad one she left on, you agree to give her complete silence for a time."

Let Jeff see his family, have time with them to assure him that they were well and still *were* his family, in exchange for total silence between him and them for a period of time afterward.

And maybe, if they were extremely lucky, Chloe would have a moment of clarity when they were all together and no longer need the time apart.

And Chloe and Jeff, seeing him and Ella together, would understand that there was going to be no reunion between them.

Logistics played themselves through his mind— the challenges first. Like convincing Ella that this was a good idea…

"You'd do that?" Jeff was saying, leaning on the bar's round high-top table, focused on Brett. "You'd be willing to spend time with Ella? From the little she's said, up until now you wouldn't see her at all."

"You were there for me at my crossroads," Brett said, meeting the other man's gaze with difficulty. He and Jeff had had some emotionally sloppy moments, back when they'd been kids and Brett had been pretty messed up. But they weren't kids anymore. "If not for you, I don't know that I'd have stayed in school, much less graduated. I could've ended up a drunk just like my old man."

"You didn't drink any more than the rest of us."

He'd never drunk at all until that first year in

college. Not while Livia was alive. And he was living at home watching out for her and their mother.

"I owe you," Brett said now, needing not to get lost in memories that he could ill afford. "And it's not like she and I would have to interact personally." He was assuring himself as much as he was Jeff. "You and Chloe and Cody will be there the whole time."

"I know Ella would do it," Jeff said. "My sister doesn't know how to say no to me, which is why I'm always so careful not to put things on her."

A true statement on all counts, as Brett knew from personal experience way back when.

And not at all the actions of a manipulative, abusive man.

"But what about Chloe? Would she be willing to leave wherever she's staying and meet up with us all?" Jeff asked, looking hopeful and worried at the same time, his beer untouched on the table. "I mean, I'm pretty sure she would if Ella asked her," he continued without pausing long enough for Brett to respond. "She'd never ask Ella," Jeff said. "She's careful not to pit my sister against me, which is why I was so glad to know that they've been in touch. Chloe still considers Ella and me part of her family."

He sipped from his beer then. And Brett waited. Being duplicitous with Jeff, for whatever reason and in whatever fashion, did not sit comfortably with him.

"But if Ella suggested a gathering to Chloe," Jeff continued as soon as he put his glass down, "Chloe would probably agree."

"I can't guarantee anything," Brett said, his mind calculating. "But I think we might be able to work something out." Once he explained the plan. "We could meet up in LA someplace," he said. Santa Raquel was definitely out, for obvious reasons.

Such as Cody somehow letting his father know that the town was familiar to him.

And while taking Chloe back to Palm Desert for a weekend might help her realize that she missed home, wanted to be there, belonged there, Brett was fairly certain that, for those very reasons, Ella would refuse to be a part of *that* plan.

"I'll go anywhere," Jeff said. "You name the time and place, and I'll be there."

"I think it might be best to suggest the idea, and then to let Chloe choose a time and place." Brett was thinking out loud now. "We want her to feel comfortable and like she has some level of control…"

"That woman has all the control where I'm concerned," Jeff said, shaking his head with a bit of an affectionate grin on his face. "Has since the day I laid eyes on her."

"I remember." Brett grinned now, too. He and

Jeff had been on a bike trip along the coast—Brett's choice for his bachelor party—and had stopped at a small but very popular diner along the ocean road. Chloe, who'd been in culinary school, had been managing the place. Jeff had seen her from across the room and had dropped his glass of spiked tea. He'd said the glass was wet. That it had slipped.

What it had done was summon the manager over to their table, and she'd helped mop him up.

They'd both ended up chatting with her. She'd asked where they were from. Jeff had told her that they were bent on raising hell one last time before Brett got married the next weekend to his baby sister.

Before they left that day, Jeff had asked Chloe to the wedding.

And they'd been together ever since.

Unlike the couple whose wedding had been Jeff and Chloe's first date.

Brett and Ella hadn't made it together, but as Brett boarded his plane half an hour later, he was determined that Jeff and Chloe would.

There had to be some happy endings.

CHAPTER FOURTEEN

ELLA HADN'T SLEPT well the past two nights and was fighting irritability when she went into work Friday morning. Chloe's constant need to have everything shiny clean, because Ella liked it that way, had bothered her that morning. While she appreciated Chloe's attempt to keep Ella's life as normal as possible, she also just wished Chloe would relax. She was tired of living with someone who walked on eggshells.

Then she ended up behind a slow driver in the passing lane on her way into work. By the time she got to work, the closest parking lot was full and she had to park in the off-site garage. And then an orderly on the shuttle from the employee parking garage to the hospital's main campus was on the phone the entire trip, talking twice as loud as he should have been.

And there was a hair in her ponytail that was pulling. She'd redone the thing twice, but still felt a little jab to her scalp when she moved her head.

Standing in the elevator, it occurred to her that Chloe's walking on eggshells in the apartment might not be as much about living with her as she'd thought, but rather another symptom of being a victim of domestic violence.

Then she was irritated with herself for taking so long to figure that out. And felt even guiltier for the ill thoughts she'd had regarding Chloe's obsessive cleaning.

The NIC unit's on-duty child-life specialist was standing in the hall just outside the elevator when Ella got off.

"I've been waiting for you," Jacqui said, though Ella was half an hour early for her shift. "Henry's being discharged this morning. Nora's taking him home."

Henry. The baby of the young abuse victim Ella had turned over to Lila.

They'd been expecting the orders to come through for the past two days. "The Lemonade Stand's ready for him," she said, switching immediately into work mode. Child services had been up the day before. Without any formal proof against Ted Burbank or Nora, they were releasing the baby solely into his parents' care.

Lila had police and lawyer members of the High Risk team working to establish proof that would help prevent Ted from having unsupervised access to his son until he got help.

In the meantime, the man wouldn't know where to find his wife and son, or be able to get to them if he did.

"No," Jacqui said, twisting her fingers together

as she walked beside Ella and, when Ella slid her pass card through the reader, followed her onto the unit. "She's taking him home, home. She's in his pod now, packing up the things she had in there for him."

Stopping in her tracks, Ella stared at the woman whose prime responsibility was advocating for the patients in her care. And secondarily to their families. "What do you mean home, home? She's going to her home at the Stand, right?"

Jacqui shook her head. "She's going home. I thought her permanent address on the paperwork was a mistake so I went in to have her correct it, and she's not going back to the Stand."

Ella hadn't gotten a call…

Pulling her cell phone out of the pocket of her scrubs, she glanced at the screen. No missed calls. No voice mail. No text messages.

Lila would have called. The High Risk team would have been notified…

"There must be some mistake," she said, turning toward Henry's pod. They had pictures of Nora's back. The woman had talked to the police and was willing to testify against her husband… .

"I thought so, too."

"Did she say she checked out of the Stand?"

"She didn't. Check out, that is. She said she just decided on the way in this morning."

Before seven in the morning? Right after waking up? She'd decided to take her baby out of a safe environment and back to a dangerous home that spontaneously?

"I'll talk to her," Ella said.

Thus began a morning that didn't improve as the day wore on.

DRIVEN BY A tension he couldn't assuage, Brett finished business on Friday afternoon and sped most of the way to Santa Raquel. Was he that worried about Jeff? Just determined to be there for his friend as his friend had been there for him? Or that eager to get the business with Ella behind him?

He asked the questions. And had no answers.

Something he didn't usually abide. There would be no unanswered questions in his life. He'd made the promise to himself when he'd left his marriage with the intention of living alone for the rest of his life.

He wasn't going to risk hurting anyone as he'd hurt Ella. Or worse, risk hurting anyone as his father had hurt his mother and him. The nightmares he'd had after finding out he was going to be a father had ceased. The memories had faded. But they'd served their purpose.

He'd spoken to a counselor about them, of course. Who'd talked to him about fear versus reality. About the residual effects of growing up in an abusive home. But he knew that statistically, abusers had very often grown up as victims. That the pattern of abuse perpetuated itself. His parents had both grown up in abusive homes, had promised each other that abuse would not enter their home. Trusting that, because they knew better and so badly needed and wanted a safe home, they'd break the pattern.

His father had failed first.

And then, according to his mother, she'd failed, too. Brett didn't agree with her assessment, knowing that when she'd lashed out at him the afternoon of Livia's funeral, beating him on the chest with blows that didn't even leave bruises, she'd been railing at life, distraught with grief, and clinging to him as much as pounding her fists against the wall he presented between her and her need to die…

She'd cut herself off from him after that day. And shown her son by example how to be accountable to the intense emotions that could be smoldering inside him. No one had been able to assure him that there was no chance he'd be capable of becoming his father. Of someday exploding. Just as no one had been able to guarantee him that those dreams he'd had after Ella had finally become pregnant hadn't been a warning from his unconscious mind.

His phone beeped with a text message, but he didn't stop to read it. He was low on fuel, noted that his dashboard computer told him he had enough miles until empty to make it home and passed on the fill-up for now.

Ella's shift ended at three. He needed a few minutes of her time. Without Chloe.

After pulling into the visitor parking lot of Santa Raquel's new children's hospital—a building he'd visited during the grand-opening ceremonies— he strode inside and had Ella paged, saying only that someone was there to see her for personal reasons. And then waited.

If she was with a patient, he could be there a while.

So be it. This was going to get done.

"Brett?" Her face was ashen as she came hurrying toward him from behind a locked door. "What's wrong?"

He'd always thought her scrubs were sexy. Something years and distance apparently hadn't diminished.

God, she was beautiful.

"Nothing's wrong," he said a bit curtly. For both their sakes. "I just needed to speak with you."

"I'm working," she said, pointing out the obvious. "A phone call wouldn't do?"

"I wanted to make certain that Chloe wasn't around." Lame. But also true. There was good reason for him to control this situation. To protect everyone involved.

Leading him over to a deserted conversation pit, Ella sat on the edge of a brown tweed couch with piping that reminded him of his parents' old sofa. "Is this about Jeff?" she asked. "Is he going to be a problem with the phone calls?"

He remained standing. But didn't want to be rushed. "You're off in half an hour, correct?"

"Yeah. There about."

"You think you'll be later?"

"Not much. Most of my charting's done."

"Go ahead, then. I'll wait. I've got some work to do." He motioned to the satchel he'd carried in with him. It contained his tablet and laptop. The hospital had free Wi-Fi in the lobby.

Frowning, Ella shook her head. "No, this is fine. I skipped my last break."

She hadn't smiled since she'd seen him. Had lines around her mouth that he recognized. Ella wasn't having a good day.

Convincing her of the viability of his plan might take a few minutes.

"I'll wait," he told her. And then had another thought. "Better yet, let's go to the Bistro and get a glass of wine." He stopped short of adding *You look like you could use one.* Or *I need you a bit more relaxed than you appear at the moment.*

"We can take my car," he said.

Her eyes lit. And then faded. But she said, "I'd rather drive myself. Besides, I'm in the garage, not the lot outside. I'll meet you at the Bistro in an hour." And he was satisfied.

As she stood, Brett turned to go. But spun back

long enough to watch his ex-wife's backside all the way through the door.

A guy needed a little vicarious pleasure every once in a while. Even a satisfied and determined bachelor like himself.

ELLA DIDN'T GIVE Chloe much of an explanation when she called to say she wasn't coming right home. Just that she'd be late and to go ahead and eat without her. Chloe had brought home food from the Stand, a casserole they were all having for dinner that night, and could easily warm Ella's when she got home.

She'd have liked to have told Brett no, she couldn't meet him for a glass of wine. But as much as she wanted to take care of her emotional health and avoid any nonessential contact with him, she also wanted to have this glass of wine with him.

But only to find out what he had to say. To make a solid plan for helping her brother, so that his wife and son could go back to living with him, go back home where they needed to be.

And then she was going to accept the dinner offer she'd received that afternoon from a doctor on the ward. Jason Everly, a pediatric pulmonary specialist, was gorgeous, a couple years older than she was and single.

He didn't want children of his own. Which was a good thing since she had no intention of putting herself and her partner through several more years of fertility efforts only to risk another heartbreak. Her body's peculiar metabolic imbalance meant that she was at high risk of another miscarriage. Not that she intended to share any of that with Jason. They were just having dinner.

Brett was seated at a high-top on the patio. The Bistro was close to the hospital, an upscale place in a lovely landscaped strip mall of equally lovely places. The patio looked out toward a row of historical homes that were now bed-and-breakfast establishments.

Feeling a bit self-conscious about her purple scrubs with pink teddy bears on them, Ella ran a hand through her recently released hair, hoping that the long curls would detract from all the pinkness, as she walked toward him.

And then she noticed that about half of the clientele was dressed like her. Clearly the place was a popular hangout with hospital staff. And there had just been a shift change.

Now slightly self-conscious for another reason, Ella glanced around to make sure that Jason wasn't there, and was relieved when she didn't see him. Because she didn't want him to see her with Brett and lose interest?

Or because she didn't want another man approaching her while she was in the company of the man she'd promised to love and cherish until death did them part?

"I ordered," Brett said as she slid onto her stool

and glanced at the bucket with a yet unopened bottle of wine on their table.

A glance at the label showed her that he hadn't forgotten what she liked.

So Brett.

Other than his inability to open his heart, or share it with anyone, the man was pretty much perfect in every way.

"Good, I'm parched," she told him, fiddling with her glass rather than looking at him.

Parched? Who drank wine when they were parched?

But to make good on her word, she picked up the ice water in front of her and took down half the glass.

As if on call, their waiter appeared before she'd set down her water glass and opened the wine.

Brett ordered a fresh vegetable appetizer for them to share, and the waiter excused himself.

"To good work," Brett said, raising his glass to her.

Don't lift your glass, a voice warned from inside her. *Don't honor the old tradition*. Brett's glass hung suspended. If she didn't tap hers to his, she'd be rude.

And it wasn't as if he'd toasted to their future, or their love, or even just to them, as he'd done in the past.

His glass remained in the air.

Ella lifted hers. Touched his. And felt as if they'd just kissed.

HE'D HAVE PREFERRED to wait until the wine had had time to make his job easier, but as soon as he'd seen Ella cross the restaurant floor, he'd known he had to present his proposal and leave.

He had some inane response to the woman. Like an allergic reaction. Quite irritating.

"I stopped in Palm Desert last night and saw Jeff," he said as soon as the waiter had poured and departed.

He had his mental agenda prepared.

"After speaking with him, I believe we need to take action to resolve this issue."

Ella gave him her full attention. But the way her fingers were caressing the stem of her wineglass was distracting.

He should have stuck to iced tea. And taken his chances with her mood.

"What does that mean, *take action*? What kind of action? You aren't suggesting that we turn him over to the authorities, are you? Because that's not what this is about, Brett. The whole point here is early intervention. To help him before it gets that far."

He'd been right about her irascibility. In a past life, at home after a hard day like hers obviously had been, he would have suggested that she drink some more wine, the words accompanied by a grin, and followed up with a kiss, to which she would have responded with all of the tension inside her and they'd have made love hard, followed by a softer, slower coupling.

They might or might not have made it to the kitchen for dinner...

"I'm sorry. I didn't mean to snap at you."

The apology drew him out of his mental fog. And made him aware of his lack of response in what was only a business conversation.

"No apology necessary," he said, pushing everything away but that meeting's agenda. "And no, I'm not suggesting we call in the authorities. Nothing along those lines. On the contrary, I'm not convinced that the root of Jeff and Chloe's problem is Jeff."

Ella blinked. "What?"

A woman from the next table looked over.

"How can you not think the problem is Jeff?" She leaned forward, her voice quieter, but no less intense. "He's been verbally abusive and now has escalated to pushing and shoving and restraining. You know as well as I do what the next step in that progression will be."

"Jeff admitted to taking out his work frustration on her," Brett said. "Much like you're doing with me now." He had a talent for getting to the point.

Sitting back, Ella took a sip of her wine, watching him.

He withstood her scrutiny with ease. He was a professional at the boardroom table.

"I asked Chloe about Jeff's behavior," he continued. "When you took Cody to play in the sand-box. She said pretty much the same thing he did. That he snapped at her, said things he'd give anything to be able to take back, simply out of frustration. That he apologized. Bad days are a part of life. Husbands and wives fight. People say things they don't mean. None of that equals abuse."

"I had a feeling she downplayed things for you," Ella said, her tone equally professional now. Equally serious, too. "She wants your help. And she thinks, as I do, that you're our only real hope in getting Jeff to see that he needs help before things get completely out of control. But she's also a bit intimidated by the fact that you're the founder of a women's shelter. She's afraid that you're going to turn Jeff in, and she most definitely doesn't want that."

Should he be straight with her? Let her know that he was working with a different set of facts? That he wasn't attempting to get Jeff to admit that he had anger issues that needed attention? "Jeff thinks that Chloe is going through some kind of emotional blip. Similar to the postpartum depression she suffered from after Cody was born."

"I know what Jeff thinks. We need to change his thinking. He has to be able to see that this is his problem, and if he keeps blaming someone else, he could very well lose his family and maybe even end up in jail."

"But what if he isn't wrong?"

"You think this is all Chloe? That she's making up the incidents of verbal abuse? The shoves and pushes? Of slamming Cody into a chair so hard he screamed?"

"I'm just suggesting that maybe she's embellished them in the retelling to you because she's slowly losing parts of herself by always putting Jeff and Cody first and is struggling with a way to understand herself and be happy."

He knew when Ella took a long breath that she was considering his words. One of the things he'd loved so much about her was her ability to take a step back and look at both sides of a situation.

With one exception. She hadn't been able to see the possibility that he could one day turn violent. Something that had, at least partially, ended their marriage.

He lost faith in her ability to hear his truth. She knew about his upbringing, of course. Understood and sympathized. And was completely certain he only suffered from abuse-based fear, not from the same latent violent tendencies that had struck his dad.

Her refusal to see, to believe in the possibility, had made it impossible for him to continue to share those fears with her. She gave them no credence. They fell on deaf ears...

But as good as she was at putting herself in other people's shoes, she'd never seemed to figure out, or understand, that if he opened up and gave her all of the emotions he kept in check, all of the passion and the love and the joy, he'd also risk exposing her to the shadowy side of all of that. The anger that had lurked inside his father just waiting for a life challenge that was too big for him to handle to trigger it. And could possibly lurk inside him, too.

The tension that had built within him during the repeated fertility treatments had been a sign to him. He'd thought, at first, that he was experiencing the normal reactions most couples in their situation experienced. He'd only realized, after Ella finally got pregnant, and he couldn't share in her joy, that his tension stemmed from something else. He wasn't prepared to be a father. Wasn't willing to have a child, as his parents had, knowing that at some point, he could turn from a loving father into a monster...

Ella wasn't aware of the danger. But he was.

"I saw the bruises, Brett." Ella's voice was completely different now. Soft. Almost pleading. And a shock to him, following on his thoughts...

"Chloe told me she was bruised when she came here." He gentled his voice, as well. Because Jeff and Chloe—they didn't fit the pattern of abuse. They were just a normal couple. "She said she fell into a doorjamb during the last argument. He'd said something to her about bombarding him with her crap and pushed past her just as she was stepping back away from him..."

Breaking eye contact, Ella took a sip of her wine. Watched as the couple at the next table, the older woman who'd stared when Ella raised her voice, paid their bill and left.

"They had a victim at the Stand a while back," Brett said. "She was young. Fifteen. She claimed that her brother had hit her. More than once. He was older, about our age. The brother had raised her from infancy…"

He had Ella's full attention again.

"He claimed that he'd never touched her. And that he wouldn't ever do so. There was no indication through medical or school records that there'd ever been an issue with him. Or her, either, for that matter. But it was clear to Sara and Lila and others that the girl was afraid of her brother. And that she'd been abused. Charges were going to be pressed against him, on her behalf. He stood to lose custody of her. And would have, if not for one person, an attorney, who believed him enough to do some checking on her own."

"You said *would have*. I'm guessing that means he wasn't charged?"

"He didn't abuse her. There were other things going on. He'd lied to his siblings about his past. His little sister found out his secret at the same time she witnessed something else that weakened her trust in him. She felt angry. Afraid. And had to get away from him."

"But he'd never hurt her?"

"More like he was father-of-the-year material."

"But her distress was valid."

She was getting it.

"Yes."

"You're saying that you think something else could be going on here with Jeff and Chloe."

"I'm saying I believe Jeff when he tells me he's not abusing his wife. I also know he doesn't fit the profile. He's never been involved in any sort of violent activity. He's never shown signs of having a temper or anger issues. He comes from a good, loving family. Your folks were respectful of you both. And still are."

Other than being gone more than they were around. Traveling through North America as full-time RVers, working in various parks as they went, going on their eighth year now.

"He doesn't have an alcohol problem, has an easygoing disposition and is financially secure. He's socially adept, confident and is clearly devoted to his family.

"All of this leads me to believe that something else is going on here."

"Like?"

"I don't know. Maybe, like Jeff thinks, Chloe *is* suffering from depression. She went from being a career person, managing a restaurant with the hopes of owning her own someday, to being a stay-at-home mom."

"That was her choice. Jeff was happy to support

whichever decision she made, to stay at home or keep working."

"And maybe it was the choice she wanted to make, the one that she believes is best, but it's an enormous life change. There could be some residual depression involved. And maybe subconsciously, Jeff is reacting to that. Maybe he's more irritable with her because of it, which feeds her feeling that his anger with her is escalating…"

"I know that she loves her work at the Stand," Ella said. "She's exhausted, but clearly enjoys what she's doing."

Ella paused and then asked, "Did you ever meet him?"

He frowned. Wondering what he'd missed.

"The brother you were talking about. Guardian to the fifteen-year-old resident at the Stand."

"Of course not. I have nothing to do with any of that. You know that."

"You still get the reports."

"Yes." The place was his responsibility. Others did the work, but ultimately the buck stopped with him. He had to read the reports.

Ella nodded and sat back as their vegetable tray was delivered with a chrome bowl filled with dip in the middle of it.

As soon as her hors d'oeuvres plate was in front of her, she filled it. He watched, knowing before she reached where her fingers were going to land.

Carrots, celery, broccoli and cauliflower. No peppers. Ever. The cucumbers weren't peeled.

She passed them by just as he'd expected.

He paid attention. And when his study—of life, of situations, of people—presented choices, he made the one that made the most sense.

CHAPTER FIFTEEN

BRETT POURED HIMSELF a little more wine and topped off Ella's glass, too, though neither of them had had much to drink, and looked out over the street of homes below them. Provincial, large and in pristine condition, the old Victorian homes stood tall and proud. And yet, intrinsically vulnerable, as well. To the weather coming in off the ocean. To a modern-day society that wanted everything to be new.

Homes that were similar to his own.

The plumbing was a challenge. Electricity had had to be rewired to be up to code and still had hiccups now and then. But there was affection in knowing the home's eccentricities so well. Security and a kind of beauty that couldn't be created overnight. Or purchased.

Like good art, he could enjoy their value.

And like good art, he could enjoy a moment sipping wine with a woman who, while young, had the wisdom of age and wore her value beautifully.

"You had a rough day today." The words came as she was down to her last stick of celery. He'd shied away from personal conversation. But he was confident that they were on the same road where Jeff and Chloe were concerned, which to him meant that getting her to agree to the plan was no more than a formality at this point.

A presentation and acceptance that would end their meeting.

Taking a short breather from the business at hand was perfectly acceptable. Maybe even advisable to further the good working relationship they were establishing.

He wished he'd held his tongue as the shadows came back over her face. Why did he have such a propensity for hurting her? Almost as though it came naturally to him.

Old feelings of guilt and frustration filled him. Panic would follow. He knew the way it worked. Brett reached for a carrot. Took a sip of wine. Distracted himself long enough for the sensations to pass.

"I'm assuming you've read the emails," Ella said while he was busy tending to himself.

"I haven't seen anything since first thing this morning," he told her. "As soon as the day's meetings were over I headed to the hospital and then here."

"Your mother didn't text you?"

"No." Pulling out his phone to check for any missed communication, he asked, "Why? What's wrong?"

"Lila must not have been in touch with her yet," Ella said. "It's not like it's an emergency as far as the Stand is concerned. Not like we can do anything, and if we all got in 911 mode for every at-risk woman we dealt with, we'd never get out…"

"El…" He reached forward and touched her hand. As he'd done a million times before when she thought out loud before letting him know what was going on.

Getting ahead of herself, he'd always called it.

"I got ahead of myself, didn't I?"

Every nerve in his system tightened as she voiced the words running silently through his mind.

"It's Nora Burbank," she continued, unaware of the discomfort he was feeling. The connection that had just been revealed to him.

Him. Her. Still of like minds.

He'd thought the divorce had taken care of that.

"What about Nora?" The woman Ella had brought to the Stand from the hospital, he reminded himself. Her infant was Ella's patient.

"Her baby was released today, and she took him home. To their permanent home."

"I thought arrangements had been made for her to live at the Stand."

"They had. She didn't tell them she wasn't coming back. We wouldn't have known at all, until she didn't show up downstairs for her ride, if an employee hadn't noticed the change she'd made to her address on the discharge papers."

He frowned. "I'm assuming the High Risk team has been notified?"

"Yes."

So there was nothing more they could do for now. Except add another name to the prayer list. Keep a close eye out. And hope.

"I can't believe she did this, Brett. I don't get it. She was desperate for help. And was so grateful when it was provided to her. She couldn't have faked that."

"I'm sure she didn't," he said, and it dawned on him. This was a first for Ella. Her first domestic-violence case. Her first case on the High Risk team. Her first flesh-and-blood introduction to the manifestations of the insidious disease.

"She loves that baby, Brett. Much more than she loves her husband…"

"But she's a victim, El."

"Not if she stays away from him."

"That's a misconception. She's a victim whether she's currently being abused or not. Much like an alcoholic is an alcoholic even when he's not around alcohol. She's mentally and emotionally vulnerable to his conditioning."

"Brainwashed, you mean." She was drawing on the table with her finger.

"In essence."

"I read about some of that, but you should have seen her, Brett. She was so glad to have a way to take back control of her life…"

"She had moments where she was able to think clearly. But in the beginning, those moments will be less frequent than the ones where she feels out of sync with herself every time she goes against his conditioning."

He heard the passion in his tone and sat back. Blamed the wine.

"I spoke with her as soon as I got to work this morning and was told of her plans. When she heard that child protective services had cleared them, she called him," Ella was saying. "She said she wanted him to know that she hadn't gotten him in trouble. That he was free and not being looked at anymore. She said that as soon as he heard her voice he started going on about how wrong he'd been, how sorry he was, how things were going to be different. He said it took her leaving him like she did to open his eyes and that from now on, she'll be in charge of their son's care. That he'll do whatever she tells him from now on."

"You don't believe him." Neither did Brett, but he was understandably biased in cases like these. He'd heard his own father make similar promises when his sister had been in remission.

And then she'd relapse again.

First thing in the morning he was going to use some of his investigative skills and do a thorough online check on Ted Burbank. Before the day was done he'd know if the man had so much as ever gotten a speeding ticket.

And he didn't kid himself about why, either. Yes, he'd do what he could to keep Nora safe, but there was no way he could keep track of every abuser of every resident they'd ever had at the Stand.

It wasn't technically legal, either, with him having access to the residents' personal information.

No, he was doing this for Ella.

Because he knew her well enough to know that she'd blame herself if something happened to that young woman and her son...

"I've never met Nora's husband," she was saying. "But based on what I've read, and seen with her, I don't believe a word he said. If he was truly sorry, he'd get himself into some kind of program. And he'd want Nora to stay someplace safe until he was confident that he had his issues under control."

Which was exactly what Chloe was telling Ella she was trying to do.

And he was back to where he'd started—knowing that getting her to cooperate with his plan wasn't going to be easy.

Knowing, too, that his idea was their best shot at reaching their goal—getting Chloe back home with Jeff. Though their ideas of what it would take to fix the situation were different—he and Jeff believed that Chloe needed time alone to find herself, while Chloe and Ella hoped that the separation would prompt Jeff to acknowledge his anger issues and seek help—the time apart was key. And the only way that Jeff was going to be able to give Chloe that time was to see her again and assure himself that their love was still there. As it stood, the last time they'd been together had been angry. If they could spend some time together and then separate on good terms, Jeff's chances of giving Chloe what she needed were far greater.

And yet, to help his friend, Brett had to put his own emotional health in the direct line of fire.

A line he'd told himself he'd never approach again.

Brett took another sip of wine, uncomfortably aware that he could well be facing the challenge of his life.

EITHER SHE NEEDED more wine, or she needed to go home to bed. Ella was wiped out.

"So, are we done here?" she asked as she finally finished her glass of wine. One glass was all she'd had. Over the space of an hour.

She could afford to have another and stared at the bottle as though it would tip itself over above her glass.

"No." Picking up the bottle, Brett poured a little more wine into each of their glasses. More than half the bottle remained. "I called you here to discuss an idea, and I haven't yet told you about it."

She thought back. They'd discussed Chloe and Jeff. It had felt as though they were on the same page for the first time since this whole thing had begun. Except that she knew Chloe's bruises were Jeff's fault. And knew that her brother needed help.

And they hadn't actually decided what to do for the other couple. Hadn't discussed ways to help.

So how had more than an hour passed?

And why had she let it? She'd promised herself she wasn't going to get sucked in by Brett's magnetism again.

"What's the idea?" she asked.

"Each day that passes without your brother knowing where his wife is, or understanding why she's gone, he gets a little more desperate. Not as a sick man with control issues, but as a man in love with his wife, who's just had his life disrupted and isn't sure it'll ever be right again."

"I know—that's where you came in. I'd hoped you'd help him see why Chloe left so that he can get help, and his world can be right again."

She still wasn't convinced that Jeff didn't have a very real and dangerous problem.

"I don't want my brother falsely accused," she said. "But I don't think Chloe imagined all of this. When you listen to her over a period of time, you hear how the fights escalate, and I think she's right to be concerned. *I* was concerned," she admitted. "I'm the one who suggested she get out of there.

She thought she could stay with him and help him to see that he needed help. I was scared to death that if she did, Jeff would really hurt her. To the point of her needing a doctor or the police being called, and then there'd be no going back."

"But if the situation continues as is, especially now that Sara's involved, he could start looking like he's stalking her when in reality he's just a desperate man trying to save his marriage."

"Regardless of what's happening, she needs time apart from him to get herself straightened out, Brett."

"I agree."

Okay. Good. She met his gaze. Almost smiled at him. That intimate, it's-me-and-you smile that they'd shared when other people were around.

"The other problem is that Cody's birthday is coming up, and Jeff has every right to see his son for his birthday." Brett's words stole the smile before it could escape.

Jeff could push things. Get the law involved. And win his birthday party with his son. But at what cost?

They'd be right back where they started.

"I asked Jeff if he'd be willing to give Chloe total silence, no phone calls, no attempts to see or speak with her, if we could arrange a weekend away first—the five of us—to celebrate Cody's birthday. A weekend would give him enough time with Chloe to celebrate their son's birthday, but also for them to reconnect. Just enough to reassure him that he and Chloe aren't becoming strangers."

The five of us. They were the only words she heard.

For a few wonderful years it had been the four of them. And then she'd gotten pregnant, and it was going to be the five of them.

Now here they were, all these years later. And Chloe and Jeff's baby made the fifth, not hers.

The five of them...

"El? I promise I'd stay out of your way." Brett was talking faster than normal.

This really meant a lot to him.

Which told her he thought it would work.

And since it meant him having to spend time with her, he must think it was the only thing that would work.

"Jeff has agreed to leave her alone," he said, meeting her gaze. "That means he's not going to come off looking like a stalker."

He knew where she hurt. And how to work her.

He'd said he didn't want to hurt her ever again. He'd had tears in his eyes at the time. The night he'd told her he was walking away from their marriage forever.

She'd believed him then. And believed him now, too.

A weekend in his company.

She didn't know if she could handle it.

She loved the man. Always had. And knew now that she always would.

But he wasn't good for her.

"El, will you talk to Chloe? At least see what she thinks about the idea?"

She didn't feel as though she had any other choice.

"Okay," she said.

And drank her wine so she didn't have to look at him again. Make eye contact. Feel that special connection between them.

How could she, and take care of herself?

CHAPTER SIXTEEN

A CABIN IN the woods, with private lagoon access, a dock, pontoon and speed boats and a fire pit in a huge backyard, had seemed like a good idea at the time.

Private enough that if Chloe and Jeff had it out, there wouldn't be outside witnesses, and yet with enough to do to keep them all occupied for the one day and two nights they'd be spending together.

Because the soonest they could all get together was on a Friday night, and to give Chloe and Jeff an entire day together without long drives eating into that time, Brett had agreed to the two nights. The night of the arrival, Saturday together with the birthday dinner that evening, followed by a quick departure on Sunday morning. The itinerary wasn't ideal, but Jeff was happy and everyone else was satisfied.

They'd arrived, Brett and Jeff in his car, Chloe and Cody with Ella in hers, at almost the same time.

The place had come stocked with linens and kitchen essentials. They'd had to bring the rest.

He and Jeff had been in charge of beverages.

Ella and Chloe had been in charge of food.

The guys took one room, with Cody sleeping with Jeff to give his father time with him. The girls took the other.

And it all could have worked out just fine if Jeff and Chloe had actually needed Ella and Brett there.

As it was, the couple spent all day Saturday together, with their son, talking, laughing, going from speed boat to pontoon to playing croquet on the lawn, while Ella and Brett tagged along, trying to stay out of each other's way.

He and Ella had barely spoken, which was good and bad. It was good…great…that he wasn't engaging with her.

But bad that it left him far too much time to notice how those curves of hers hadn't changed in four years' time, nor had her penchant for bikinis.

She filled out the black one she was wearing far too well, which soured his mood. The only good thing about the string-and-Lycra contraption was that there were no other men around to see her in it.

Except Jeff. Who didn't notice anyone but Chloe in her colorful one-piece suit. And didn't matter anyway since he was Ella's brother.

"What's got you so boned up?"

Brett took the beer that Jeff slid along the deck railing to him Saturday evening as his friend posed his question. He hadn't heard the other man come out of the cabin. Now that the sun was down, there was a definite chill in the air.

The women were inside bathing Cody and getting ready to put him down for the night while Jeff did the dishes. Brett had been on grill duty all weekend and had been excused from cleanup.

Once the baby was down, they were going to play cards.

A nice, intimate family holiday. The things memories were made of.

He wasn't there to make memories.

"I'm worried about you," he said, which was partially to blame for his cantankerous mood.

"What's to worry about?" Jeff sounded like the happy-go-lucky guy he'd been in college again. "We're going to beat the girls at cards and call it a night."

"And you're going to be okay leaving Chloe tomorrow? And then leaving her completely alone?"

Because he was damn sure that the couple hadn't had a single conversation about their situation in the time they'd been there. Nothing had been resolved. While the couple had had moments alone, Brett and Ella had been close enough to have noticed if there'd been any lengthy discussion.

"I wanted to talk to you about that," Jeff said now, taking a long gulp of his own beer. It was the first one he'd seen him with all day.

Brett was on his second.

And still had the night to get through.

"You can't be thinking about reneging on the deal, Jeff," he said, his shoulders heavy with dread. He could just hear the spin Ella would put on that.

Unless Chloe was agreeable to moving home.

And Ella would be fine with it—realizing that the problem had been Chloe's, not Jeff's...

"No, if Chloe needs to leave tomorrow and have her time apart from me, she can have it. Truthfully, if she needs that time, I need her to have it," the other man said, and Brett relaxed. "I want her healthy for her sake, but for mine and Cody's, too. We can't constantly be living in fear that she'll need to take off again."

"I agree."

"I'm just glad that Ella's sweet enough to go pick her up from wherever she's staying and bring her here for these two nights. It's been great. And whatever this blip is, at least we'll have good memories of Cody's second birthday, rather than a yearly reminder that things weren't so good."

They'd had birthday cake and presents at dinner. Brett had spent the event behind a camera lens.

"So what did you want to talk about?" The girls would be out soon.

And he'd have to sit at the table with Ella. Interacting, even if just as competitors in a game.

"I want to spend the night with my wife."

Good thing Brett hadn't been holding his beer. Chances were it would've spilled all over him.

"I can't ask Ella to ask Chloe to spend the night with you, man." The regret in Brett's voice was real. "I feel your pain—" and then some "—but there's no way."

"You don't have to ask." Jeff was grinning. Not sharing Brett's pain. "I already did."

"You asked Ella to ask Chloe?" And she'd agreed to ask?

Because Ella never said no to her older brother? Because he so seldom asked for anything?

Did that mean that Ella wasn't opposed to spending the night with him? Because the only other alternative would be for one of them to sleep on the couch.

His blood started to race. And he hadn't drunk enough beer to blame it on the alcohol.

"No," Jeff said, dousing Brett's flames before they'd fully ignited. And then he continued. "I talked to Chloe. She agreed."

He was on fire. An inferno. Burning out of control.

"I just want you to smooth the way with Ella. Chloe's afraid of upsetting my sister and…"

Brett was trapped.

"Just like that she wants to sleep with you?"

"We're husband and wife, man. I don't have to spell things out for you, do I? It's not like either of us can get any on the side while we work through our problems."

He supposed not. But...

"You talked to her about having sex, but not about the issues between you?" Brett took a sip of beer wondering how Jeff and Chloe had pulled that off. And when? They'd been chaperoned the entire weekend.

"Yeah, we—"

"And when did you do this, by the way?" He couldn't tell a guy he wasn't allowed to sleep with his wife.

But he absolutely could not spend the night with Ella. No way.

Hell would have to freeze over, and that definitely wasn't happening. The heat surging through him was proof enough of that one.

"In the boat. When Cody was on Ella's lap and you were driving."

The speed boat. Cody had wanted to help him drive, and Ella had sat in the passenger seat with the toddler on her lap hollering with glee the entire time. They'd had all of ten minutes to converse out of earshot of their chaperones.

"So you had a few minutes, and you chose to use them to get in her pants rather than to figure out what was going on between you two."

He'd have done the same. But he wasn't any less pissed because of it.

"I want in her pants so that I can get her to tell

me what's going on." Jeff leaned in to speak softly. "You know how women are. They trust you more, open up more, after you make love."

Brett nodded. But didn't want to think about what he knew about women after making love. Because that led to thoughts of making love with Ella.

"Besides, I think I know what this is about," Jeff said, his congenial self.

If the guy didn't wipe that grin off his face, Brett might have to go inside. Or better yet, take a walk. A long one. That lasted all night.

Maybe he should just get in his car and go.

Except that he knew his ex-wife well enough to know that she'd pull the plug on the weekend if he did. She wasn't going to leave Chloe alone with Jeff where things could turn bad. Not without Brett there to help her defuse the situation. Or to call the cops while she saved Cody from harm.

And chances were Chloe wouldn't agree to stay, either, if Brett bailed.

"You really think one night in bed with her and you'll have figured out what's going on with her?"

"I'm fairly confident that'll be the case. I know my wife, Brett."

"What do you think it is, then? Her depression?" He'd do what it took to help them.

Jeff knew that.

"Because, you know, I've been thinking," Brett continued on as though if he kept talking, he wouldn't have time to think about the night ahead. Him on the couch and Ella alone in the next room.

With a toddler sleeping in a porta-crib close by.

"You've been thinking..." Jeff held the same beer he'd had when he'd come out. It was still mostly full.

"Yeah, I'm wondering if the problem is that Chloe needs to go back to work. She's extra sensitive right now, we know that. So maybe, without even realizing it, she's a bit jealous that you're out working every day while she's at home. There's no question that the work she's doing is valuable, but she's not getting outside validation from those who don't love her. Maybe she sees her chances of having her own restaurant sliding further away." He was on a roll. And was experiencing the first couple minutes that hadn't been uncomfortable in the last several hours. "Ella was talking about how happy Chloe seems to be, working..."

"Chloe's working?" Jeff's smile turned into an immediate frown.

And Brett caught himself.

"Just volunteering. In a kitchen for people down on their luck." He quickly improvised while sticking with a semblance of the truth.

"She's in LA, isn't she? With those college friends of hers. Her sorority sisters. I had a feeling that's where she'd gone..." Jeff was smiling again. Apparently approving of the sisters.

Brett couldn't answer the question.

Jeff didn't seem to take offense as he continued. "Anyway, no, I mean, maybe that's part of it and I'll certainly take it up with her, but I still think she's struggling with some kind of emotional phase. And now I'm pretty certain that there's something else going on, too. At least from what she hinted at today."

"What did she hint at?"

"I just have this hunch that Chloe is trying to get you and Ella back together."

For the first time since Ella had contacted him, Brett had doubts where Jeff was concerned.

"You're kidding, right?"

"No. It's crazy, I know, but think about it. She adores you both. Ella especially. And, I hate to say it, but you have no idea how close my sister came to breaking down completely after you left. Maybe if she hadn't lost the baby, too, I don't know…" Jeff finally took a drink of his beer. A long one. "And really, it's water under the bridge. Don't get me wrong. Chloe clearly wanted to get my attention. What I said that last night, about her burdening me with her crap—" The other man stopped. Swallowed. "It was unforgivable. I'll never forget the look in her eyes…"

Brett would have liked to save Jeff from himself, but this time, he couldn't. So he did what guys did in situations like these and sipped his beer instead.

"I'm just wondering now, though, if this time

with her sorority sisters—I'm pretty sure that's where she's staying because it's something she's been talking about doing for months—has given her another goal, too."

"Another goal." He watched his friend, seriously contemplating the idea that Jeff was hiding from his own truth. The man was facing the fact that his wife would be leaving him again in the morning and he was smiling.

Jeff nodded.

"What goal would that be?" Brett was almost afraid to ask.

"Keeping you and Ella in the same room long enough for you to figure out how much you love and need Ella."

"That's ludicrous…"

"No, think about it. She goes to to LA but calls Ella to let her know where she is. Ella then calls you, you come see me and suddenly she sees her family whole again…"

Brett knew that Chloe wasn't in LA. But the sorority sister part wasn't really necessary to the plan Jeff was laying out…

"She gets to teach me the lesson I most definitely needed to learn. Has some time to come to grips with her own emotions and, in the midst of all that, sees that she can help you and Ella, too…"

Brett shook his head, came up with nothing to say and took another sip of his beer.

"Ella's getting older," Jeff said now, completely

serious. "And as much as she's made to be a mother, her biological clock's ticking away. With everything she has to go through to conceive, Chloe says Ella's adamant about never trying to have a baby again."

That he hadn't known. The part about never trying again. The knowledge was like another nail on the coffin that held his marriage. Had he made the fertility treatments and eventual pregnancy so hard on her, with his coldness and his inability to celebrate the eventual pregnancy, that she couldn't face the thought of going through it all again?

"Anyway, she's not even dating, and Chloe's certain that she never will because Ella's heart isn't hers to give away. It's yours."

No. That just wasn't true.

Wasn't? Or he didn't want it to be?

He could control his own emotions. His own heart.

He couldn't control hers.

Still… "Chloe has seen me and Ella. She knows there's no chance of us getting back together," he said.

"It's far-fetched, I agree. But I know for certain that she staged that time with the two of you in the boat with Cody. I was heading up front to watch Cody and she pulled me back. Wanted me to give you two time alone with him."

Chloe really thought she could get him and Ella back together?

The whole idea was preposterous.

And Jeff was completely side-stepping the fact that his wife was flinging accusations—serious allegations—around that could put him in a certainly uncomfortable and possibly life-damaging situation.

A memory of the report he'd relayed to Ella sprang to mind, the one pertaining to a fifteen-year-old sister accusing her older brother...

Sometimes people were emotionally confused. Not thinking clearly.

"Don't get me wrong," Jeff said. "I think Chloe left for the exact reasons she says she did. I was angry and acted out of turn. With everything else she's obviously going through, it was too much for her. But then you and Ella came to the rescue and maybe she's seen an added benefit to our time apart."

Good God, could Jeff be right? Or was he really in denial as Ella thought? And so far gone that he'd concoct a seemingly positive reason for his wife's continued absence.

Unless...could it be the way Jeff thought? That Chloe was struggling, but could also see an upside to her time with Ella?

Was she trying to help Ella while she helped herself?

Did Ella know?

She couldn't possibly know.

She didn't want him.

She'd made that quite clear.

He'd made certain she wouldn't.

She'd hardly looked at or spoken to him all day.

"So, will you talk to my sister and get her off Chloe's back so I can have a night with my wife? I swear, I'll do all I can to get the truth out of her and hand it to you on a plate for breakfast."

"I don't expect you to make me breakfast," Brett said, his mind reeling. "But yes, because I owe you and want your family home with you and happy, I'll talk to Ella."

After all, he was a man experienced at digging his own grave.

CHAPTER SEVENTEEN

ELLA COULDN'T SLEEP. She'd never slept in a room with a little one and, although she needed to toss and turn because she couldn't get comfortable, she lay stiffly, afraid of waking Cody.

She couldn't leave the room because Brett was right outside her door, sleeping on the couch in the living room. The only other room in the cabin, other than a bathroom and the bedroom currently occupied by her brother and sister-in-law.

And God, she hoped Chloe wasn't making a mistake. Would she, after spending a night in her husband's arms, be strong enough to leave him in the morning?

Chloe had said that, on the contrary, it would be easier to leave him if she had that bonding to hold on to. If they could share some kind of personal closeness in the midst of the turmoil.

She'd also said that she hoped sleeping with her would remind Jeff how valuable their relationship was to both of them, how much they loved each other and maybe spur him to seek help more quickly. She'd thought lovemaking would bring him to his senses.

And if nothing else, she would be gaining his

full cooperation on a complete separation. No more phone calls.

Neck tight and body rigid, Ella felt the beginnings of a migraine and knew she had to get up. A sliding glass door led out to the back deck.

Moving stealthily, she pulled on a pair of thick socks, exchanged her pajamas for the jeans and sweater she'd worn that night, grabbed her sweater coat to ward off the fall chill and slowly and carefully lowered the latch to the door. The baby stirred when she slid open the door, and she froze. He settled and she slipped outside, shivering, and quickly got into her sweater, wrapping it around her and securing it tightly at her waist.

They were in the crazy time of year when days reached the high seventies but nights could drop to the forties.

The deck had been built a story above ground and was gated at the top of the steps leading up to it, hopefully precluding any wildlife from sharing the space with her.

It was dark, the moon almost completely hidden by the trees, but she knew her way around enough to find the padded lounge furniture and settle into a chair. Cool air chilled her face and fingers, the only exposed parts of her, but not enough to drive her back inside.

"Disclaimer. I'm here."

Ella turned with a jerk toward the whispered

sound. Brett was upright in a chair angled away but not two feet from her.

Her heart pounded out of fear, shock at finding herself not alone, and continued to pound even after the shock wore off. Brett had a way of eliciting that reaction from her.

"I'll go back in," she said, arms wrapped around herself as she started to rise.

"Don't go on my account," he told her. Still fully dressed, he lifted a beer to his lips. The same one he'd nursed during the game of cards they'd played before Jeff and Chloe ran off to have sex?

Or was he breaking his self-imposed limit? Not that three beers would even put a man his size over the legal limit, but Brett didn't break his self-imposed limitations.

Not ever. She'd noticed that the couple times they'd had wine he'd stuck to his two-glass limit.

And why was he sitting alone in the dark?

None of her business. Or concern.

She should just leave him to it.

But she couldn't do it. That had always been part of their problem. Her need to share his life with him.

"Would you be interested in taking a walk down to the boat?" he asked. "I left a small cooler of bottled water down there, and I'd like a chance to speak with you," he continued as though they met like this every night.

She couldn't say no to that request, either. So

she got up and walked silently with him down the yard to the dock and even took his hand to steady herself as she stepped onto the pontoon boat that was swaying on the water.

The lagoon was dark, occupied only by docks from other summer residences. But because it was fed from the ocean, it was alive and even sometimes rocky as waves came into shore.

The boat had a couple of seating areas. Couches and chairs. She went to the back, where she was somewhat sheltered from the night air by a canvas half wall, and dropped into a chair.

After grabbing the small cooler at the front of the boat and bringing it back with him, Brett took the chair across from her, still with his beer in hand.

Silently he offered her one. Jeff had stocked the on-board refrigerator earlier in the day.

She shook her head.

"What's up?" He'd been right to lead them away from the house. At least out here they wouldn't have to worry about waking anyone. Or being overheard.

"I think after this weekend it's pretty clear that the problem isn't Jeff."

Ella stared out in the direction of the ocean, watching for lights from ships to pass by their alcove. "How so?" she asked, carefully assessing. Carefully guarding.

Herself. Her heart. Her future. Chloe. She didn't know what.

"I know the signs of abuse, El, and he doesn't show any of them. He's not controlling of Chloe—quite the opposite, really. He allows her to call the shots. He caters to her now as he always did."

She'd noticed. And noticed, too, that she was alone, on a boat on the ocean, with the man she still loved.

"There's no change that I can see in either of them," Brett continued. "Personality-wise, or in their relationship, other than a certain emotional distance Chloe keeps from him. Timidity, maybe."

Clearly he'd given the situation a lot of thought. He'd been sitting in the dark alone, with a houseful of people in bed behind him.

So Brett.

So heartbreaking.

"That's a sign of abuse," she had to point out.

"Not by itself, it's not. It's a sign that she's struggling. Jeff doesn't overdrink. He's not short-tempered. Hasn't shown anger once in this whole situation. At least not that I've witnessed, and certainly not even a hint of tension since we've been here."

"We're on vacation, Brett. Time out of time. There's no responsibility. Nothing to stress about." Other than the situation itself. One divorced couple and another one, estranged, sharing a cabin.

It was soap-opera fodder for sure.

But they'd all done great. As Brett had said, it had been a wonderful weekend. If she didn't count the tension building inside her. She was tight enough that she could snap with the smallest provocation. A sensation she hadn't experienced in ages—but one that had been her constant companion for the first year after Brett turned his back on her.

She'd thought she'd left that part of her behind. That she'd recovered from it. From him.

Brett tipped his bottle to his lips. Maybe he felt some of the tension, too.

"He's a great dad. Patient. But firm, too. Cody was clearly happy to see him. I think back to vacations with my dad and, even when we were having fun, there was always this underlying sense of being on a tightrope that could snap at any moment." Brett was definitely focused on Jeff and Chloe.

While Ella sat there filling up her senses with him.

He was right, though. Cody had shown no signs of being afraid of his father. Or even hesitant around him. To the contrary, he'd begged to ride on his daddy's shoulders. "Up! Up!" he'd cried again and again since they'd been here. Whether they were walking down to the dock at the bottom of the yard or just to the bathroom for a bath, Cody had wanted Jeff to carry him.

But Ella had another memory, too. One she'd

forgotten about until that afternoon. The boat rocked and she held on, riding the small swell. "I was at their house about six months ago. Jeff had asked Cody if he wanted up, and Cody ran behind his mother and hid. I just thought it was because he was going through a phase where he was afraid of heights, but I asked Chloe about it this afternoon."

"What'd she say?"

"That Jeff had grabbed Cody by the arm the day before and shook him once, asking him couldn't he just leave him alone for a damned minute, when Cody had asked to be picked up. Jeff had just come home from work, and Cody had run to greet him."

"We all get impatient. Most particularly after a hard day at work. And clearly it's not something that Cody remembers."

"According to Chloe, Jeff shook him so hard, he cried."

"Did he leave a bruise?" The question sounded more informational than doubtful.

"Chloe said no." But she'd looked away when she'd said so. And Ella had sworn she'd seen guilt in the other woman's eyes. But then Jeff had called to her to get the life vests so they could go out on the boat, and the moment had been lost.

"I'm worried, Brett," she said now. "I think Chloe's in denial, too. That maybe things are worse than she let on."

Brett shook his head. "Sometimes you worry too much, El." He spoke with a strange hint of affection in his voice. A familiar tone that sent a tingling through her. "I'm telling you, I know the signs. I lived with them for too many years to miss one."

"And Jeff knows them, too. Through you. He also knows to be on his best behavior with you because of that."

"Jeff is a good man."

"So are you. And you're the last person he'd want to disappoint."

He sipped his beer.

There might have been bugs out, if they'd been there a month or so earlier. And there were still no lights out on the ocean. She needed them there. Needed something to look at besides him.

Because out on the water, alone with Brett, all she wanted was to crawl on his lap, have him wrap his arms around her, grab her sides with fingers that could work magic on her body and never let go.

But of course he would let go.

And she'd fall.

"If Jeff was struggling with anger issues, he'd do something about it. Like me."

Ella froze. Not because of the chill in the air, but from the inside out. Like him? The words were so random she couldn't help but stare at his silhouette in the darkness.

"What do you mean, like you…and struggling with anger issues? You didn't even act out in anger, Brett. Not ever. Heck, you never even raised your voice. You were afraid you'd be like your dad, sure, but you never were, Brett. Not ever."

While she could hardly believe her brother would hurt his wife or child, she knew, with every ounce of her being, that Brett could never be that man. He had a shut-off valve that would stand up to anything.

He sipped again. And she wondered, with guilt and a small bit of hope, too, if he'd had so much beer that his tongue would be loosened.

If maybe, this one time, Brett would open up to her about the residuals left behind by his father's anger. To her knowledge only her brother and his mother had ever been that lucky.

"What do you think you did?" she asked. Because she knew damn well he'd never stepped out of line. Hell, for that matter, he'd never even stepped up to the line. There'd been a time, in one of her lowest moments, when she'd wished he had lashed out. At her. At the world. Even if it meant slamming his fist through a wall. At least then he'd be fully alive.

"I went to see a divorce attorney while my wife was pregnant with our child," he said.

She was on a precipice. She couldn't see. Didn't know how she'd gotten there or where she was going. Holding on to the arms of the chair, she rode the water with the boat.

"Because you were struggling with anger issues?"

"Yes."

Ella's jaw dropped. Leaning forward she reached for his beer. Took a swig and handed it back.

History had a cruel way of reinventing itself. "No, Brett, you left because you didn't want to be a father to the child I was carrying. And truth be told, you'd been leaving me slowly long before I got pregnant. I think it was because I wanted more than you could give me," she said softly, but very clearly. Because one thing she'd learned over the years was that she had a right to be heard. "I needed you to be all in and the more I needed from you, the more emotionally distant you became."

He didn't say a word. And she knew she'd said too much. So she took another sip of his beer. It was still more than half-full.

"You used to tell me how you feared being like your father," she said to the night air. Unable to look at him again. "But that was just fear talking. A result of having grown up in an abusive home. You told me so yourself. And I've done a lot of reading since then."

She could smell him, though. That aftershave… she wished she'd never chosen it.

He reached down beside his chair, and she

heard the refrigerator open and then shut, followed by the sound of a beer cap twisting.

"I wanted to share your daily ups and downs. You didn't," she told him, sorry if he didn't like the truth, but intending to get it out anyway.

He'd started this.

She'd been prepared to go back inside, sleep on the couch he wasn't using and leave him in the room with a sleeping toddler.

Their marriage was long over. What she'd once thought they'd had, if they'd had it, had been destroyed a long time before. Facts were facts. She'd learned to accept them. He couldn't come along now, all these years later and suddenly try to rewrite the script.

"I believe in helping others," she said now, taking the cold beer he'd retrieved and opened as he handed it to her. Finding a sad humor in the knowledge that he must not have wanted her to share his. "And I believe in asking for help when I need it. I think people being there for people is what life is all about."

He didn't respond for a third time. Déjà vu. As usual, she was talking to herself. But when, in the past, she'd have fallen silent in response, she didn't this time. She wasn't speaking for his benefit. She was speaking for her own.

"You're just different," she told him. "All those years of infertility treatments and you never once told me you didn't want to be a father. Don't you think that's something I should have known? Instead, after I finally get pregnant, you go see a divorce attorney without even talking to me first. And look at The Lemonade Stand. You're its founder, and no one there knows who you are. Because you can't get that close. Can't let anyone share the emotional parts of your life. Even your career… You don't do charity work yourself—you check up on those that do to make sure they stay honest. It's commendable work. Necessary work. You're a great man, just one who's chosen to live life from the sidelines."

She'd figured it all out a couple years ago. Once she'd come through the haze of hurt and disbelief after her world had fallen apart.

But she was fine now. Or thought she was until she heard him say, "I'm not denying any of that."

Somehow she managed to stay upright. To sit there without dropping the bottle of beer she held. Inside she crumbled.

She'd been right!

And only in the confirmation did she realize that she'd subconsciously been hoping that someday he'd tell her differently. That she'd spew her accusations and he'd dispel the hurtful assumptions and tell her…what?

"However," he continued, "it's important for you to know, in light of Jeff's situation, that I tried to talk to you about my issues, but you refused to believe me."

"What?" If he'd told her he was a Martian she couldn't have been more surprised.

"I told you I struggled with the very real possibility that I could be like my father."

He had. Several times. "In the beginning, yes, you did. You were completely honest with me way before you even asked me to marry you. But that was it, Brett. I assured you that I wasn't afraid. That your fears were just that—fears. Not reality. And our years together proved me right. Even in the worst times, you never once showed any sign of violence."

"Why do you think I grew more and more distant?"

Confused, Ella stared toward his shadow in the moonlight. Was this really happening?

"You want me to believe that you were struggling with anger issues?"

She sat. Welcomed the air cooling her hot skin.

"The first time I noticed a burning need to lash out was your freshman year in college when we were all at the homecoming party at the Delta house and that lecher, Danny Simpson, had you up against the wall, pawing you…"

She'd forgotten all about that. Danny, while pretty much a loser slob, hadn't been a mean guy. He'd been attempting to come on to her and had been too drunk, falling against her and trapping her against the wall. He'd also apologized a thousand times over the next day and had appointed himself her silent slave for the rest of their years in college.

"I didn't even know you saw that," she said now. She'd been at the party as Brett's date. From the moment she'd stepped foot on campus as a freshman, in his and Jeff's sophomore year, she'd been Brett's date.

"I was heading over to save you from him, but you disentangled yourself and led him to a couch before I could get to you."

She wished she could see Brett's face. It sounded as though he might be grinning.

And her belly flip-flopped. She'd given him a memory that made him smile.

"I'm not seeing where the anger issue was in all that," she said. She knew for certain he hadn't gone after Danny. The guy had passed out minutes later and hadn't come to until the next day.

"Inside me," Brett said. "It's not what I did. It's what I felt."

Light flashed behind her eyes. Almost as though the sun had suddenly started shining through the night sky, and then was gone again. Leaving her sitting beneath the canopy in the dark.

"You saw an injustice. You saw me at risk of getting hurt, and you got mad."

That thing with Danny had been before they'd ever made love. Long before he'd asked her to marry him.

"You're doing it again."

Another jolt. Her stomach turned, and nausea was there. "Doing what?"

"Making light of what I'm trying to tell you."

"I'm not…" Ella replayed his words in her mind. Brett saw himself as someone he wasn't. His inability to trust himself came from his youth. Her job was to help him see himself as she saw him. Right?

But… "Why do you say that?"

"Ah, El, this isn't worth going into. You were a great wife. I failed. Can't we just leave it at that?"

In some ways she really wanted to.

"I don't think so." Because his words, if he didn't explain them, were going to give her sleepless nights she couldn't afford. She'd already had more than her share. And she told him so.

"In the first couple years of our marriage, during those first fertility treatments, I'd tell you about my fears. You'd basically pat me on the head. You didn't believe me when I told you I was struggling."

Well, of course she hadn't believed him. If he'd told her he was afraid he was going to fly to the moon in the morning, she wouldn't believe him about that, either. But…

"All you ever told me was that you were afraid of becoming like your father, Brett. You never once told me that you were struggling with anger…"

"I feared being like my father for a reason, El. You should know me well enough to know that."

"Yeah, the reason was that you grew up in an abusive home and your fear was left over from that..."

"No, I struggled because you brought out the most intense emotion in me. A love that was bigger than I was. More than I could control. And for every good emotion, there's a shadow side. I came face-to-face with that over the incident in college, but didn't think much of it at the time. As you say, most guys would have been pissed enough to get violent in that situation."

Understanding teased at her in a horrifying sort of way. She *had* made light of Brett's fears. Because to do otherwise would have given them a weight they didn't deserve. She'd been trying to help him.

But in the end, would it have made any difference? Whether the fears were based in reality, or simply imagined, they'd still come between them.

"The longer we tried and failed to get pregnant, the more tense I grew," he was saying. "Not because of my need to have a child. Exactly the opposite. Each time, I'd feel more relieved. But you...you got more and more depressed, took longer to bounce back each time. I was losing you to your need to have a child. At the same time, I was growing more and more certain that I wasn't meant to be a father. But I loved you so much and didn't want to be without you. I just kept hoping the treatments wouldn't work, and you'd eventually see that we could be happy just the two of us. But that wasn't right, either, because I knew, deep down, that you needed more than I'd ever be able to give you. Before I could figure out what to do about any of it, you got pregnant…I felt like I was being crushed between steel walls with no way out. I saw the attorney because I had to be prepared in case I got to the point where I couldn't handle things. And then later, after you lost the baby…"

That was the one that hurt too much for her to handle alone. She'd needed someone who could share her grief, not someone who'd made it clear that having their baby wasn't what he'd wanted. When she'd started bleeding after her eighth week, she'd called Chloe long distance in Palm Desert, not Brett, who'd been forty-five minutes away. And then she'd called an ambulance to take her to the hospital in Santa Barbara.

"When I got the call…when I got to the hospital…"

It had been too late. He'd been in LA, at a board meeting. By the time he'd made it up the coast, she'd already lost the baby.

Brett had come to her room. She'd woken long enough to see him sitting there. And remembered hurting because he'd been in a chair along the wall, watching her. Not close. Not holding her hand.

She'd needed so badly to feel his touch. To

know that he was hurting for their lost child. To know that he felt anything at all for her. And hadn't been able to ask him anything before losing consciousness again.

She found out later that they'd given her high doses of sedative that first day because she'd been so inconsolable.

"I couldn't help you," Brett said. "You knew by that point that I hadn't wanted us to get pregnant. I blamed myself, like I'd somehow tempted fate by not appreciating the gift we'd been given…"

Sad thing was, she understood. Brett couldn't help how he felt. Any more than she could help how she felt. Her heart ached for him.

She tried to stay on that road again, now, with Brett. He was finally talking to her. But she couldn't travel with him. He'd arrived too late. Living in the moment was how she'd learned to cope.

"I left before the love you felt for me turned to hate."

His words called her back.

CHAPTER EIGHTEEN

BRETT SAW ELLA slide forward on her chair—to reach out to him? Or go in?—and panicked.

He blurted what was on the tip of his tongue before she did, either. "If you wanted so much more than I had to give, why did you stick with me all through college?"

He was curious. And curiosity killed the cat. Much better to have understanding and move on.

"I don't know." She gave the nothing answer, but she sat back again. So he waited.

"You exude." She'd gone back to sipping from her beer. And he was glad.

"There's an energy about you, Brett. A goodness that permeates the air around you."

He should have asked the question long ago.

"And, as we've already said, before we were married, and for the first year or two afterward, you shared more. You used to talk to me."

They used to discuss the world's problems. And find solutions for a lot of them, too. He remembered the conversations. Missed them.

"I never quit talking to you," he said. But he had, of course. In the way she meant.

Until the last horrible few months of their marriage they'd had great discussions about anything and everything that didn't pertain to intimate, personal emotions.

And they were back where they'd started. He was a man who could be a potential domestic abuser. As his dad had been.

"My dad was a great guy once. I told you that." The boat swayed, and he shifted. Unbuttoned the top of his shirt as he started to sweat in the cool night air.

"Yeah." The man was a first-class dick, and Ella knew it. She also knew that discussion of him was off-limits. Even in college, he'd refused to talk to her about his old man. What she knew, she'd learned from Jeff, and he had it on good authority that Jeff had told her very little.

His beer was more than half gone, and he wasn't tired.

But maybe he could talk himself to sleep. Maybe he owed Ella this—understanding. A way to set her free.

"He and my mom, they were high school sweethearts." He'd never told her that, either, though he knew that Jeff had done so.

"Both of them products of abusive homes."

He drank. "Time out of time," she'd called their weekend. He damned sure hoped she was right. That he'd be himself when he got home the next day.

Himself with one hell of a headache—not from

three beers, but from the tension climbing up the back of his neck.

"That's what brought them together." He wasn't as careful about his word choice as usual. "The dark secret they shared. The shame."

Shame. Brett could feel it, even now, descending upon him. Like humidity from the air, it clung to him. Making him sticky. Heavy.

"They promised each other that they'd never have an angry word in their home. Because they both knew the cost, the pain, they trusted each other like neither of them would ever have trusted anyone else, to keep the violence away."

He heard an intake of breath. And knew that he was giving Ella something she'd deserved long ago.

"It worked right up until I was ten years old."

There were so many ways that it had worked right. Little League. Summers at the beach. Dinners at Uncle Bob's. His father had taught him how to in-line skate. And let him ride behind him on the back of his motorcycle...

"What happened when you were ten?"

He knew she already knew the answer to that question.

But he didn't want her to go up to the cabin. To leave him out there all alone.

He did, of course. But he didn't.

"My little sister was diagnosed with leukemia. And because my dad was spending so much time with Mom and us, while they figured everything out, he lost his job."

"What about the Family Medical Leave Act?"

He forgot. He was talking to a nurse.

"It had just been signed into law a couple years prior to that, and I don't know what happened. I was only ten.

"The story's a classic from there," he said. "Dear old Dad started drinking, and anytime he found out Mom had another bill to pay or Livia needed another test, he'd hit something. Started out with the wall. Then Mom."

And eventually him.

But never Livia. That was the only hope the old man had of ever meeting up with a saving grace. He'd always been good to Livia.

"I thought he just started getting physically violent when you were in high school."

He'd forgotten that she just knew basic facts.

"After a couple years of tests and treatments, Livia went into remission. And Dad found another job. A guy we met, whose kid was going through the same treatment as Livia, offered him a job. It lasted as long as her remission did."

And the second time around, life had been pure hell. For all of them. Ending with Livia's death. His mother's unbearable grief. Her anger. His father a drunk who eventually ended up in jail.

An imploded family.

ELLA COULDN'T SPEAK. Her throat was choked up with an effort not to cry, even as her eyes filled with tears.

"Without help, boys who witness domestic violence in their homes growing up are far more likely to become abusers." Brett's quote was uttered without inflection of any kind.

That's when she found her voice. "You had help."

She wasn't ready for his fountain of words to dry up. Not by a long shot. He owed her a good ten years' worth of them. At the very least, another ten minutes.

"So what you're saying, then, is that every boy who grows up in an abusive home is destined to live life alone, or become an abuser?"

"Of course not." She heard the disdain that time.

"So why are you putting that on yourself?"

He didn't respond. Typical. But disappointment filled her anyway.

Along with a load of compassion she couldn't afford to carry.

If Brett had talked to her about this even a little bit years ago, so many things would have been different.

Not everything, but maybe the process of splitting up wouldn't have been as hard.

Maybe she'd still be married, or married again, instead of on her way to spinsterhood.

"Do you have any idea how hard it is to live

with the fact that your husband didn't trust you enough to be completely open with you?"

The pain that filled the darkness scared her. She hadn't known there was so much of it left.

"Do you think I wanted to hurt you? That I felt good about it?" Brett sat forward. Lifted his beer and set it back down again without drinking.

She wanted to drink. Seemed to be the way of dealing with the darkness. Which was why she put her bottle in a cup holder on the next chair.

"I saw what I was doing to you, and the sadness in your eyes ate away at me until I couldn't stand to live with myself anymore. I had to do something…"

His hands were inches from her knees. She stared at them. With very little effort, even a rocking of the boat, she could be touching him.

"You could at least have told me before you talked to a divorce attorney."

"You're right, of course." Not the answer she'd been expecting.

"So why didn't you?" Not a question she should have asked.

"Because you would have understood and loved me anyway," he said, his voice raw with honesty. "I couldn't trust myself not to be as selfish as my old man and let you talk me into staying."

She'd asked. Maybe forgetting that nothing with him had been easy.

"You knew I loved you enough to do that, and

then turned your back anyway. Why throw it all away when there was as much chance that it would be good as that it could go bad?"

"Because it was already bad, El. I had a knot in my stomach every single morning. I couldn't be the man you wanted me to be and the more I tried, the more tense I got. And with the baby coming… It certainly wouldn't have been the first time an abusive situation started when a pregnancy was thrown into the mix."

She'd read about triggers. Some men with control issues—and out-of-control jealousy issues—sometimes felt threatened by the introduction of a child into the relationship. This could trigger the start of a domestic-violence situation. And didn't describe Brett or their relationship at all.

"The tenser I got, the more chance there was that the tension would get the better of me someday," Brett was saying.

"If you'd talked about it, we might have been able to work through it. Loving's not easy."

"No, and it's not a guarantee of happy-ever-after, either."

Had he just said what she thought he had? That he *did* love her? At least that he *had*?

Was it possible that someplace, locked away in that heart of his, he'd loved her the way that she'd once believed he had?

He'd asked her why she'd stuck with him through college.

A better question might have been *why had she married him*?

She knew the answer to that.

Ella had tied her life to Brett's because his life was the only one that felt as though it was the other half of hers. She'd married him because she'd believed he loved her as much as she loved him.

It had taken years to crush that belief. Even after his initial rejection of their child. He'd been unprepared when he'd come home from work one day as usual to find her there, gushing happy tears, holding a home pregnancy kit result out to him. He'd seen her tears, not understanding they were happy tears at first, and then, in the confusion of her explanation, had been unable to mask the look of horror on his face. Still, she'd told herself that it was just the shock. That it was normal for a man to be nervous about being a father. It wasn't until he'd told her he'd seen a divorce attorney, that he'd lost her.

Up until then, she'd believed that, deep down, her injured warrior needed her to believe in him.

You'd have thought that moment, the one when her husband had so backhandedly told her he wanted a divorce, would have been the one to sever all her faith in him.

But no, it had taken another couple years for that to happen.

She'd lost too many years of her life to this

man. She couldn't afford to go back. To care if he'd ever loved her.

She couldn't afford to lose her heart to him ever again. He was who he was. A product of his childhood, just as he said. She was listening to him now. Believing him. Oh, not that he'd ever lift a hand to her, or would have to their child, but believing that he'd been irrevocably scarred by his father. Emotionally scarred. She might have continued trying to work on him the first time, if he'd given her a chance, but not now. Because she was older, wiser and knew that there were some battles she couldn't win.

CHAPTER NINETEEN

HE WASN'T GOING to sleep. And didn't much want to spend the night sitting on the porch.

"Let's take her out," he said, standing.

"Take who out?"

Brett was already at the front of the boat, reaching for the key they'd left in the ignition.

"The boat?" Ella asked, joining him up front. "Are you kidding? It's almost midnight. We'd wake up the neighborhood."

He heard one thing. She hadn't said no.

"It's not the speed boat, El. It's not going to be any louder than a car starting. We're far enough away from the cabin that the noise won't carry, and who else is in the neighborhood besides us? In case you hadn't noticed this afternoon, most of the places around here are closed up."

"It's dark. We can't go out on the ocean this late. Who knows what's out there? And no one would know where to look for us if something went wrong."

When had she become so cautious? The Ella he'd known had had a wild streak that he'd found captivating.

He suspected he was in large part to blame for its loss.

Which made it vitally important all of a sudden that he get her to agree to do something slightly crazy.

That and the fact that it seemed clear to him that neither of them was going to sleep, and the cabin was way too small for them to pretend the other wasn't close by. Taking the boat out seemed the safest option.

"We'll stay in the lagoon."

She stood next to him by the driver's seat, looking up at him. If they didn't get going, he was going to kiss her.

"Move over, I'll drive." Ella touched him, but not in the way his mind had been imagining. She pushed him aside and sat down.

Standing behind her as she reached for the key, Brett waited until he heard the engine start before jumping onto the dock to free the pontoon of her restraints.

THE WIND CHILLED Ella's face and fingers and blew softly through her hair, tossing it lightly around her arms and back. She'd had it tied back earlier in the day when they'd been out on the water, but had taken out the ponytail for bed. Brett stood wordlessly beside her, watching the front of the boat.

Her lookout, she assumed.

He gave no direction. No suggestion. Just rode where she took him.

The ocean beckoned. They'd taken the speed boat out earlier in the day, only for a few minutes and within sight of their alcove, but not the pontoon.

"It's suicide, taking a pontoon on the ocean," Brett said from above her. Before she'd even headed in that direction.

In some ways he knew her so well. There was comfort in that.

The lagoon was over a mile long. She had plenty of space to travel.

And knew that she would never have enough room on earth to get away from him. Brett Ackerman was her one and only.

She'd known so. Had spent years convincing herself she'd been wrong. But now, after seeing him again, she could no longer doubt herself. Or the truth her heart had made clear that day on her college's campus when Brett met up with her and Jeff as they arrived with a carload of stuff, and helped unload Ella's in her dorm room before heading off to the apartment they'd agreed to rent with two other guys.

She understood something else, too. Just because she'd found her one and only didn't mean that she had a happily-ever-after in her future.

Brett was damaged goods. He'd never convince Ella he was as damaged as he believed he was, but that wasn't the point. He believed it. And so, in any way that it counted, that made it true.

It didn't change the fact that just being near him made her want to be connected to him in every way possible. She drove. He watched. So close if she leaned her head back, it would rest against his thigh…

Eventually he took the seat next to her, his unfinished beer left behind in the back of the boat as he looked out into the night.

Tears sprang to Ella's eyes, seeing him there. Farther away from her.

He was such a good man. Deserving of love. Needing love.

And alone.

No. She swiped an arm across her face, getting hair out of her way—and tears—at the same time. She couldn't help loving him, but she could control where she let her thoughts take her.

She could control the choices she made.

For his sake, as well as hers, she had to let him go. To block any empathy she might feel. Any desire to help.

All hope.

Hurting her hurt him. She understood that now.

And somewhere in that knowledge, she'd have to find some peace.

BRETT TOLD HIMSELF the boat ride was doing the trick. He was relaxing. Having a seat, he wanted to think he could just fall asleep out there.

Anything was better than going up to the cabin.

Where his best friend was having sex with his wife. And then sleeping cuddled up naked beside her.

Where his own wife—ex-wife—was lying in bed just feet away from him. They had never, not once, spent the night in the same place without spending it in the same bed together.

He'd barely slept the night before, and he'd been shut in a room with Jeff. But tonight? With Ella sleeping all alone? He was supposed to just curl up on the couch and relax? He couldn't do it.

The boat had stopped.

He sat up. Glanced around. They were in the middle of the lagoon.

"I'm sorry." Ella was standing by the crank that would lower the anchor. "I thought you were asleep and was just going to let you rest."

She stood there, her hands raised as though she didn't know what to do with them. Lower the crank. Drive.

Touch him?

God help him, he'd been reliving the touch of her fingers on his skin since they'd arrived at the cabin last night.

Hell, who was he kidding? He'd never stopped having fantasies about the woman.

He'd known he couldn't be married to her. Had no doubts on that one. Even now his resolve didn't waver.

But making love had never even come close to bringing out violence in him...

"I'll just get us going again and head to shore," she said, leaving the anchor. She turned, and the light of the moon gave him a bounteous gift.

A clear view of two things. Ella's lips. And her nipples showing against her sweater where her wrap had dropped open.

She was chewing on her lower lip. All the sign he really needed.

But the hard points of her nipples were added fuel for his raging fire.

"Don't do that with your lips. It makes me want to kiss you." She'd wanted openness.

"Brett." She chewed again, staring at him. Ella never had played coy with him. She knew he knew she wanted him.

Just as he knew she now knew about him, too.

"Would it be so awful, El?" He heard the craziness come out of his mouth. She was still standing closer to the crank than the steering wheel. She hadn't made up her mind to go back, or she'd have walked away from that crank.

"It would just make it that much harder to get over you a second time."

"Unless you don't have to." He was known for

his instant solutions. But why in the hell hadn't he thought of this one before?

With a stumble, Ella fell into one of the back seats. "What do you mean by that?"

He heard the hope in her voice. And rushed to quell it before this got out of hand, and everything was ruined.

"We don't have to be married, or live together, to have sex."

She didn't say anything for so long, he wasn't sure what to think.

She'd changed. In some ways he didn't like.

For instance, this ability she'd developed to close herself off from him. He wanted that for her. Understood that it was necessary. Didn't mean he had to like it.

"You think you could be satisfied with that? Sex without commitment?"

He couldn't tell a damn thing about what she was thinking.

"I think that sleeping with you would be better than not sleeping with you."

His penis was hard. His heart pounding. "I'm not seeing anyone," he continued when she remained silent. "Jeff tells me you aren't, either. It's not unheard of, you know. Two people who can't live together, but still care about each other, being attracted to each other, seeking each other out for physical company now and then."

Leaving her in the morning was a given. He

had full confidence on that score. Had proved his resolve to himself—and to her—enough to know that it was rock solid. It was the next hour he was concerned about.

"I'm asking seriously, Brett. Can we really have sex and walk away without scalding ourselves?"

She wanted it as badly as he did. The fact that she wasn't driving them the hell out of there was proof of that. That peculiar little tremor in her voice said so more quietly. It was that tremor that called him to his feet, to cross the carpeted expanse between them. Keeping his hands to his sides, he leaned over and placed his lips against hers. The choice was hers. She could grab hold. Or step back.

Ella opened her mouth. The boat lurched.

And Brett didn't think of anything but getting them naked.

THE SPLASHING SOUND woke Ella from her doze. She hadn't been deeply enough asleep to lose awareness of the fact that she only had a few hours left in Brett's arms.

But the rest of the world had ceased to exist.

There it was again. That splash. She blinked against the darkness.

And that was when she remembered… "The crank!"

Jumping up from the bed of clothes on the floor of the boat, tripping over them, she rushed to lower the anchor. And saw that they'd docked against the edge of the lagoon that led into the ocean. A few feet more to the right and they'd have floated out to sea.

"I'd say fate was smiling on us tonight." Brett's low tones, soft and sexy and relaxed behind her, had her instantly wanting him all over again.

"Or you could say that we were just incredibly stupid," she whispered, holding on to the crank for dear life.

She no longer felt like the Ella Ackerman she'd been before meeting Brett again. She was hot and desperate and willing to do anything to keep him with her.

In the dark.

As long as it stayed dark.

Which would only be another couple hours based on the moon's position in the sky.

"Can you go again? Or are you too sore?" He was rubbing his penis between her legs from behind.

She couldn't answer him. Because her mind was screaming no. So she nodded. Felt Brett nudge against her. His kisses on the back of her neck.

And when he offered himself to her, she took him.

CHAPTER TWENTY

MORNING CAME. IT always did.

Brett hoped the weekend hangover didn't kill them all. No one had even come close to getting drunk. It was the emotions that had flowed too freely that might do them all in.

He and Ella had made sure to return to their respective sleeping places by dawn.

Chloe got up first and made breakfast while Ella and Brett got up separately, avoiding each other.

Ella cleaned up the cabin. And then showered.

Brett packed the cars. He'd shower later. After a long, hard swim in his pool.

As planned, Chloe said goodbye to Jeff—with a long hug and trembling lips—then buckled her son into the car seat in the back of Ella's vehicle, before climbing aboard herself.

Ella pulled away. She didn't glance back.

He couldn't tell if she was crying.

"Let's go get drunk." Jeff had made the suggestion before. In another lifetime. They'd been kids then.

"Can you stay over at my place?"

"Yeah."

So Sunday was taken care of, then.

Monday he would go back to being a man.

A WEEK PASSED with no word from Jeff. As promised.

And no word from Brett, either. He hadn't come right out and said he was serious about them sleeping together on anything more than a one-time basis. But Ella knew he was.

She'd certainly known what she was doing.

And like a masochist, she'd hurt herself again.

At least this time, she knew she'd survive. She hadn't lost her heart to Brett all over again.

How could she have? He'd never given it back the first time.

By Saturday, she was able to smile again without feeling as if she was going to cry. She'd finally accepted a dinner date with Jason Everly, the pediatric pulmonary specialist on her ward. Chloe wasn't thrilled about the idea, but Ella figured it might help take her mind off Brett.

Turned out that Jason was the type of guy who wasn't opposed to going to bed on the first date.

He tried his damnedest to get Ella to go home with him. And she was tempted. Just to get Brett out of her system.

But in the end, she turned him down.

Maybe the next time.

Jason asked her out again for the following

weekend, accepting a chaste kiss good-night, so she figured there really would be a next time.

No word from Jeff meant there was no need to be in touch with Brett. There'd been a case brought forward to the High Risk team earlier that week, but it hadn't involved Ella. She'd read the report. Assumed Brett had, too. Wondered what he thought about the date rape, death threat and ultimate arrest of the victim's boyfriend.

And then tried not to think about him at all.

The task was made a little more difficult by the fact that Chloe was at the Stand six days a week now. In counseling. And setting up a permanent menu and kitchen-duty schedule. Ella could see that Chloe was getting stronger every day.

Enough that Ella believed her when she said she wasn't in contact with Jeff at all. On Friday night, two weeks after their weekend getaway, they went to Uncle Bob's for dinner with Cody.

Chloe looked over at Ella with her burger poised halfway to her mouth. "Thank you."

"For what?"

"Dink!" Cody squealed and kicked his legs, reaching forward, and Ella reached for his sippy cup without breaking focus.

"For bringing me here. I'll never forget everything you've done for me."

Ella shrugged. "You and Jeff, you're my life. I couldn't sit by and watch as Jeff slowly unraveled."

"He still might, you know." Chloe's eyes took

on a sheen of tears. "We have no way of knowing if he's getting help. He could just be sitting there, waiting for me to call and say I'm coming home."

"Didn't you two talk at all when we were at the cabin?"

It was the first time she'd asked her the question. Some things weren't her business. Unless Chloe needed to talk about them.

"Yeah, we talked. I told him what I thought. He told me what he thought..."

"Which was?"

"That while he'd been out of line, I was overreacting. He wants us to go to marital counseling together. I told him I'd think about it. That first I had to have this time to myself to figure out what's going on inside of me with all of this."

"And have you found any clarity?"

She asked only because she'd been noticing the difference in her sister-in-law.

"Yes." Chloe gave up pretending to eat. "I know that Jeff pushed me into that doorjamb on purpose. And that's all I need to know to be certain that I can't go back there, can't take Cody back there, until he's able to admit what he did and get some help."

"Are you going to tell him that?"

Cody stuffed his last piece of hot dog into his mouth. Chloe watched her son and then leaned on the table, looking at Ella. "I told Sara that I'm going to tell him. I'm just not sure I'm ready yet.

I need to do it in person. And I need to be certain that when I see him, I can stand strong."

"You left him two Sundays ago."

With a sad smile Chloe nodded. "I know. That was the turning point for me," she said. "I knew in my heart that I couldn't go home. And I found out that I was strong enough to do what had to be done."

Chloe was going to be all right.

Ella smiled. Squeezed her sister-in-law's hand. Told her she could stay as long as she liked, that she'd always be there for her, no matter what, and prayed that her brother would get his shit together.

JEFF CALLED BRETT four times over those same two weeks. In Boston. In Atlanta. And twice at home. They didn't talk long. Only long enough for Brett to know that Jeff was slowly losing hope. He was drinking more.

And had mentioned a woman in his office on a couple occasions.

He'd somehow convinced himself, in spite of Brett's warnings, that once he and Chloe slept together, she would come home.

With another two weeks of their lives gone, with no word from her, Jeff was running out of explanations for his wife's behavior.

Brett was a bit surprised himself. He'd expected Chloe to leave with Ella that day from the cabin.

But he'd also thought she'd be back home in Palm Desert within the week.

He hadn't called Ella. Because he was pretty much obsessed with thoughts of her. He thought about her on the plane. In the airport. On the road. And even at the boardroom table, when a gesture, a sound, a smell or some other woman's hair reminded him of her. He couldn't trust himself to hold on to his resolve feeling that way. And to do anything else would be opening them both up to the nightmare of the past.

His mother seemed to be more absent than usual, as well. Used to getting a text or email at least once a day, he'd gone three in a row with no communication.

But when he'd finally called her, leaving a message insisting that she let him know she was okay, he received an immediate reply. Reminding him that she'd been in his house to see to the cleaners the day before.

He'd told her he'd seen Jeff. Whom she knew to be his ex-brother-in-law.

She'd never met him and didn't respond.

He didn't mention Ella to her. Didn't mention the High Risk team at all. She didn't, either.

And then on Saturday night, two weeks after he'd spent the night with his ex-wife, he saw her. He'd stopped in at the Bistro after a game of golf, not because he knew she'd be off her shift soon, but because they had the wine he liked, and no one knew him there.

No one but Ella.

His nerves tightened when he saw her car in the parking lot, and he almost pulled back out to the road and went to the little pub on the corner by his house instead. But then he thought about Jeff and figured he could ask Ella how Chloe was doing, and then leave her alone.

Determined to decline any invitation she might extend to join her for a glass of wine, Brett waited for his gaze to adjust from the bright sun to the restaurant interior before he walked all the way into the room.

His pause had given Ella time to notice him, he observed, as he finally stepped forward. And then stopped. The look of pain on her face was unmistakable.

She was sitting not far from the door. And she wasn't alone.

ELLA DIALED BRETT'S phone the second she was in her car.

She owed him nothing.

But that didn't mean she wanted to hurt him.

"Brett?" Why she said his name when his voice mail picked up, she didn't know. It wasn't as if cell phone voice mail blasted out into the room and gave the listener a chance to pick up. "This is Ella."

No kidding. Her hands were shaking as she sat there. Jason drove past, waving goodbye, and she waved back. Wondering if he was curious who she was on the phone with so soon after they'd parted ways.

"Listen," she said, rubbing her head with the hand that had waved. "I... Just call me, please. I mean it, Brett. Don't make me chase you down."

She clicked the phone off.

Wondering why she'd ever thought Brett Ackerman was worth all the trouble he brought her.

And when, less than a minute later, her phone rang and she recognized his number, she knew.

Just knowing that he'd called when she asked him to gave her a modicum of peace.

"Why didn't you come say hello?" she asked, getting straight to the point.

"I didn't want to interrupt."

"We were in public, Brett. That opens up the expectation of possible interruption."

Were they really having this inane conversation? They'd spent such an incredible night together, she could hardly believe it wasn't a dream, followed by two weeks of complete silence and now they were arguing about expectations surrounding privacy in a public establishment?

"So, what did you want?" she asked.

"I was just stopping in for a drink after golf."

In the bistro so close to the hospital that it had become the unofficial after-work gathering place for hospital personnel? When Brett lived across town?

"So why not have the drink?" She knew why she was pushing him.

Because he wouldn't have come inside if he hadn't meant to see her. She knew him. Brett was deliberate about everything he did. If he hadn't wanted to see her, he'd have checked the parking lot to make sure her car wasn't there.

"I wanted to ask—casually, without putting you on the spot—how Chloe's doing. I have no intention of pressuring you to give up confidences, Ella, and don't want you to think, because we... Anyway, I just wondered if there's been any change on your end."

"Chloe's doing well. She started daily sessions with Sara the Monday we got back."

She started her car, but didn't pull out of the parking lot. Her phone wasn't charged enough to waste the battery on wireless or Bluetooth. Dusk had set, leaving a gloom over the mostly full lot.

Saturday night. There were lots of people out on the town. Going on dates.

She and Jason were going to see a movie Sunday afternoon. Because she wasn't ready to go to bed with him.

But she liked him, and she'd told him so tonight.

Then she'd seen Brett.

And the guilt that had swamped her took her breath away.

"You still there?" she asked when enough time had passed for her to figure out that Brett wasn't going to respond.

"Yes."

"Where are you?"

"Pulled over at a lookout."

"Are you okay?"

"I'm fine, El. Just had a bit of wind knocked out of me back there. Seeing you with someone."

"I..." What could she say? She was moving on.

"Is it serious?"

"In two weeks?"

"It could have been going on before."

"You think I would have slept with you if I was seeing someone?" For some reason that really hurt.

A lot more than it should have.

"No. But if you weren't exclusive with him at that time, there's no reason why you shouldn't have..."

If she was someone else, maybe. Brett knew her. She didn't sleep around. But didn't bother to respond.

"Anyway, I'm happy for you. It just caught me by surprise, you know?"

She'd loved him so much once. "Brett..."

"No. It's fine. Good, really. Best for all of us. Just... Is he good to you, El?"

"Yes, very." Insofar as it went with only two dates between them. And seeing him at work.

But he made her laugh. And right now, that was a huge plus.

Also, Jason wasn't getting impatient with her, in spite of her not going home with him. He wasn't giving up on her.

"Who is he?"

"A pediatric pulmonary specialist who has a couple patients on my unit."

"Someone you met relatively recently, then?"

"Brett, why all the questions? What do you want to know?"

He waited so long she thought he was going to stand her up for an answer again. "I want to know you're happy, El."

She believed him. And said, "I'm on my way there—to being happy."

Because she wasn't going to live the rest of her life without joy.

Even if she had to live it without Brett.

CHAPTER TWENTY-ONE

ONE GOOD THING came of Brett's disastrous stop at the Bistro Saturday night. He was able to tell Jeff that progress was being made. That Chloe was in daily counseling and doing much better. He'd had to tell Jeff that, no, he hadn't spoken to Chloe personally, and no, no one had said whether Chloe had asked about him.

They'd all agreed that Chloe would have this time to herself without contact with Jeff. And Jeff agreed that it should be left at that.

He and his college roommate had scheduled a golf game near Anaheim for the following weekend, and by the time Brett hung up Sunday evening, he was convinced that Jeff was doing better.

Work awaited him in his hotel room Sunday night. With a 6:00 a.m. flight out of LAX to New York, he didn't have time to waste. Flipping open his laptop, he turned it on. Turned on his tablet, too.

And picked up his cell phone.

Ella might be out. He just needed to know.

So he'd quit thinking about her.

"Hello?"

"It's me."

"I know."

The lights blazed brightly in his luxurious hotel room. He closed his eyes against the glare and was back on a boat, in the dark...

"I just wanted to apologize. If I made you feel awkward, I had no right..."

"You're right, you didn't."

Okay, good. "So...you're having a good weekend?"

"Yes."

"Are you with Chloe?" It was a reasonable question. To know if, when she answered his questions, she had an audience.

"No. But I was going to call you tomorrow. Chloe would like to see Jeff, just for a visit, sometime in the next couple weeks."

They arranged a meeting for a week from the coming Thursday—almost two weeks away. At Brett's house. Jeff would expect Chloe to be coming in from LA. Chloe wanted the meeting to be someplace private, but also neutral.

And clearly, it couldn't happen at Ella's. Jeff would know instantly where Chloe was staying. He'd also know that his sister had been lying to him all this time.

So...fine. They'd had business to discuss. It was good he'd called. Now he could get to work.

"Why did you call, Brett?"

As he sat, bent over, elbows on his knees, staring at his shoes in the plush beige carpet, he measured his words. "Just to know that you're okay." He was sure about that.

"No, what do you really want? Clearly it bothered you to see me with Jason last night. You want to talk about it?"

The man had a name. It was *Jason*.

Not a bad name.

"It just…"

"Look, it's okay to admit that you didn't like seeing your ex-wife with another man. You're human for God's sake, Brett. You're going to feel emotion every now and then."

"I just…"

"Just tell me one thing."

"If I can."

"Did it change anything for you? Where we're concerned? Seeing me with Jason. Are you interested in exploring any kind of a relationship with me at all?"

He was interested in having sex with her again. As soon as possible. And then again after that. And maybe for the rest of his life.

"The only reason we've been back in touch was for Jeff and Chloe. You didn't even know until you called that Chloe was ready to see Jeff. Which means there was no reason for your call…unless something's changed…"

She knew him well. And was calling him out in a way she never had in the past.

"No, El." He heard the words he knew were true. "Nothing's changed."

He heard the click on the other end of the line and realized he didn't even know where she'd been talking to him from.

Or if she'd have someone there to wipe away the tears he'd heard in her voice when she'd asked him that last question.

ELLA DIDN'T HEAR from Brett again during her day off and told herself that she was firmly over him as she dressed in yellow scrubs with kitty cats Tuesday morning. Brett hadn't called, but Jason had. He invited her to lunch in the hospital cafeteria on Tuesday. A big step. They were going to be seen together in a nonworking moment in front of their peers. Some had already seen them together at the Bistro. It wasn't like there was anything to hide.

Still, Ella hadn't really been ready to broadcast their dating status to the entire hospital. It wasn't as if they'd agreed to be exclusive or anything.

But she accepted the invitation. It was all well and good to talk about getting on with her life, but the words meant nothing if she turned her back on opportunities to do so.

Which was why she greeted Jason with a more intimate smile than she might have otherwise when he arrived to pick her up, ten minutes later than scheduled. He leaned forward, as though he might kiss her cheek, and her pager sounded. A 911.

From the emergency room.

Which meant that someone had asked for her specifically.

Jason went with her to see what was wrong.

Ella's heart raced the entire time she stood in the elevator. Standing beside her, Jason waited for other staff members to exit the car when it stopped on the sixth floor, and then, when they were alone, held her hand the rest of the way down.

"The page was from a nurse," she said.

"Someone you know?"

She shook her head.

There'd been no callback number given.

Just a 911 to emergency.

"Maybe it was a mistake."

She'd already tried Chloe. Had been sent to voice mail. So she'd sent a text, just checking in, she'd said, not wanting to alarm her sister-in-law if she wasn't involved.

She was in a children's hospital. She didn't know any other children but Cody.

A nurse was waiting for her when Ella got off the elevator. "We have an adult female. We tried to get her to the hospital," the young woman said, referring to the Santa Raquel general hospital, as the children's hospital couldn't treat adults except in cases of severe emergency, "but she wouldn't budge until she saw you. Dr. Johnson has her in triage, just until we get her out of here. She just walked in off the street, and she's got a baby…"

Chloe?

At a run now, beside the other woman, Ella made it to the examining room first. She pushed inside.

Horror immediately followed relief. It wasn't Chloe.

The woman was Nora Burbank. One eye swollen shut. Her mouth misshapen. Her nose obviously broken. But she clutched her son to her and wouldn't let go.

"You need to take him to The Lemonade Stand." The words were obviously difficult for Nora to speak, but clear for all to hear. "Please. I'm asking you to babysit him for me. Just for tonight."

"What happened, Nora?" Ella took the baby, but didn't break eye contact with his mother.

"Who did this to you?"

She wanted it on record. With Jason and the other hospital staff present as witnesses.

"Ted did. But I saved him," she said, looking at her baby. "I saved Henry, Ella. Ted didn't touch him."

The baby put his finger in Ella's mouth. And when she grinned at him, he grinned back.

"Okay," she said, making an instant decision. "I'll take him home with me. I'll babysit him. But I'm also going to call the High Risk team, and you're going to let these people get you in an ambulance and straight to the hospital."

Nora nodded. "I'll go. I just need you to keep Henry. I saved him. I'm a good mom. And I want to live at The Lemonade Stand until I can get us back on our feet."

Ella had some phone calls to make. Detective Sanchez first, to get Ted Burbank in custody. Their child protective services delegate. Lila McDaniels. But first, she put an arm around Nora, kissed the woman's head and told her that she was, indeed, a good mother.

She waited until the ambulance arrived. Unwilling to take Henry out of his mother's sight until she had to go. And then made one last promise.

"He'll be waiting for you," she said.

And knew that she'd do whatever it took to see that it happened.

So much for second chances. Ted Burbank be damned.

BRETT WAS IN bed in a hotel room in Wisconsin Tuesday night when he read the report. Nora Burbank had been treated and released into the care of Lynn Bishop, the nurse practitioner at The Lemonade Stand. Her son, Henry, was with her. Both were in protective custody. Meaning that until Ted Burbank was found, Santa Raquel police were stationed at the Stand, guarding Nora's cottage.

Off-duty police. Volunteering their time in four-hour shifts.

Ella's name was on the case.

He read it all.

And noticed one thing more than anything else.

Throughout the entire episode, High Risk team member, Nurse Ella Ackerman, had been accompanied and aided by Dr. Jason Everly.

Brett wanted to hate the man.

But couldn't.

He didn't hear from Ella, not that he'd expected to.

But as soon as he was back in town at the end of that week, he went to his mother's house. Lights were on. House lights, not the timer ones. She was in there.

He texted her to let her know he was out front.

No response.

Out of his car, leaning back against it in case she looked out, he waited. And half an hour later, texted her again.

I have to see you. To talk to you.

This time, his phone buzzed a text. Brett's hands were sweating as he opened the message.

Go.

Why couldn't she ask if something was wrong? Wonder, at least?

I'm not feeling well.

His fingers flew over the tiny keys, and his thumb punched Send. It was bunk. And shamed him. But he needed her, dammit. She was the only one who would understand.

You're fine. I saw you leaning against your car.

So she was watching him through the window. Ella's seeing someone. A doctor, he typed.

I hadn't heard.

Why should she have? Did she think a date would come through on a High Risk team report? She was just blowing him off. And he knew it.

I'm struggling with it. Don't know what to do.

He was a powerful businessman. Known and respected across the nation. And here he was, standing outside his mother's house, feeling lost and unsure of himself.

Dammit. He was what he was, incapable of having a normal relationship, in part because of her. She'd raised him in that home...

No. Brett climbed back in his car as his thoughts deteriorated. He didn't blame his mother for anything his father had done. Or for keeping them in that home. She'd stayed because as long as she was there, his father looked for jobs and eventually found work. Those jobs had not only eventually provided the insurance that paid for Livia to have the best care, but it had also allowed his mother to be a stay-at-home mom, there to care for Livia 24/7. And not once had his father inflicted his violence on Livia. Not once. His mom had stayed for Livia. And Brett would have done the same.

He turned the key in the ignition. And his phone buzzed.

Would you marry her again if you could?

He read the question twice.

No.

His answer to her was unequivocal. She'd understand that, too.

Because it hadn't just been his father who'd broken the vow to keep violence out of their home. She'd broken it, too.

Then you have to let her go.

Just as his mother had let him go.

Because she was afraid she'd take her anger out on him again.

As she had the last day he'd seen her. The day of Livia's funeral.

The day any hope of a happy life for him had ended.

He just hadn't known it yet.

CHAPTER TWENTY-TWO

BRETT HADN'T HEARD from Ella at all since he'd told her that nothing had changed.

Nor had he tried contacting her, other than a brief call to finalize Jeff and Chloe's meeting plans.

As his mother had said, he had to let her go.

And still he hoped, as he flew into LA and drove home to Santa Raquel the following Thursday in time to meet Jeff at his place, that when Chloe showed, Ella would be with her.

"What time did she say she'd be here?" Jeff paced from the living room to the formal dining room and back again, his heels sounding on the hardwood floor with each step. Still in black pants and a white dress shirt with small black pinstripes, he'd taken off his tie.

And looked...wrinkled.

Jeff knew the designated time. But Brett told him again anyway. "Seven." After dinner at the Stand, but Jeff didn't know that, of course.

Chloe was a couple minutes late.

"She could be caught in traffic," Jeff said now. "You know what LA traffic is like at rush hour."

He did know. He drove in it a lot. And commiserated with his friend. More than Jeff knew. Loving a woman you couldn't have—for whatever reason—was difficult.

"She's bringing Cody with her, right?"

"That's what she said." Or rather what Ella had said when she'd spoken with him briefly to finalize meeting plans. He hadn't actually spoken to Chloe. "She wants you to see him."

He knew the mistake of his words as Jeff swung around, a look of horror on his face. "I thought... hoped...with Thanksgiving coming up and all... but if she's bringing him so he can see me, that would imply that she's not planning to come home." He flopped down on the couch. "Where he'd see me every day."

"You don't know that," Brett said. But he'd drawn the same conclusion. "Could be she didn't want to leave him wherever he's staying. Could be that she wants to ask for just a little more time."

All Ella had told him was that Chloe needed to speak to Jeff.

A car turned in, coming up his drive. Ella's car. Was she with them?

"You sure we can talk in your bedroom?" Jeff stood, dangling his hands at his sides, rubbing them together and dropping them again, as though he didn't know what to do with them.

"When you're ready, I'll take Cody into the living room, turn on the TV while you two talk.

There's a conversation alcove in the suite, and you'll have privacy there."

It was the only place he could think of where the couple could talk without being overheard. The walls in his house weren't well insulated, and sound traveled through the old register ducts.

And the fact that there was a bed in the room, if they needed it…well, he'd changed the sheets.

ELLA DIDN'T SHOW. After playing with his dad for half an hour or so, Cody had fallen asleep on the blanket Brett had laid on the wool rug in the family room, watching a Blu-ray about a dog named Blue. Something Chloe had brought with her.

Jeff and Chloe had been in the bedroom for over an hour. With the little one asleep, Brett could concentrate on his agenda for the next morning's meeting in Phoenix—a fifty-page booklet of motions—and research every item on it.

He was more than a quarter of the way through when he thought he heard his bedroom door opening.

The knob was old—had a bit of a squeak to it. Saving his work, he set his laptop on the coffee table, turned off the television and reached to eject the disc so that he could pack up the bag Chloe had brought with Cody's things in it. The boy had fallen asleep before he'd had the graham cracker snack his mother had brought for him.

A snap and he turned. Had that been the door

closing again? He heard a thump and, disc forgotten, Brett moved across the family room, through the kitchen to the hall leading back to the master suite. "Let me go, Jeff."

Brett heard the words as he started down the hall. Chloe's tone was firm. Not frightened.

"Chloe, wait! Just give me a second. I listened to you. I heard everything you had to say. I just want you to understand my perspective …"

A fair request. Brett stopped. Thinking he'd turn and go back to work.

"I listened to you, Jeff. For over half an hour. I understand that you think this is all me—but who, when he says he wants to reconcile, calls his wife a stupid bitch?"

What? Had he heard that right? Moving forward, Brett stood outside the door, his hand on the knob.

"I know, that was completely wrong," Jeff said in a tone that told Brett his friend was truly sorry. "I apologized. It's just…you have no idea how hard it's been with you gone and me not knowing where you are. Not being able to see you or Cody. My son is learning new words, and I don't even understand them because I'm not there…"

"And telling me I'm not very bright just because I don't agree with your take on our problems?"

"Frustration, Chloe. You know I don't mean it. Hell, you're smarter than I am by far, and we both know it."

Nerves tense, heart pounding, Brett slipped into old habits, zeroing in on the mundane. The thoughts and words that were least threatening.

Jeff had been an average student. Chloe had excelled. But that only made one a better student than the other...

"And it's not like you've never lost your cool, or said things you aren't proud of," Jeff said.

Brett's shoulders relaxed. Maybe he should go...

"I've never called you an effin' liar." Chloe stumbled over the words.

"Would you just stop?" A new tone had entered Jeff's voice. A tone Brett had never heard before. One that kept him standing at the door. "Why do you have to go on and on and on? It's like you remember every bad thing I've ever done!"

"I'm only talking about the past hour, Jeff. You've threatened to divorce me if I don't come home. To have me charged with fraud for saying that our home is my address when I'm not living there."

"Stop!"

Brett heard the word just as Chloe screamed out, "Jeff!" and Brett burst through the door.

Jeff had been closest to him and the force with which Brett pushed into the room knocked him back, stopping him just before his raised hand made contact with his wife's face.

Like a slow-motion movie, everyone just stood there. Frozen.

Jeff's hand suspended, Chloe ducking and Brett breathing fire.

In the next second, or countless seconds later, Jeff's hand fell slowly to his side. Brett could feel every inch of the descent. Chloe, crying, ran from the room.

And Brett...couldn't leave.

The look of horror, of utter terror, on his friend's face held Brett in place.

"Oh, my God, what have I done?" Hands over his head, Jeff fell to the bed. Rocking back and forth. "What have I done? Oh, God, what have I done?"

Brett couldn't comfort him. If he hadn't come in when he did, Jeff would have hit his wife.

That wasn't okay. Jeff wasn't okay. His marriage could very well be over.

The man rocked. His body shook, and Brett knew he was crying.

And remembered a night more than fifteen years earlier. He'd been a freshman college student, had had a call from his father who was in jail, wanting him to bail him out. He hadn't done it. For his mother's sake.

His father had been crying, too. Asking for Brett's help. He'd turned his back. On his own father.

But he'd called his mother. Thinking she'd be thankful enough that she'd start talking to him again. Let him back in her life.

She hadn't responded.

He'd just lost his sister, and that night he knew he'd lost both of his parents, as well.

He'd started to cry. Jeff had come in. Brett had pretended to be asleep. Praying that Jeff would either go to bed or get what he'd come in for and leave.

It turned out that he'd come in for Brett. Because he'd known that Brett had refused to help his father. He'd known, even though Brett hadn't said so, that leaving his father in jail—no matter how much the asshole had deserved it—made Brett feel dirty.

Jeff hadn't asked Brett to go get drunk. He hadn't made a joke or shrugged off the situation. He'd laid a hand on Brett's shoulder. Told him he'd get through it. And he'd sat with him for the rest of the night, listening to the horror stories of the previous eight years of Brett's life.

Moving slowly, worrying about Chloe, wishing Ella was there, Brett approached the bed. Sat down. Put his hand on Jeff's shoulder.

"You need help, man," he said. "You gotta get help."

Jeff stilled. He quit crying. But he didn't meet Brett's gaze. "The tension…it just gets… I tell myself everything will be fine. I remind myself that everyone else works and raises a family. That my challenges aren't the end of the world. That there are others so much worse off. Others who handle so much more. I think of the good times. And still…the tension builds."

Brett wasn't a counselor. As Ella had said that night on the boat—he paid others to do the work.

"What causes the tension?" he asked because Jeff seemed to need to talk.

Shrugging, Jeff shook his head.

"Is it money?"

"Maybe. I'm definitely more irritable when stocks are down."

Not uncommon after a bad day at work.

"Look at me," Brett said.

Jeff slowly turned his head. But he didn't hold Brett's gaze for long. Clearly his shame was too great.

"Jeff?"

The other man turned his head again. "Are drugs involved?"

"No."

"And there's no pressing debt? Are you gambling?"

"No! Of course not! If I knew I had a problem, don't you think I'd tell you? Tell myself, for God's sake? I'm losing the only thing in the world I care about!"

"Okay. Okay." Stereotypes, profiling, weren't going to help here. Because the answers weren't always easy.

Weren't always clear or neat or clean.

"So when did it start? What caused you to lash out the first time? How long has it been building?"

Jeff sat for a long time. Brett heard the front door open and close. Hoped to God that Chloe was going straight to The Lemonade Stand. Or to Ella, who would take her there.

He needed to call Ella. To warn her.

"You know…" Jeff sat up a little straighter. "I'll tell you exactly when it started," he said. "It was after Cody was born. Chloe was really struggling with her postpartum depression. I had to take time off work to stay home with her and take care of the baby. She'd follow me from room to room. Lie on the floor beside my desk when I was trying to get my work done. I get paid on commission, and I see money going out the door right and left, my marriage is pretty much empty and now I've got this tiny little human being who needs me 24/7. It's like there wasn't enough of me to go around…"

Reminded of how he felt when Ella had handed him the home pregnancy test results when he'd come through the door all those years before, Brett wished he couldn't relate.

But he could.

"I wasn't ever going to be able to do enough," Jeff was saying. "I couldn't provide enough. If Chloe wasn't going to be able to contribute, I'd need a cleaning person, a babysitter, and I had to start a college fund, too. The pressure was always there, pushing me harder and harder."

"But things got better. Chloe got better."

"I know. That's why I didn't think we had a problem. Everything was fine." Jeff hung his head. "Or I thought it was."

"I'm guessing you've got some anger built up over it all." Brett said the only thing that made sense to him.

"I know that every time the stocks go down now, even when I know the recovery is going to follow, I get that same feeling I had right after Cody was born. Like I'm strangling, and there's nothing I can do..."

"You need help."

"Yeah."

"You can get through this, Jeff. You and Chloe."

He shook his head. "She's never going to stick with me now. Not after what I did tonight. I don't deserve her."

Maybe not. And maybe Chloe would file for a divorce. Maybe she needed to.

"Ella told me once that all Chloe wanted was for you to see that you were having problems and get help. Just like she got help after Cody was born. You stuck by her then..."

"Yeah."

"And you didn't hit her, man. You've never hit your wife. Have you?"

Brett forced his fingers to loosen.

"No."

Brett breathed.

"But I've shoved her," Jeff said. "Pretty hard that last time. I didn't mean to. She stepped up just as I was passing through the doorway, but when she got in my way, I reached out with both hands and shoved her into the doorjamb."

Ella had been right.

"Have you ever hurt Cody?"

Jeff turned, meeting Brett's stern look. "I've never left a bruise on my kid, Brett. I swear to God."

"I believe you." He did. No reason why he should. But he did.

"I was a little rougher than I should have been, once or twice," he said. "I made him cry, and I swore to myself that I'd never do that again. That if I did, I'd hang myself. I'm not doing to my kid what your dad did to you."

"Don't do to your wife what my dad did to my mom," Brett said.

"You think I should let her go?"

Brett couldn't give advice on this one. This was Jeff's row to hoe.

But he could empathize. He could be a friend.

"That's for you to figure out, man," he said. "Not every abuser or abuse situation is the same. And you have the advantage of growing up in a loving home. You aren't starting out from behind, having to fight the pattern of abuse."

He could guide Jeff to the help he needed. They had resources—people he trusted who could find a support group for Jeff to join in Palm Desert in addition to individual counseling.

"I'll do whatever it takes," Jeff said. But the man looked beaten.

Because nothing—no amount of counseling or time—would ever change what had happened there that night. Nothing would erase, in Chloe's mind, the memory of her husband raising his hand to her.

And suddenly, as he looked at Jeff, Brett knew that there, but by the grace of God, went he.

CHAPTER TWENTY-THREE

ELLA SAT WITH Chloe until she finally fell asleep. When Chloe had called from Brett's, as soon as she'd determined that Brett was with Jeff and that no one had been physically harmed, she'd told her to stay put while she took a cab over.

They'd gone straight from there to The Lemonade Stand. Sara had been at home with her fiancé and his daughter, but she'd come in. Lynn Bishop and her sister-in-law Maddie, both of whom had small children and lived on the premises, came up to the main house, too. Lynn, in case Chloe needed any medical treatment, and Maddie, to help watch Cody.

It had been nearly eleven by the time they arrived back at Ella's apartment. Thankfully, Cody fell asleep in the car on the way home, and Chloe had been able to get him from the car seat to his bed without waking him.

Lila McDaniels had not notified the police, for which Ella was thankful. The only thing that could have made the night worse was to see her brother arrested.

But there'd been no reason to make an arrest.

Thanks to Brett. The timing of his intervention had been seemingly divine.

And Chloe wouldn't have pressed charges anyway. Although she'd been understandably shaken, she was holding up well, thanks to Sara's counseling over the past weeks.

She'd handled the situation with Jeff just as she'd been coached.

And could have been physically hurt, regardless.

The whole situation left Ella feeling sick. Confused.

And out of hope.

JEFF WENT HOME. Put himself in anger-management counseling. Joined an anger-management support group. And went back to church. He talked to his pastor, asking him to keep an eye on him and to pray for his family.

And every night he wrote to his wife—letters that stayed with him since he had no address for Chloe.

A couple weeks after the incident at his house, Brett called Ella to ask if Chloe would be open to a supervised conversation with Jeff.

Thanksgiving had come and gone. Ella had called Jeff, who'd just come back from spending the day with a family he'd met through his support group. A middle-aged couple with three children. The husband had hit all of them at one time or another.

And hadn't lifted a hand to them for more than eight years. Jeff told Ella that he'd never seen such a close, caring family.

She'd heard the hope in his words. But hadn't relayed either the words or her interpretation of them to Chloe as the three of them drove to The Lemonade Stand to share with the rest of the residents the full turkey dinner Chloe had planned.

Jeff hadn't asked about Chloe, and Ella hadn't mentioned her, either.

According to Brett, when he'd called to relay Jeff's request to speak to Chloe, Jeff had been making good progress and was at a point where there were some questions only Chloe could answer for him. Like when did she first notice the change in him? How long did the progression take from irritability to verbal abuse? He didn't remember many instances, but had been told to expect her to remember many more. He needed her perspective. But only if she could give it without causing undue stress to herself.

Ella talked to Chloe, who asked if Ella would go with her when she talked to Sara about Jeff's request. Chloe said she wanted Ella's full support if she decided to speak with Jeff and figured Sara could help Ella understand what Chloe couldn't always put into words. Sara advised that Chloe was certainly, in her opinion, healthy enough to speak with her husband, but strongly believed that the session should be supervised.

Sara seemed to think that Chloe had an interest in saving her marriage.

Ella hadn't asked. She still didn't.

But when she called Brett that night—the first Wednesday in December—she told him that she thought Chloe was leaning in that direction.

She'd waited for Chloe to go to bed and was in her own suite on the other side of the apartment, in her bathroom, with the fan blowing.

Speaking as softly as she could.

"You sound as if you don't think them getting back together is a good idea," he replied, as though they had all night to chat. He'd picked up on the first ring. His voice sounded good to her. Too good.

She didn't think it was a good idea for Chloe to speak to Jeff yet. Just as she didn't think it was a good idea for her and Brett to talk. It was too soon. For both of them. She'd been dating Jason for seven weeks. He'd made it clear he wanted to take things to the next level. And anytime he tried to get intimate with her, she pictured Brett and pulled back.

"I think it's too soon for them to be together," she told Brett, referring to Jeff and Chloe, wondering where Brett was. And not wanting to know. Not wanting to be able to picture him in real time.

"I mean, Jeff's my brother, and I love him and

want him happy. I don't want him to lose his family. I don't want to lose Chloe as a sister-in-law, either. But more, I don't want Chloe hurt and my brother in jail. Just the thought of how close he came…"

"He's in a twenty-four-month program," Brett reminded her. "And he's already making progress. He's been able to take an honest look at himself. He's taking moral accountability, and has a strong support system set up already and an even stronger desire to change."

"I was reading…" Ella stopped. Swallowed. Started again. "Only three to eleven percent of abusers actually recover…"

"Jeff's issues haven't escalated as far as many of those accounted for in those statistics, El. He was heading there, but he didn't live the life of having to cover his actions over and over. He doesn't carry around the memory of actually hitting his wife. And his lashing out wasn't out of a need to control Chloe, or some lacking in his own self-concept. The only manipulation he's guilty of is trying to get her to believe, as he believed, that he wasn't heading down a wrong path. He has no drug or alcohol problems to fight…"

"You believe he can do this. That he can be one of the three percent."

"Three to eleven percent. And I guess I do."

With her knees to her chest, she wrapped her arms around her shins and cradled herself. She'd missed a period and was feeling cranky. While she'd had unpredictable and difficult periods, it had been a long time since her body had acted up on her. Not since she'd lost the baby.

"A key factor to recovery is that there be separation," Brett added. "At least a year is recommended, but because Chloe acted before Jeff's behavior escalated into full-on physical abuse, their time apart could be shorter."

"I told Chloe she could stay with me until she and Jeff get things figured out. We're doing fine here now that we've settled into a routine, and that way I can help with Cody.

"Anyway, Chloe said she was fine with a meeting. She wants to help. And if all goes well, she'd like to set up regular meetings with Jeff, one every couple weeks to start, so that he can continue to be a part of Cody's life."

She heard a squeak in the background. "Where are you?" The question slipped out before she could remember she didn't want to know.

"Home. I just got in from LA, and I'm heading into my room to get comfortable."

He was going to be undressing, he meant. Too much information.

"I heard a squeak." The explanation sounded lame.

"The doorknob on my bedroom door sticks. I was going to get it fixed, but I've decided not to. If not for the squeak, I'd never have heard Chloe trying to get out of the room that night, wouldn't have been outside the door…"

"I wondered how you happened to burst in at just the right moment…" So much rested on his having been there. Jeff's whole life. His marriage. Chloe and Cody's lives, too. "Your instincts are well honed to prevent abuse," she said, thinking out loud.

But the words were true. Growing up as he had, Brett was always on alert.

She heard his belt buckle clink. And realized what was supposed to have been a two-minute call had already gone on too long.

Without an extra word getting in anywhere, she made plans with Brett to arrange an afternoon meeting with Jeff a week from that Friday—nine days away. She'd take time off work to drive Chloe to Palm Desert. Brett would let Jeff know to alert his counselor to the plan.

Brett would be in Texas at the end of next week so couldn't be present himself, Ella was glad to hear.

And disappointed, too.

ELLA DIDN'T EVEN consider that something other than food poisoning could be wrong with her when she threw up suddenly at work Thursday afternoon—the day after she'd spoken to Brett.

Jason happened to be on the unit at the time. Told her to take the rest of the day off. She couldn't figure out what she'd eaten that didn't agree with her. With Chloe serving dinner at the Stand all week while she honed the menu, Ella had eaten out with Jason two of the past three nights. And had what the rest of the residents at the Stand had the other night. No one else had taken ill.

Jason checked in with her again the next morning, though he didn't generally do Friday morning rounds, and she was glad to tell him she was fine.

Until that afternoon when she experienced another violent bout of nausea that caused her to run out of the room while she and Jason were in with a patient.

Jason found her half an hour later, in her office, going over notes for a staff meeting she was holding the next morning. He walked in, put a hand on her neck and then picked up her wrist, as though taking her pulse.

"Anything wrong, doc?" she asked, a twist to her mouth. She wasn't worried. She knew her body. And nothing was seriously wrong.

She might have a minor bug.

Or a case of the nerves. Worrying about Jeff's emotional state. His marriage.

Torn between Brett and moving on.

Dating a man she liked but knew she didn't love. Wanting Chloe to be happy...

"Are you prone to nausea?" Jason asked, sounding all doctor-like as he looked at her.

"No. I don't think I've thrown up since I was a

kid." Back when she'd first started her period, her cramps were so bad they sometimes made her sick to her stomach. She later found out that her system basically told itself to ovulate and menstruate at the same time. Which was why she couldn't conceive without help.

"Food poisoning doesn't last more than twenty-four hours and doesn't just come in once-a-day bouts."

"You think I have the flu?" She'd been concerned about it herself, after this afternoon's illness. She obviously had a bit of a bug that her body was mostly fighting off. With a bit of nausea as the only symptom. Which was why she was in her office, away from the patients. Since the initial Ebola scare in the United States, she'd been more aware of the viruses that could catch you unawares. More aware of her chance of catching something, working in a hospital. And more aware of her ability to spread, them, too.

"You don't have the flu," he said. "You aren't the least bit flushed, have no fever and, by your account, aren't feeling lethargic or achy."

The way he was looking at her, eyebrow raised, he seemed to have something else on his mind.

Not that she knew him that well yet. He'd agreed to take things slow. She'd told him a bit about Chloe and Cody staying with her. About Jeff. As reasons why she couldn't jump into anything with both feet at the moment.

They had dinner a couple times a week. Saw each other at work.

And he still made her laugh.

"I hate to ask this, especially in light of my hope that we're on our way to being exclusive, but have you... Is there any chance you could be pregnant?"

"No!" Her response was immediate. And followed by another severe bout of nausea. She made it to her private bathroom. But just barely. And was embarrassed as hell when she took the moistened towel he handed her when she was done.

He was a doctor. He dealt with bodily functions every day.

But not hers.

Ella wiped her face, sitting on the floor of the bathroom, leaning back against the wall. She didn't trust herself to stray far from the commode. And the cold tile felt good.

Jason stood along the opposite wall, his lab coat giving him a sense of authority that she didn't need right then.

"I can't be pregnant, Jason."

"I can't tell you how glad I am to hear that."

He didn't want kids. It was one of the things that had drawn her to him in the first place.

She told him about her medical condition. About the years of treatments that had been necessary to help her conceive. About losing her baby. Leaving out the part about Brett not wanting the baby and retaining a divorce attorney.

"Have you had normal periods since you lost the baby?" He was frowning. And sounded so doctor like.

Her stomach felt sick again. "Up until recently, yes."

"As you know, metabolic irregularities cover such a broad range, you don't always hear or understand everything about them," he said, looking more serious than ever. "But you should have been told…sometimes—not always of course, but sometimes—pregnancy corrects the irregularity in certain hormonal imbalances, allowing a woman who couldn't conceive on her own prior to the pregnancy to conceive quite naturally afterward. Regular periods could indicate such a correction."

Oh, God. She might have been told. She couldn't remember a lot about the time immediately following her miscarriage. She'd been too busy grieving. And divorcing. Paralyzed, Ella sat on the floor, staring up at Jason as he said, "Doctors don't always mention the possibility, depending on the circumstances, because there's not enough known about why it does or does not happen, but, there are enough marked instances that we know that it can. Anyway…I find it interesting that you tell me you can't get pregnant, not that you haven't been with anyone recently."

She knew the exact second that realization dawned

on him. Knew, too, that he'd probably read the truth in her expression.

The timing had been right when she'd been on the boat with Brett. If she were a woman who ovulated normally, she could have conceived...

Afraid she might be sick again, she leaned her head back against the wall and said, "It's not what you think."

She wouldn't have blamed him if he walked out on her. She'd been free to sleep with Brett. But when Jason had asked her if she'd been in a relationship recently, she'd told him the truth. That she hadn't.

"I'm assuming this is why you've wanted to go slowly with us? Because there's someone else?"

She didn't hear any recrimination in his voice.

"There is no one else." But yes, the fact that she'd slept with her ex-husband seven weeks and six days ago did probably sway her decision to take things slowly with Jason. Mostly, it had been the fact that she was still in love with Brett that had done it, though. And sitting there on the bathroom floor, Ella told Jason about Brett. The divorce. And his recent advent into her life. When Jason reached out a hand to her, suggesting with more kindness than she felt she deserved, that they go do a blood test, Ella had a feeling, as she knew he did, that they weren't going to get the answer they wanted.

CHAPTER TWENTY-FOUR

OH, GOD. SHE was pregnant. For the second day in a row, Ella took half a day's leave and left work before she was scheduled. She didn't go anywhere in particular. Just drove around.

Alone.

Jason had asked if she wanted company. He'd offered to spend the evening with her. But she had a feeling he was going to be distancing himself from her life fairly quickly.

He was a good guy. He'd be a friend.

But he didn't want children of his own, let alone another man's child.

And that other man—the one whose child this was—didn't want anyone.

SHE ENDED UP at the beach. She'd driven by The Lemonade Stand. Needing to go in. To see Chloe. The place was crawling with compassionate women and she needed someone to talk to.

She'd even settle for Lila McDaniels. Would prefer the older woman, actually, with her quiet, but firm, motherly way.

Ella's nerves needed a firm talking-to.

But she couldn't tell anyone else until Brett knew.

She'd already made an appointment with an obstetrician she knew from the hospital for Monday—having explained her situation. Her hormonal imbalance. The loss of her first child. The woman had worked her in.

She'd had a doctor's confirmation. She was pregnant.

At the moment, all that made her feel was fear.

She was all alone.

What if something happened and she lost this baby, too?

Shaking, she stared at the ocean. Jason had assured her that if her body had reversed itself, there was every chance she could carry this baby to term.

This baby. She was pregnant.

She, Ella Ackerman, was going to be a mama.

If all went well.

And...Brett...

She had to tell him. Right away. But she wanted nothing from him. And was clear on one thing. She wasn't going to give him the chance to reject their baby a second time.

BRETT HAD NO idea why Ella wanted to see him. But he didn't ask her any questions, either, when she texted him on a Friday afternoon eight weeks after their weekend at the cabin and asked if she could see him right away.

He assumed it had to do with Chloe. She was

supposed to be taking Chloe to Palm Desert to meet with Jeff the following week. But hadn't liked the idea of a meeting so soon after Jeff's explosion. Maybe she'd talked Chloe into waiting.

Still, a phone call would have done in that case. What could she have to talk about that had to be done in person? Ella had asked if they could meet at his place. Out by the pool. She'd said it made her feel good out there. Peaceful.

He was expecting her at six. By quarter to he was pacing. The tea was freshly brewed. With lemon. But there was a bottle of wine chilling, too.

For the first time in history, he'd cut out of a board meeting before its conclusion when her text had come through late that afternoon. The meeting was continuing the next day, and there'd be a full video transcript. He'd wanted time to change out of his suit into khakis and a polo shirt. He always ended up acting like a stuffed shirt around her.

Probably made her uncomfortable.

Was she coming to tell him she was ready to have a purely physical relationship? That it hadn't worked out with her doctor friend?

Or that it had and she was getting married again?

Maybe it had nothing to do with them at all.

She hadn't bought a house yet. Had she decided not to stay in Santa Raquel after all?

He wanted a beer.

But had sworn off beer after that night on the boat. Though he'd only had three drinks that night, he'd made a mistake in sleeping with Ella.

He'd known that she couldn't make love with him without investing part of her heart.

He'd known and done it anyway. Because he'd wanted to touch the heart of her one more time.

It hadn't been fair to her.

And if she'd give him a chance, he'd apologize…

The doorbell rang.

Brett was ready.

HE WASN'T READY. Studying the staunch expression on Ella's face, unable to glean even a hint of what was going on with her, he started to panic.

Like he hadn't panicked since high school.

She sat across from him at the table by his pool, sipping tea. In black pants and matching black-and-white tweed jacket with silk trim. Looking professional and gorgeous and untouchable all rolled into one. Had she carried the clothes to work or gone home to change before meeting him?

"I need to talk to you," she said, obviously uncomfortable.

"That's what you said."

He'd like to believe her odd tension was just nerves, but didn't think so.

"I… Something has been on my mind, Brett, and I need it cleared up."

Why did he have the feeling that hadn't been

what she'd planned to say? Breathing more normally now, Brett said, "I'll do what I can."

"That weekend…when we were on the boat…"

So this *was* about sex! If she was ready all she had to do was say so. Should he make it easy for her?

"You drew a correlation between your dad and you. Talked about how your parents vowed to keep violence out of their home—trusting each other to do so because they both came from violence and knew how damaging it was."

He remembered Ella reacting strangely when he'd said that. As if she'd finally understood something.

Remembered, too, specifically not asking her about it.

He hadn't wanted to know, then. And didn't want to know now, either.

She didn't seem all that surprised by his lack of response. Or deterred by it, either.

She also wasn't drinking much of her tea.

"You said that I'd quit really listening to you. That I *patted you on the head* when you tried to talk to me about your fears. And so you quit talking."

He nodded, feeling far too much at the moment. He wasn't good at being vulnerable.

"Tell me how you felt, Brett. Really felt. When you came home that day and found out you were going to be a father."

"Why?" He'd spewed his frustration at her. His tension. He'd told her he wasn't like her. Wasn't ecstatic. Wasn't even happy about it. He'd accused her of never stopping to find out what he wanted. Somehow blaming her for his inability to celebrate with her.

The past was past. He wanted to leave it there.

But sitting there on his patio with Ella, noticing how much better it felt having her in his space than occupying it alone, it hit him why she was there. She'd come to him looking for a way to leave the past behind her and be free to love another man.

Jason.

He thought about telling her that he knew, thought about preventing this whole conversation— sparing himself from it. But didn't.

Ella had the right to say what she'd come here to say. Had the right to get this closure.

He also knew, without doubt, that he had to give her what she wanted...

"Please, Brett, tell me how you felt."

She didn't answer his question. Didn't tell him why.

But she didn't owe him that. He owed her.

"I was scared to death," he said, meeting her gaze in spite of what it cost him. His chest tightened to the point of pain. If he didn't know better, he'd have considered the possibility that he was having a heart attack.

But Brett knew better. The sensation was all too familiar to him.

And one he'd been having since junior high.

"Of what?"

He drew in air. "Of having someone look up to me, looking to me for example and guidance in matters of life, and me, damaged goods, ruining them. Putting the family curse on them."

"I was going to be there, too."

"Yes, but it only takes one person to bring misery to a whole family."

"You were afraid you were going to be your father."

"There's no guarantee I wouldn't be."

"Because he showed you the way, right? He showed you how a man can be absolutely, completely certain he'd never bring violence into his home and then…he did."

"Maybe."

"My father was a great dad, El. A great husband. For well over a decade there'd been no sign…and then, he just snapped."

"Maybe there were signs. Maybe you were too young to recognize them."

"I have a lot of memories of me and him when I was a kid. None of them bad."

"Kids have ways of forgiving things, forgetting them. They adjust. Adapt."

"There's no guarantee I wouldn't do the same. And I can't let that happen. I'd rather be dead than abuse someone. And the thought of creating an abusive streak in another human being...of continuing the pattern..."

"But there's no guarantee you *would* do it." Her words were a cry from the heart. Even he recognized them as such.

"Didn't you ever wonder why, after we knew you were pregnant, I'd started wandering the house in the middle of the night?"

"You were having trouble sleeping, obviously."

He hadn't planned to tell anyone other than the counselor he'd spoken to about that time in his life. About the nightmares that still haunted him when he allowed their memory to surface. Had thought that was a shame he'd carry with him to his grave.

But Ella needed his help. Needed to understand. And her comfort was more important to him than his own. At least these days. He'd grown up a bit since staying with a woman long past the time when he'd known he should get out.

"I was having nightmares, El. Every night. I'd close my eyes and there they'd be, waiting for me..."

He swallowed. Couldn't meet her gaze.

"What kind of nightmares?" The softness of her voice reached him as surely as if she'd reached out a hand and stroked his cheek.

"I'd dream about things that had really happened. About times my dad had come at me. But in mid-dream his face would change to mine. And the boy in the dream would be my son, and I'd be lifting my hand to hit him. I'd see the fear on his face. And in those eyes, the love he still felt for me. I'd want to stop my hand from coming down, but I just couldn't. Not ever. Not one single, damned night…"

He looked straight at her as he fell silent. Needing her to know the truth behind his words. The tears in Ella's eyes weren't a surprise to him.

"Didn't you ever have a good dream about him? Something about us together? A family? You said you had good years with your dad."

"Not one good dream, El."

She nodded, dislodging the tears that filled her eyes. They dropped to her cheeks. "So…the fear… it was greater than the joy? Greater than the idea of you and me making a baby together?"

She was reaching for her future. He had to help her let go of her past.

"You want the truth?" he asked, knowing that now was the time to give it to her.

"Yes."

"When I found out you'd lost the baby…my first conscious feeling was…relief. I'd been saved from what I saw as my fate—finding out too late that I was like my father."

There. Now she knew his dirtiest secret. His darkest shame. He'd felt saved when his child had died before ever being born.

Now she could leave him, the phantom in the cellar.

Brett wasn't surprised at the horrified pain on Ella's face. The fresh spate of tears in her eyes. He wasn't surprised when she stood and left him sitting there, in his beautiful garden, alone.

The only thing that surprised him were her parting words.

"I love you, Brett Ackerman."

Sad truth was he loved her, too.

CHAPTER TWENTY-FIVE

ELLA RAN FOR her car. Got around the block before she pulled over and gushed a river.

For herself. For Brett. And for the precious little child who was just beginning to form in her womb and would never know his or her father.

She'd gone to Brett's to tell him about the baby.

Chloe was going to know soon. She'd probably think it was Jason's.

And she'd be happy for Ella.

She couldn't tell Chloe, or anyone else, the truth without Brett knowing.

She had to tell him. She just hadn't been able to stay with him another minute.

She'd been sitting there, wishing she belonged. And knowing she never would. Not with Brett.

No one would.

She cried until her stomach cramped and her tongue was dry. Cried for the baby she'd lost. For the life and dreams she'd lost.

And then, when her stomach cramped, she stopped.

She had a child to think about now.

A new life.

Cradling her stomach, she sat there in the darkness and rolled down her window so she could hear the waves in the distance.

She was going to have to move.

It wouldn't be fair to Brett to have his child grow up right under his nose.

And she owed him. Because he'd done this for her. He'd given her his child.

He couldn't give her his heart. Or his life.

But he'd given her a piece of himself. A new life.

One that would be a connection between them Brett could never sever.

She just had to get herself under control enough to let him know what he'd done.

BRETT WAS OUTSIDE, still in his khakis and polo shirt, skimming the pool in the shadows cast by the landscape lighting when he heard his doorbell ring. He glanced up, a bit confused by the sound. In all the years he'd lived there, he'd never had unsolicited visitors and now it was happening a second time.

Still, it wasn't a summons he could ignore. And when he pulled open the door, he saw Ella standing there, looking exactly as she had when she'd walked out of his home an hour before except for her tear-ravaged face.

"I have to talk to you," she said, stepping forward so he had to either let her in or block her. He stepped back.

"El, I'm so sorry…" The words stuck in his throat. It was closing in on him. He'd sworn he was done hurting her. And he was doing it all over again.

With a wave of her hand she dismissed his apology. And anything else he might say.

"I came here today to tell you something. But I had to understand the past first, and then that got in my way."

She walked toward the kitchen, but before he could follow her she was on her way back to him. Looking at the floor. Not him.

"I know you don't want this, but I still have to tell you. Brett, I'm pregnant."

He was busy watching her pace, trying to get a good look at her face so he could figure out if she was pissed or beside herself with pain. It took an extra second for her words to register. She'd come to tell him she was pregnant?

Dear God, don't let it be true.

That was why she'd been asking questions about the past?

Because she was pregnant?

No. Oh, God, no. Please…no.

She couldn't be. They'd made love one night with no thermometer. No test tubes, or small rooms with a command to him to perform. No artificial insemination. Or fertility treatments. It had been physical desire, period. No baby making involved.

His thoughts flew like snowflakes in a blizzard. Mixing with mental repeats of the words he'd said to her earlier.

"I understand that you don't want a child in your life. And I'm absolutely certain that I don't want you in this baby's life. You're right—he doesn't deserve a father who would be relieved by his death. The damage that would do to him would be irreparable…"

She paced. Still not looking at him. "But as his father, you had a right to know. I had an obligation to tell you. So there. You've been told. Now I have to go…"

She headed for the door and Brett, arms crossed, barred her way.

"Wait." The word was short. Softly spoken. And filled with more emotion than he could decipher. But panic was definitely in there.

"The baby's mine." His gums hurt with the force with which his jaws clamped down on the words.

She looked up at him. And he saw the anger lighting a fire in her eyes. "I haven't slept with anyone but you since we met." How words that were so cuttingly delivered could ease the storm inside him he didn't know, but they did.

Just not enough. "I wasn't asking a question," he clarified. She wouldn't be there if the child wasn't his. And then continued. "How dare you set me up like that? You come in here asking me to be honest about our past pregnancy, knowing full well that you're about to tell me about a current one?"

"Exactly." She was still staring him down in the front hallway of his home. "Because I needed to know the truth, Brett, not whatever obligatory or accountable thing you'd come up with. We know our situation. No matter how much we care about each other, we aren't good for each other. A baby doesn't change that. If anything, it makes any personal association between us even more out of reach because any risk I take now would involve the baby, as well."

If she'd reached out and slapped him it would have hurt less.

His worst nightmare had just been reborn. With a twist. Ella wasn't going to let him be involved with his child.

Why wasn't he relieved? And what in the hell was he going to do?

"Is that all you've got to say?"

She nodded. But didn't leave. If she was done talking, she should leave.

No. It was his turn.

There were questions he should ask. His mind was frozen.

"I'm sorry. I shouldn't have been sharp with you." This was no more her fault than his. And he couldn't blame her for needing answers. "You have every right to ask whatever questions you need to ask. To make sure the past doesn't repeat itself."

He noticed her lips trembling. And felt shaky, too. All over. His thoughts. His body. His heart. The ground he stood on. Everything was shaky.

"I'll pay for everything."

That felt right.

His words brought tears to her eyes, and she shook her head.

"I told you, Brett. I'm doing this on my own. I don't want this child to be supported by someone who isn't in his or her life. There will be questions. Inferences drawn—you know, 'he really loves us or he wouldn't have supported us all these years.' I know you can't help how you feel, Brett. I don't blame you or think any less of you. I just can't set this baby up for the kind of heartache I've felt all these years." Her voice fell as her eyes continued to glisten.

The words cut into him with a sharpness he could hardly withstand. And even then, he knew she was right. Knew there was nothing he could do to change things.

She was right on all counts.

For once in his life, he wanted to be angry. Wanted to fight back.

There was nothing to fight.

"You were right about one other thing," he told her as she turned to go.

"What?" She paused at the door, looking back at him.

"Nothing's changed."

He meant between them. Her needing things he couldn't give. Him trying to do the right thing and hurting her in the process. It wasn't until later, after he'd calmed down enough to think and was replaying their exchange over and over in his mind, that it dawned on him that she could have taken his statement another way.

"Nothing's changed," he'd said. Had she thought he was referring to how he'd felt the last time she'd told him she was pregnant? Referring to the things he'd told her by the pool that afternoon? About him not wanting the child? Not wanting to be a father? The panic and dread.

He hadn't been. And didn't ask himself if those same feelings even applied. At the moment, they were moot.

He tried to call her. To apologize. And explain. She didn't pick up.

BRETT WAITED FOR Ella after work on Saturday. He'd rescheduled a dinner meeting and given away courtside basketball tickets to be back in Santa Raquel by three so he could find her car before she got to it and drove away. Luckily she'd found a spot in the on-site lot. He didn't have access to the garage.

He wasn't going to call and just be sent to voice

mail. And he didn't want to risk having to make small talk with Chloe at the apartment.

She stopped short when she saw him standing there among all the vehicles lining the lot. She'd made it to about five feet from her car.

"It's okay," he said, holding up both hands as he went to meet her. Her scrubs were purple again, with primary-colored teddy bears, and her hair was up in its usual ponytail. "I'm just here to apologize. And to explain. When I said that nothing's changed, I was referring to me trying to do the right thing and hurting you instead. I wasn't talking about the baby or my feelings about the pregnancy in any way."

She nodded. Looked toward her car but didn't leave.

"Ella? Can we talk about this?" he asked, following her. "I was up most of the night and don't imagine you got much sleep, either. We're having a baby. We need to figure this out."

Her expression closed to him, Ella tilted up her face. "You're right. I was up most of the night and after a full shift, I'm exhausted. But I know this, Brett. I'm going to be happy. I'm sorry for the cards you were dealt. I'm sorry for me that you are my one and only. But I'm not going to spend my life unhappy because things aren't different. I've been given a second chance. I'm embracing it for what it is. Thrilled that it's here at all. And I can't afford to deal with your issues anymore. I can't keep opening myself up to being hurt when you can't come through for me. And I can't keep hurting you, either, making you feel like you're doing something wrong all the time, just because you don't need the same things I do, or feel as I do, or think like I do."

Her blows bounced off him like arrows against steel. He stood and took every one of them. Because he'd spent one of the most uncomfortable nights of his life. And that was saying a lot. Because Ella's shocking news was forcing him to face up to the life he'd been dealt.

"I withhold affection when you need it most. You can't trust me to be caring when you need to be cared for."

"Maybe. Probably."

"When you miscarried, I thought I'd been given a sign. A reprieve. I could be a selfish bastard and stay regardless of who got hurt because it was what I wanted. In spite of the fact that you knew I'd seen a divorce lawyer, you weren't going to kick me out. But I saw what it was doing to you, El. Every time I got quiet, your shoulders would hunch. Your face got tight. It's like a little more of you died every day. I'd try to think of something to say and just came up blank. And I knew my reprieve, my second chance, was to set you free."

"Maybe, but you wanted out, Brett. That's the truth that finally dawned on me. You didn't try to get help. You just saw an attorney. And later, just left. You aren't your dad, you know. You're your mom. You check out. And maybe you can't help that. I just know I can't do it anymore.

"I'm sorry," she said then, her eyes warming and glistening, as if she might cry again. But then her shoulders slumped and the softness came back into her eyes. "I'm sorry," she said again, giving her head a little shake. "I'm not myself right now. I don't mean to be so hard on you. Or so harsh. It's just…I'm… I have to be strong, Brett."

He nodded. Wanted to take her in his arms and promise her that everything would be all right. That he'd be strong for her when she couldn't be.

But he knew he couldn't.

Ella couldn't take any more empty promises.

"I was going to call you," she said, her voice gentle. "I was wrong yesterday. So wrong. I want you to know that as far as I'm concerned, you have no obligation here, at all. I'm perfectly okay and capable of doing this on my own. But I have no right to keep you out of your child's life. This baby is yours as much as mine and you are welcome to whatever involvement you want to have. If that's financial, then so be it. This baby is mine, but only on loan. I can't control every aspect of his or life—including his relationship with his father. And I just can't do…you and me…anymore."

She was beautiful. And so far away. And so right. Again.

"Let me ask you something…"

She waited.

He stood in the employee parking lot of a children's hospital and felt as though he was somehow fighting for his life.

"Knowing what you know about me, if I was around, would you really trust me not to abuse my child?" The question was purely hypothetical, but one that had repeated itself over and over as he relived the last time she'd carried his child.

"Of course I would. It's not a matter of what I think of you, Brett, it's a matter of what you think of yourself that's always been the problem."

The arrows hit flesh that time.

"Who knows, maybe with you living separately from us, if you are involved in the baby's life, you won't feel so afraid of getting out of control. You'll have your own place to go to when you're angry, so maybe you won't be so paranoid about what you might or might not have in you. All I know is that you've taken almost thirteen years of my life, Brett. You can't have any more."

Unlocking her car, she flung her bag over to the passenger seat, climbed in and drove away.

But not before Brett had seen the tears in her eyes.

And he knew she meant every word she'd said. If, upon hearing the night before that Ella was having his baby, he'd had even half a hope that they might find some kind of future together, she'd just snuffed it out.

ELLA WAS CLIMBING into bed the next night—Sunday, one day after Brett had met her outside work—when her phone rang.

Recognizing his number, she slid her legs under the covers and sat back against her headboard while she answered.

Best not to deal with Brett lying down.

"Is this too late?"

"No."

"I'm in a little town in Kansas, getting ready to attend the meeting of a potential new client in the morning, a nonprofit delegation of farmers, and my concentration is not what I need it to be. I want to help you. And it occurs to me that I don't know how. I know that I can't give you what you need most, but surely there are ways I can help."

Oh, God. Her emotions were too vulnerable right now…she couldn't let herself get soft. But soft was exactly how Brett's words made her feel.

"I don't have the answer to that, Brett," she said, giving him complete sincerity when what would have been better for both of them was more of her stiff upper lip. "You are who you are. It's not fair to you that you try to be anyone else. None of this is fair."

"So…I was thinking…I would like updates on the baby. I want to know everything. Every step of the way. I just don't want to make things more difficult for you."

He sounded so stilted. So unnatural. Because he was trying to be something he was not?

Was trying too hard?

Biting off the words *this is difficult for me*, she said instead, "How about if I text or call when I have something to report?" she asked, picturing a relationship similar to the one he shared with his mother.

"That would be good."

"Good…so…good…"

"I'd like to start now," he said before she could get the "'night" part of her salutation out of her mouth.

"You're two months along. Based on what my memory's telling me, you'll soon be hearing the heartbeat and having an ultrasound. At some point, you'll be able to choose whether or not you want to know the sex. And you need to be thinking about birthing classes…"

Whoa. He'd remembered all that? She started to smile. And then sobered. What was she getting herself into here?

He was the baby's father. What choice did she have?

"I have my first appointment tomorrow. And when the time comes, I'm thinking of opting not to know the sex…" At least not until she was further along and had more assurance that she was actually going to carry the baby to term. "And

I'm thinking about having the baby here, in the apartment, in my garden tub."

"At home? Is that safe?" She wanted to be able to ignore his concern, not to be warmed by it, but failed. Miserably.

And spent the next ten minutes discussing details of the birthing process as she'd heard it described by the mother of one of her patients a few months before—an option many women were choosing these days.

"Can I be there?"

Heart pounding, she took a deep breath. "If you want to be." This was his child. He had rights, though not the right to be present at the actual birth if she didn't want him there.

"I think I do."

He felt that way now. But she knew him. If he started to get too uptight, he'd change his mind. When Brett's emotions started to get out of control, Brett got going.

Just as Jeff was learning ways to be accountable to and responsible for his negative emotions, Brett had been learning to avoid his since he was a little boy.

She'd finally started really listening to him.

He couldn't help how he felt or what he needed. Not any more than she could help loving him. She got that now, too.

And wished him good-night.

CHAPTER TWENTY-SIX

HE STOOD NAKED and let the water sluice over him. Eyes closed, arms raised with his hands splayed above him on the porcelain tile in his hotel room, Brett dropped his chin to his chest. Monday morning after the longest weekend of his life and he wasn't ready to face the week ahead. Water pressure that was fine for cleansing, wasn't strong enough to wash away the tension knotting the muscles along the back of his neck.

He knew how to stay in control. Of himself and of his life. He had his rules clearly established. When emotion threatened to get the better of him, he headed for a hot shower. A completely private and personal relaxation that would allow his emotion to dissipate without hurting anyone else.

The water swirled down the drain. But it didn't take his emotions with it.

He stood there anyway. Planned to let the hot water run out and then to remain in the cold for as long as he could take it.

Anything to ease the tension.

Maybe if he'd been home, in his own shower, his own space, he would have found some peace. He'd shaped his life, made his choices, so that he had a place he could always return to when he needed to find calm.

His phone rang. Brett wanted to let it ring. To stay right where he was and give every drop of that water a chance to help him feel better.

But Ella was pregnant. And Jeff was in therapy. And they both might need him.

His phone was always ringing. Because he'd given his life to the outside world, rather than creating one in his own space. Another conscious decision.

He stood with droplets running down his body, a towel held to his front side, when he saw the name on his caller ID.

"Hello."

He prepared himself for a cryptic message. Followed by a hang-up.

An important message. But one he could get from the voice mail she'd leave if he let the phone ring.

"How are you?"

Trembling, Brett almost dropped the phone. Almost fifteen years he'd waited.

And on a normal day, out of the blue...

I'm fine, Ma. How are you? The millions of words he wanted to say were there, but none of them came.

With the silence hanging on the line, he pulled on his robe. Avoiding looking at himself in the mirror as he left the bathroom part of his suite.

"Ella's pregnant." He finally said what mattered most and choked up.

He was ashamed. She'd told him to let Ella go.

"I know. You're going to see the announcement in this morning's High Risk report. She sent in a notice by email early this morning. She'll be taking a leave from the team after the baby is born."

His mother's voice. Speaking a full sentence to him. He'd begun to think he'd never hear that sound again. Tears filled his eyes, and he felt like a fool.

"It's mine."

"I wondered."

He stood at the French doors in his room, looking out at the artificially lit garden beyond his balcony. The sun had not yet risen. "It was one night," he said, his hand squeezing the back of his neck. "Jeff is having anger issues. You know Chloe, the cook at the Stand. She's his wife. She left him until he gets help."

She'd have seen all the paperwork regarding Chloe. Approved everything on his behalf.

It was all so damned complicated.

"I didn't believe Ella at first when she told me how Jeff had been treating Chloe. Ella asked me to look into it. We ended up spending a weekend at a cabin on the lake, all four of us. It seemed like Chloe and Jeff were going to be fine. I drank more than normal. Left the cabin. Was going to spend the night outside by myself. Then Ella came out."

"You loved her once."

"Yes."

"And now?"

"More than ever."

"How does she feel?"

"I think she loves me. I'm afraid she's never going to love anyone else. But she doesn't want a relationship any more than I do. She's been hurt too much. She knows my limitations."

"What limitations? Have you done something, Brett?"

"No! Come on, Ma. You know every move I make. You know how I live, what food is in my fridge, what flight I'm on and probably what I order from room service since you do the expense accounts."

"So what limitations?" She was his mother. And she wasn't. She was something ethereal. Not real. Like talking to an angel in a dream.

"She calls it my inability to be all in. I call it being accountable to the dangers that lurk within me."

"So you have them?"

"I'm sure I do."

"Have you felt the burning rage?"

"I think so." The night he'd thought Ella was being accosted. "I don't let myself get that emotionally invested," he said now. And then he told her about the tension that had built within him during his marriage. A tension that had had him snapping at Ella more often than not after they'd found out she was pregnant. The nightmares that had felt so real to him.

"Did you ever feel like hitting her?"

"No. Unlike Dad, I got out before it got to that point."

"Burning rage doesn't listen to reason."

Which was what made it so frightening.

He had so much to tell her. To ask her. And was afraid that every sentence she uttered might be followed by a click.

"Can I see you?" If they could just sit down. Have a real talk. If he could give her a hug and tell her—

"No. Nothing's changed, son."

"You're talking to me."

"I just found out you're going to be a father. I thought you might have issues with that."

Okay. He got the parameters now. It was a start.

"I do."

"Can I help?"

Yeah, come into my life. Meet the mother of my child. Be a grandmother.

Thinking of Ella reminded him of that horrible conversation when she'd asked him his true feelings about the first time she'd been pregnant. He'd told her about his father being a wonderful father all those years...

"Were there signs, Ma? Before Livia got sick? Every memory I have of Dad back then is good."

"He was a good father, Brett."

"And a good husband."

"As good as he could be."

"What does that mean? Are you telling me he hit you when I was little? How could I not have known that?"

"No, son. He didn't. But he'd fly into rages. Say horrible things. Call me names. Threaten to leave me. He told me once that he understood his father's need to hit something."

"I never heard any of it."

"Because I learned his triggers. Learned how to manage them."

"Manage them?"

"I'd get you kids out of the house. Or I'd leave a room, and he'd follow me."

"This was before Livia got sick? Why'd you stay with him, then?"

"A lot of reasons. I loved him, for one. I understood that he was only spewing what had been spewed at him. I knew he didn't mean any of it. He'd scream obscenities, accusing me of all kinds of horrible things, and I'd hear the translation, you know, it would go something like, 'Help, I'm feeling in over my head here. I'm afraid I'm not good enough for you. As smart as you. I'm bad and you're going to leave me. I need to know you love me.' He also acknowledged afterward that he'd been wrong. He'd beg me to forgive him and promised that he'd learn to keep his mouth closed when he started to feel like he was losing control."

He'd never known. "How could a kid live in a house with that going on and not know?"

"It didn't happen often."

"And the rest of the time?"

"He was just as you remember. A great father. A good provider. And for the most part, my best friend."

"So what are my chances?" Might as well just put the problem right out on the table.

"They are what you make them, Brett."

"You told me to let her go."

"Because you weren't going to marry her."

"Do you think I should?"

"Only you can know that."

"What would make you proud of me?" What the hell? Where had that come from?

"Ah, Brett. You are above and beyond anything I could have ever hoped to produce. It goes way beyond pride, son. You make me a better person just by getting up in the morning and taking the next breath. I can't tell you what to do because I don't know the answer. But there's one thing I do know."

"What's that?"

"Whatever choice you make, you'll make it for the right reasons."

"I love you, Ma."

"I love you, too, son."

"Will you call again?"

"I don't know. Probably not."

He'd known her answer before she gave it.

There were some things that would never change.

ELLA WAS AT work Monday, eating crackers for lunch, when her pager went off.

She'd had her first checkup with the obstetrician. Everything looked perfect. She could expect to give birth to a healthy son or daughter in thirty weeks.

Other than Ella's medical history, the doctor didn't know the circumstances of the baby's conception.

Ella didn't share them with her. There was no need.

Rounding the corner into the B pod, the area to which she'd been paged, she expected to see a nurse there waiting for her.

Instead, it was Jason. Standing with a charting tablet.

"How are you?" he asked, his glance more intimate than she'd have expected.

"Good." She smiled. Because she was going to have a baby. She was being given a new life. One she desperately wanted.

"I've been…well, thinking…" He looked down at the tablet, dropped his hand, tablet dangling at his side, and said, "Did you speak to the baby's father?"

A couple of the people at work already knew what was going on with her. Partially because she'd been sick at work. And because a doctor on the ward—Jason—knew. She walked Jason into her office.

"Yes."

"And?"

"He wants to help where he can."

"Are you getting back together?"

"No!" When she heard the sharpness of her response, she tempered it with a softer one. "We aren't getting back together. I told you, it was a one-night thing," she said. Adding that she'd had her first appointment and that everything was fine.

"So...I guess this is kind of strange, but...would you be willing to have dinner with me sometime?"

Her mouth fell open. "I'm pregnant, Jason."

"I know. I was there." He blushed. And grinned. "When you found out, that is."

"You don't want children."

He shrugged. "There is that."

So what was he doing?

"The thing is I want you in my life."

"I'm pregnant." She repeated the obvious, but only because he didn't seem to be getting it. Or she wasn't.

"Yeah, and I'm not as appalled by that idea as I'd thought I would be."

Really.

A small flower bloomed inside Ella. Right alongside the baby that was growing there. She was wanted. Her baby wasn't appalling.

That concept shouldn't be so unfamiliar to her.

But it was. And in that moment, standing there, Ella realized just how much of an effect Brett's inability to love fully had had on her.

"I'm not in love with you, Jason." She couldn't do to him what had been done to her. Couldn't promise something she was incapable of giving.

"I figured that out as soon as I knew you'd just slept with someone else before going out with me," he said. "You aren't the type of woman who has sex lightly. You're still in love with your ex."

"Yes."

"Who doesn't want you."

"Correct."

"Well, I do. And I'm willing to take my chances that when you've gotten over him, you'll see that I'm quite lovable, too."

Her eyes filling with tears, Ella hated to tell him no when, once again, he asked her out to dinner.

BRETT DIDN'T SLEEP WELL. He wasn't sure he slept at all. He spent the rest of that week and much of the next flying around the country, airport to airport, city to city, convincing himself his life was perfect as it was.

From Chicago to Philadelphia, Texas to Miami to Memphis, he did good work. Helped others help others. His life was full. Challenging. And he was making a meaningful contribution to society.

And in his hotel room at night, when he finished preparing for the next day's meetings and turned out the light, he replayed those early days of Ella's first pregnancy. She'd shared her every thought with him. Every feeling. Every fear. He hadn't realized how much he'd stored away until that week.

He dozed. In bed and on planes. But he couldn't find a place of restfulness. Nervous energy pushed him forward. From responsibility to responsibility.

He heard about Jeff's meeting with Chloe. From Jeff and from Ella. By all accounts the meeting had been a success.

And he was glad.

He actually spoke to Jeff.

Ella, he let go to voice mail.

And then replayed her message three times.

She'd told him her doctor's appointment had gone well. Gave him her due date. And told him she'd heard the heartbeat already.

She'd sounded excited. And he was glad for her.

Glad that things were finally working out.

And yet, when he landed in LA the third Wednesday night in December, and drove home with Christmas lights glittering on homes and businesses in the distance, he couldn't find any of the joy that was supposed to come with the season.

All he felt was alone.

Sad.

Cut adrift.

Jeff and Chloe were going to be spending the holiday with Ella at a hotel in LA. Ella and Chloe's room would be on a separate floor—and there'd be no question about changing sleeping arrangements.

Jeff was thrilled to know he'd get to see his family over the holiday.

He'd invited Brett.

Brett had told him he was busy.

If Ella wanted him there she'd have asked. At least that was what he'd told himself.

Brett spent the holiday at home. Working.

He texted his mother.

She didn't text back.

CHAPTER TWENTY-SEVEN

IN JANUARY, CHLOE invited her husband to Santa Raquel for the weekend, on the grounds that he either stayed with Brett or in a hotel.

She told him that weekend, when he was there, that she'd been staying with Ella all along, leaving Jeff feeling stunned.

"It's not that I blame El," he said Saturday evening as he lounged with Brett at the poolside fireplace in Brett's backyard, watching the flames and drinking a beer.

Brett had started drinking beer again over Christmas. It had been his present to himself.

And only so long as he limited his intake.

"It's just...I feel kind of betrayed, you know?" Jeff's frown spoke of confusion more than anything else.

And still Brett asked, "Did it make you mad?"

"You know—" Jeff turned to look at him "—it didn't. I didn't really think about it until you asked, but no. I'm hurt. I feel stupid, really. I encouraged Chloe to confide in El. And I know my sister was looking out for my best interests. It's just...she's *my* sister."

"Who was looking out for your best interests,"

Brett reminded. "She was trying to keep control of the situation to give you time to get help."

"Yeah. I think I'm most upset with myself," he said. "Knowing that my little sister had to do that for me, that I put her in that situation…I can't stand that." He shook his head and took a sip of beer. He was still on his first one, and they'd been out by the pool for over an hour. Brett asked Jeff about the counseling. About his support group. And knew that Jeff was being completely up front with him when he told him that the therapy had saved his life.

"What do you think your chances are for getting complete control over your anger issues?" Brett asked, studying Jeff closely. Three to eleven percent. He knew the statistical answer. Wasn't sure Jeff did.

"So here's where my expected response would be that I anticipate a full recovery," Jeff told him. "Most abusers are going to say that while they're in the program, right? A lot of them probably believe it, too. Why be in the program if you don't think it's going to work? Unless you're doing it for the wrong reasons to begin with, and then there's no hope for you anyway…"

Jeff leaned forward, his elbows on his knees, and turned back toward Brett. "But in my case, I think I have better chances than most. I'm not fighting years of alcohol or drug addiction or a gambling or debt problem." Standing, Jeff put another log on the fire. "In some ways I almost wish I did have some concrete problem to blame this all on. But mostly, I'm just so thankful that I have such an incredible family, and friend, who saw what I couldn't see and forced me to get help."

"So you really think you can beat this?"

Brett needed to hear the answer.

"I do. I'm going to stay involved in the support group—even after I complete my therapy. I've already been approached about the possibility of facilitating a group, and I think I might like to try that, later, if I can do it without creating stress at home."

"So what's the magic secret?" Brett asked. He'd read all the books he could find. He'd been through counseling as a kid and as an adult, too. He knew the rhetoric. The facts.

"For me, it's self-awareness. I know what I want and need. I see what I became, which has made me aware of my vulnerability. And I'm arming myself with tools to prevent me from falling into it again. I know how stress feels inside, and I know now that if I'm feeling that way driving home, I shouldn't go home. I'm going to drive out to the golf course, park and call Chloe."

Something told Brett that Jeff's confidence didn't just come from the thought of the idea. "You've been doing that already, haven't you?"

"Yes. But only at her bidding. She wanted to know if it helped."

"And has it?"

"Weirdly enough, yes. I love to golf. The course, even just the smell of it, relaxes me. And talking to Chloe usually clarifies whatever it was that was building up inside me."

The way a shower relaxed Brett?

"So what happens if sometime you guys disagree, and talking to her only makes you angry?"

"I hang up and calm down. If I can't, I go home and sleep in the guesthouse. And if there comes a day when this doesn't work, I find something else that does."

It sounded so…doable.

But there were those statistics. The three-to-eleven-percent success rate among abusers who sought treatment.

Brett listened. He was pleased for his friend.

And he'd never felt so incomplete in his life.

ELLA'S MORNING SICKNESS WORSENED. She texted Brett. Told him she was throwing up a lot, and that the doctor said it was normal.

She went for her regular monthly visit and texted a healthy baby report. She'd passed the first trimester and was well into the second with no sign of fetal distress. He was like her insurance adjuster. She just had to keep him informed of facts.

Nothing more.

She told herself she was happy. And only let

herself think about the baby she was carrying, not the man who'd fathered it.

Nora Burbank had filed charges against her husband. And filed for divorce, too. She was working at a computer center owned by The Lemonade Stand. She'd be living at the Stand for a while. Nora had suffered too long without any kind of support.

Ella was thrilled to know that she'd helped give the woman another chance at a happy life.

She wanted the same for her brother, as well.

Jeff was a regular visitor in her home these days. Chloe had asked for weekly visits, clearing it with Ella first, and her brother now slept over every Saturday night and made them all breakfast every Sunday morning.

The second Sunday in February, Ella walked into the kitchen to find her brother there alone.

"Chloe's packing," he said, turning potatoes that she'd just seen him drop into the pan. He didn't look in her direction.

"Where's she going?" Ella asked, grabbing hold of the small distention of her stomach as she felt a flutter. The sensation had been happening on and off for a couple days.

"Home."

She'd known, of course. Chloe hadn't said anything. But she hadn't looked Ella in the eye for the past few days.

Was she that much of a stick in the mud? So

rigid that people were constantly worrying they were going to disappoint her?

"Did she talk to Sara about it?"

"Yes."

"Do you know what Sara said?"

"She said that I had to make my own decision," Chloe said, joining them, fully dressed. She smiled at her husband. "She also said that she thinks I'm ready to make my own decisions."

Ella felt the words as a jab to her. But knew they weren't. Ella looked at Jeff. "Did you talk to your therapist?"

She loved them both so much. And they might not get another chance if they screwed this up. Moved too quickly.

"I did."

"And?"

"I'm going to be okay, sis," he said. "I'm coming to terms with the fact that I'm not perfect. I can't handle everything. And that doesn't make me less of a man. I always thought I could do anything I put my mind to. But when Cody was born, all that wasn't easy. I didn't know how to cope."

"You could have asked for help. I'm a nurse, Jeff. I'd have been there in an instant," Ella said.

Jeff yanked on a strand of her hair. Kissed the top of her head. "I know that now," he said, going back to his potatoes. "I'd just never had to ask before. It didn't occur to me that that was what I was supposed to do. My natural instinct was to believe I could handle it. That I was supposed to be able to handle it."

Looking at her brother in her kitchen—making breakfast for them, mixing pancake batter for Cody and making lovey eyes at his wife—Ella fully believed he could handle anything.

That was the Jeff she knew.

The man he'd always been. It stood to reason that he'd just take for granted that he could handle whatever came his way.

Just as being the son of an abusive man, being a victim, having his mother turn on him, were all things Brett knew about himself. And Ella had expected Brett to fit her concept of what a husband would be like in a normal, loving relationship. She'd expected a partner who could be open with her. Because that was all she'd ever known because of the relationships she'd witnessed. It was what she wanted and needed.

No wonder they hadn't been able to stay together.

"We're going to make it," Jeff said now, putting his arm around Chloe's waist as she joined him at the stove, watching as he cracked eggs into the pan over the potatoes.

"I hope so."

What he said made sense. Ella wanted to believe.

She just wasn't sure she had it in her anymore.

BRETT WAS HOME Sunday evening, having just hung up the phone from Jeff, who was also at home, his family settled back in with him, when his phone indicated an incoming text message.

He'd heard happiness in Jeff's voice, but an equal amount of apprehension, as well. Because Jeff feared that he could slip back into his old ways again.

Truth was he could. But in Jeff's case, Brett didn't think so. Now that Jeff was aware of his problem, now that both he and Chloe were tending to it, now that they were around others who knew to watch for the signs, he was going to be fine.

He'd told Jeff to text him anytime he had doubts. But this text wasn't from Jeff.

I think the baby's moving.

He read it again. And realized his hand was shaking. Not out of panic. Or fear. He wasn't feeling tense. Just…nervous.

They'd never reached this point the last time. Movement indicated life. A growing human being.

He pushed speed dial.

"Hello?"

Was she at home alone? He wanted to share the moment with her. It was theirs.

And he wanted to make certain there wasn't anything wrong. For her sake. Ella couldn't take another miscarriage. Didn't deserve one.

"What does it feel like?"

"Like air bubbles. It's been going on for a couple days—a lot more today than before. The way I'm feeling is exactly how the internet describes first baby movement. You said you wanted to be kept informed."

Yes, and there was a warmth to her voice that had been missing from her recent communications.

"When you put your hand on your stomach, do you feel any movement against your hand?" And how did that stomach look? He hadn't seen her in weeks.

She'd lost their first child before she'd started to show.

"No. Apparently it will be a bit before he gets that big and strong."

Brett had an image of very tiny arms and legs trying to stretch. Thoughts raced through his mind. All of them coming at once. Good ones. Bad ones. His breathing got shallower.

And he said, "I'm giving you my house."

"What?"

"I said I'm giving you my house."

"I don't want your house."

"Yes, you do. You love it here. The backyard." The way he blurted the words made him sound like a petulant child.

"Brett, you are not giving me your house."

"You can't really do anything about it," he

said. The idea was brand new to him. But he was warming to it. "I mean, you could choose to sell it after I gift it to you, I guess…"

And she'd have enough money from the sale to buy whatever she needed. But if she didn't sell it—she'd be living in a place designed for peace.

"There are four unused bedrooms upstairs. You can design the nursery however you want. Or use my downstairs office for the baby and have an office upstairs if you want to. And a couple guest bedrooms. For when Chloe and Jeff come to stay with you."

He felt as if he was in a boardroom. Selling what he believed in. "The baby's mine, too, El," he said, calming now. He'd found a solution to the problem of what he could do to participate. To help her. "Let me give you what you want. Let me make you happy. Let me provide for my child."

He had a way to make her happy. To give her the beauty she needed in her life.

Like Jeff, he was bringing his small family home.

"Where will you live?"

"In your apartment until I can find another place. I'm gone most of the time anyway." He was making things up as he went, but it all made sense.

He was giving up his space. His lifeline.

To her. Their child.

And it was right.

CHAPTER TWENTY-EIGHT

ON MONDAY, ELLA'S day off, she was in a big-box store, buying moving boxes. In their conversation the night before, Brett had indicated that she could move as soon as she was ready, and so she was getting ready. She didn't want to leave the unpacking for when the baby was bigger.

It had all made sense to her when she'd gotten up with a smile on her face that morning.

But as she was going to load her boxes in her cart, she caught a glimpse of herself in a mirror. In a baggy shirt and jeans, she didn't look like herself at all. She looked like a pregnant housewife. Someone she'd once been.

Someone she desperately wanted to be.

And she stopped.

What in the hell was she doing? Moving into Brett's house? How would that work if she ever managed to fall out of love with him and meet someone else?

Was she, by moving into his home, resigning herself to a life without a mate? A life without romantic love?

When she started to shake, she knew that she was in over her head. She had to talk to someone.

And the only people she felt she could comfortably confide in were at The Lemonade Stand.

Leaving her empty cart for the next customer, Ella left the store. It was her turn to admit she needed help.

BRETT TRIED TO call Ella on his lunch break in Seattle. When she didn't pick up he left a message for her that the paperwork to transfer his house over to her would be complete by the end of the week. If she wanted to move in prior to that, she was simply to let him know, and he'd accommodate her.

She was welcome to whatever furniture of his she wanted. What she didn't want, he'd either move to the apartment or have put in storage until he found another place.

He wasn't in a hurry.

The house, the yard—they'd all be ready and waiting for her.

And when he hung up, he wasn't feeling nervous about the plan at all. He wasn't worried about finding another perfect house for him to live in. He just wasn't fueled by a need to do so. He had nothing to prove to himself.

To prove to himself? Was that what his life had become? A series of accomplishments that were all designed to prove...what?

That he could control his life and thereby control himself?

He texted Ella as he finished lunch, just to tell her he'd left a voice mail.

There was no response.

During the afternoon break he called Ella's cell phone. Monday was her day off. And she always responded to him, at least with a text. When she didn't answer, he tried his mother. If there'd been an emergency with the High Risk team, she'd know.

At the same time, he texted Jeff, just to ask how things were.

Jeff texted back immediately. He and Chloe and Cody were spending the afternoon at a carnival that was in town.

If there'd been an emergency, Jeff and Chloe would have known about it. They were listed as her next of kin. She'd already told him that.

And Brett forced himself to calm down. Ella was fine. Brett just wasn't a priority in her life.

Because that was the way he'd wanted it.

"I THOUGHT I was over him." It was late afternoon. Ella sat with Lila in her little apartment at The Lemonade Stand. She'd already spent an hour talking with Sara, telling the other woman her life story, or at least the parts that pertained to Brett.

Neither Sara nor Lila knew, of course, that the man she was talking about was the founder of The Lemonade Stand. She couldn't betray Brett, even now.

"I went through all the counseling," she said again now. Repeating herself because no matter how many times she explained things, she couldn't find the road that would take her out of the past.

Lila had been sitting, mostly silent, for the past hour.

"It's not like I don't want to say no to him," she said. "I do in my mind. But my feelings don't follow my head. I want to move into his house. I want to live there. I want him in my life."

"Because you love him."

"Yes, but it's destructive. Because he's right. I wasn't happy with him. I needed more. I could have done more, too. I see that now. I didn't accept him for who he was, but for who I thought he could be—in terms of our relationship. But even if I had accepted him for him, I still would have been incredibly lonely. Because I need more than he can give."

"Can or will?"

"What?"

"You need more than he *can* give. Or *will* give?"

"I think with him that's one and the same. He can't let himself open up because he's afraid of experiencing the full strength of his emotions. So the will is the choice not to let himself, but the fear makes it so he can't."

"But this…you being here…it's not really about him. Is it?"

Ella shook her head.

"I'm ashamed," she said.

"Of what?"

"I'm so busy thinking of my own life, of how hurt I've been and how to prevent being hurt again, and in doing so, I'm hurting him."

"Sometimes pain is inevitable."

"Yes, but I was so certain when I came here that I was strong enough to move on with my life. But the truth is, I'm not strong enough to stop loving him. I say I will, but I don't. We've been apart all these years and here I am, pregnant with his child and ready to move into his house. Just accepting what he decides he can give in spite of the fact that I know it won't be enough."

She stopped. Her words hanging in the room. Scaring her more than she'd thought possible.

"I'm weak where he's concerned," she said. "It's like my feelings for him have some kind of power over me and I let them manipulate me. And not only do I get hurt, but he does, too."

The pattern was slowly showing itself to her. The books she'd read. The things she'd told Chloe. The loneliness she was trying to run from.

"And then how do you hurt him?"

"Because I need what I need. Want what I want. I tell him how much I love him, but I don't accept him for who he is." He'd said she'd been so busy telling him what she saw in him, she'd quit listening to what he saw. Who he was inside. So he'd quit talking to her about it. "I set standards he can't possibly meet."

"Maybe so. But your needs and wants are a natural part of you and speaking about them, asking for them, is healthy."

"I didn't come to Santa Raquel for my new job, did I?"

"Why did you come here?"

"Because I knew he lived in town. I came here to be close to him. I'm like a pathetic groupie. I don't get mad at him, I just hang around and let him make us both miserable. I just can't believe it took me so long to figure it all out."

"Our minds have a way of presenting things to us when we're ready to accept them," Lila said. "It's called getting clarity, my dear."

Her mind went blank.

And then started racing.

"Growing up in an abusive home, not having stability or security even in the simplest of things, instilled in him the need to be in control above all else. And he and I both suffer because of it."

It was all so clear.

So frighteningly, horrifyingly clear.

"And because I love him, I put up with his inability to open up, to love and share a life with me. I know he can't help it, so I hang around. But I feel helpless. And eventually hopeless."

All these months, she'd been thinking she was proving her ability to be over Brett. To help

Chloe and Nora and others take back ownership of their minds. Their hearts. Themselves. And while Chloe had grown stronger, Ella had fallen prey all over again...

"He must be a pretty fine man, this ex-husband of yours," Lila said, her eyes glistening as though she might be holding back tears.

"He's a great man, Lila. And I don't just say that because I love him. I look at what he's done with his life, apart from me, of course. He is a man who has a national reputation for honesty. He got a lot of press at a young age due to a business he'd developed and sold. He was the golden boy everyone could trust. And still is. Believe me, some would love to find dirt on him, but it's just not there.

"He has never once given me cause to doubt his integrity."

"It sounds like he's a man worth fighting for."

The words stopped her.

Again.

"I thought the plan was for me to be free of him once and for all."

"The plan is for you to be healthy."

"How can I be healthy while I'm controlled by the love I feel for him?"

"Are you sure that's a bad thing? If you were in an abusive situation and continued to go back to it, that would be unhealthy. But from what you've said, that's not the case here."

"It can't be healthy, though. It's like we're both beating our heads against the wall. We just keep hurting each other."

"I'm suggesting that maybe love is pushing you toward him for a reason. You love him. And maybe it's that love that keeps sending you back to him. Love isn't easy, my dear. Nor is it always wrapped in pretty packages. Sometimes it's hard. Sometimes you have to go through hell to get to where you need to be. But the love is strong enough to carry you through."

The words were softly spoken, but they exploded inside her.

She felt as if she was fighting a losing battle. Because she was. She was trying to fight love, and there was no way she was going to win that one.

And still, settling into a relationship where she'd never be happy or fulfilled didn't feel right, either.

"So what do I do?" Ella rubbed her hand over her growing belly. Taking comfort from the being who nestled there so trustingly.

Lila glanced at Ella's hand caressing her baby, a sad expression on her face, and Ella wondered again about the woman. Word through Chloe was that no one really knew much about Lila's past. "I'm not an expert on love, sweetie," she said. "But it seems to me that when love is your guiding force, then you need to listen to your heart, not your head, to find your answers."

Her heart started to thud. The air cooled. It heated. Ella wanted to grin. And to cry.

"You think I should do whatever I can to get him to try again?" It was what she wanted, wasn't it? In her deepest heart.

"I'm not a counselor," Lila said. "And I can't tell you that. From what you say, he's probably facing some very real issues. I'm only saying that your heart is not accepting the choices your mind is making. You might want to find out why."

Her heart would have her running to Brett. Her heart would have her willing to accept whatever crumbs of himself he could give her. Her heart would have her hoping that someday he'd trust himself enough to love her back.

She couldn't take any more chances on hope.

CHAPTER TWENTY-NINE

THERE WAS STILL no word from Ella when Brett shut down his phone and boarded the plane home that night. He must have scared her, offering her his home. Perhaps it had seemed like nothing more than a grand gesture.

He'd meant only to give her every part of himself that he could. Because he couldn't give her what she wanted...

Brett had come full circle. Sitting on the plane after his meeting, he was grateful for the physical restraint holding him in his seat.

He'd upgraded himself to first class. He needed the space.

And ordered a cocktail. To calm his nerves.

Realizing his hands were once again clenching the armrests, he forced his muscles to relax.

He was a little boy again, a month after his tenth birthday. His little sister had been sick. His parents had just come home from the doctor. They were fighting. His father was saying things Brett didn't really understand. Using words that had never been spoken in their home before. His mother had started to cry.

Livia, seven at the time, had whispered to him, "I'm scared, Brett."

She was on the couch, where their father had set her when he'd carried her in. Brett was with her. He'd been reading, but put the *Baby-Sitters Little Sister* book down and told her, "Don't worry, I'm here."

He'd really believed he could protect her. His folks had given him the job when she was born. Before they even brought her home from the hospital. "You're the big brother," they'd said, assuring him that his role was as important as anyone else's. That he wouldn't get any less time and attention from them.

He'd been only three.

But he remembered hearing that.

In the end, it hadn't mattered. Nothing he'd known during those first ten years of his life had mattered.

He hadn't been able to help Livia. She'd been scared of dying, and he'd sat there and watched her die.

He'd told his mother he wouldn't let his father lay another hand on her, but the old man had just knocked him out cold and hit her anyway.

He'd made a silent promise to Ella that he'd never hurt her.

And that was just about all he'd done.

His plans...they hadn't worked.

Which left him with...nothing.

No plan. No action to take. No solutions.

The engine droned. A lady across the aisle snored. He was like his mother. He shut down. Cut people off. He couldn't open his heart to the woman he loved more than life.

He dared anyone to sit there with a sick little girl who was looking to you to make it all better. To listen to his mom get the crap beat out of her because another medical bill had come in, and they didn't have the money to pay and be too young to get a job.

You have to make your own choices, Brett. How often had he heard his mother say those words?

She'd been so certain he'd make the right ones.

And how could she believe that? He'd made one wrong choice after another.

You aren't your father, Brett, you're your mother. Ella's words came back to him. Brett closed his eyes. Tried to sleep.

Rage is distorted anger. Usually resulting from internal shame. He'd read that someplace.

Rage triggered fight-or-flight tendencies. Which triggered chemicals in the brain to see everyone in sight as an enemy. To distort thought.

To lash out at everyone.

He knew all of this.

Knew it.

Your instincts are honed to prevent abuse. Ella had told him that when he'd saved Jeff from hitting Chloe.

You're a great man, just one who's chosen to live life on the sidelines. He could see Ella standing on the boat in the dark, looking so damned sexy in jeans and that big bulky sweater.

I'm scared, Brett.

Don't worry, I'm here.

Livia had trusted him.

It's not a matter of what I think of you, Brett. It's a matter of what you think of you that's always been the problem.

Ella had taken a chance on him. Married him. Loved him.

I'm scared, Brett.

You've taken thirteen years of my life. You can't have any more.

And that was really it, wasn't it?

He'd had his chances. And he'd blown them.

The overhead speaker crackled. The captain's voice came on asking the flight attendants to prepare the cabin for arrival.

A good man was all he'd ever wanted to be.

He'd taken control of his life, of his behavior.

And now the only thing he could do, was being made to do, was return his seat back to its full upright position and hand over his first-class tray table.

ELLA CALLED LILA on her way home from work on Wednesday.

"I want, first of all, to thank you," she said. "For listening the other day."

"You're welcome, my dear," Lila said. "You do understand that it is not my job, nor my training, to give advice..."

"You listened. I think that's what I needed most."

"I think so, too."

She'd spent the last couple nights home alone. Cleaning. Listening to music. Talking to her unborn child. Trying to quiet her mind so she could hear her heart. Brett had been back in town Monday night, and would be again that afternoon. Ever since she'd told him she was pregnant, he'd been keeping her up-to-date on his schedule. He would be calling at some point. Wanting to switch homes with her. She had to know what to tell him.

"Do you think, maybe, we could get dinner or something sometime?"

"I don't go out much," Lila said. "But let's not rule it out."

Ella took a breath. Wiped her sweaty hand on her scrubs.

"I have one more favor to ask," she said, resting her hand on the baby mound beneath her shirt.

"So ask."

"I need to know how I'd go about scheduling a visit for someone at the Stand. Not a woman. Or a child."

"You want to bring a man here?"

"Yes. My husband. Ex-husband. My baby's

father…" She was blabbering. Talking too fast. Brett was probably never going to agree to the visit.

"I'd like him to meet you and Sara…"

"I'm happy to arrange a visit," Lila said. "I can't guarantee I'll be available, but certainly one of the counselors can be. We don't often deal with adult male victims since we aren't equipped to house them here, but we've counseled a few."

"I'm not even sure he'll agree to come with me."

"Don't be disappointed if he doesn't. From what you tell me, it could be a harder sell than he's able to take on."

"Believe me, I know."

"But if you can get him to agree, you call me. I'll arrange something."

"Tonight?"

Lila's pause prompted her to say, "If I can get him to agree, I want to get him to go before he has a chance to change his mind. I need to try this, before I can move into his home."

She was listening to her heart.

Brett wouldn't be allowed down in the bungalows. But that wasn't what she needed him to see.

"Oh. Okay, fine. Yes, if he agrees, you call, and I'll get him in."

"Could you see if Lynn and Sara have plans for tonight? And Maddie? And Darin and Grant?

Since they're the only two men living in the complex? I know they aren't victims, but… And some of the residents, too? If not, that's fine, but I thought…I might only get this one shot at this, and I want him to meet some of the others who know and understand and are like…"

Him, she'd been about to say. And stopped herself.

She wanted him to meet the people whose names he'd recognize. People she believed he'd grown to care about—even without having met them.

"I'll see what I can do," Lila told her.

And Ella crossed the easiest part of the plan off her mental checklist.

BRETT HAD HAD a meeting in San Francisco first thing Wednesday morning. Just a stop in to go over the monthly books at a local nonprofit gay and lesbian support house. He flew in and out of Burbank and made it home by midafternoon. But as tempted as he was to drive by the hospital, look for Ella's car and then wait for her to get off shift just so he could assure himself she was fine, he took a roundabout way home to avoid the hospital altogether.

Changing into his golf clothes, he thought he'd take himself out to hit nine holes. Saw his bike and changed his mind. And his clothes.

In black jeans, a black leather jacket and shades, he felt free, and completely innocuous as he took Coastal Road One and sped along the ocean for more than an hour. He'd always loved riding. From the first time he could remember being on the back of his dad's bike. He'd been given the ride—which he'd been begging for for what seemed like forever—as a gift for his seventh birthday.

He'd ridden with Jeff for a while in college.

And then quit.

Because eventually, he'd shut out everything in his life that reminded him of the good times he'd had growing up.

Because every single time he revisited them, they led to the bad times. And the pain of their loss served no purpose.

He'd been a fool.

He hadn't had to lose the joy of riding.

He pulled into his driveway just as the sun was starting to set. Maybe he'd go out for dinner.

Go down to the corner and have a sandwich and a beer.

He hadn't seen Ella's car as he'd gone roaring up to the garage. She'd parked it in the gravel parking area to the side of the house—put there by the former owners who'd used the old home as a bed-and-breakfast.

But he saw her as she stood up from a white

wicker rocker on his front porch and came toward him.

He stared. Felt his jaw drop. And just kept staring.

In jeans that hugged every inch of her long legs
and a tight, short-sleeved T-shirt, the evidence of
their child was on display for him to see.

She'd left her hair down, and it curled around
her arms and shoulders, her breasts.

"It's not polite to stare."

He'd give anything to change his past. And be
able to scoop her up and carry her to bed.

"You…look…beautiful."

"I've come to ask a favor, Brett."

He'd give her the moon if he could. Problem
was, most of what she needed, he didn't have.
"Ask. You know I'll do what I can." Hooking his
helmet over the handlebar of his bike, he smoothed
a hand over hair that was too short to stick up far,
and walked toward her. Intending to take her into
the house.

She stopped on the driveway.

"I want you to trust me. Completely trust me,"
she said.

Frowning, Brett studied her face, wishing he
still had the ability to read her. "I do trust you.
Trust has never been an issue between us."

"I mean *really* trust. As in, you'll go along with
whatever I say—whatever I ask of you over the

next hour or so. No matter what. Just for an hour. Not a lifetime."

An hour he could do. Couldn't he? An hour was only sixty minutes.

Even he wasn't convinced by his own nod.

"I mean it, Brett. But we'll take it slow. If you really can't handle it, as in you're going to have a heart attack or throw up or start seeing stars or something, you tell me and we'll stop."

He had no idea what they were talking about. And Ella's expression was as serious as he'd ever seen it.

He nodded again.

"So, just so we understand each other, in this exercise, if you start to struggle, you have to tell me."

He got it. Loud and clear. She was trying to force him to share himself with her.

Standing toe-to-toe with her, Brett, careful not to allow any part of his body to touch any part of hers, looked her straight in the eye. "Just so we understand each other," he echoed, "I will do my utmost to try to do as you ask." He could only give what he had to give. But he had to give all of it.

Nothing had changed.

And there was no room for game playing between him and Ella.

Life had been serious from the day they'd met.

Because he'd come to her with issues.

And she'd loved him enough to take them on.

He'd give anything to be able to love her back that much.

CHAPTER THIRTY

ELLA WAS MORE nervous than she'd ever been as she took the shortest route she knew. A five-minute drive.

Brett had never been to The Lemonade Stand. Not even to the land he'd purchased to have it built on.

He'd paid for it. Others had done the work.

It was time for him to stop paying and start reaping some of the benefits.

She hoped.

The exact location of The Lemonade Stand was known only to those who'd had occasion to be there. Brett's mother actually owned the two city blocks housing the shelter and its holdings—gifted to her from Brett much as he'd planned to gift Ella his house. She hadn't missed the connection.

Her sweaty palms slid along the leather steering wheel, leaving a visible sheen behind. She wondered if he noticed. Three more minutes and they'd be there.

"Your hands are shaking."

"I'm nervous."

"Me, too."

Well. There, then. They were off to a good start. And were a couple minutes away from the possibility of all hell breaking loose.

"I've been an ass, El. I confused controlling my actions with controlling destiny."

She had no idea what he was talking about. And couldn't focus. Which upset her more because Brett was finally doing what she'd always prayed for.

He was talking to her. Not all stilted as though he was choosing every word, but just like a normal person.

She turned the last corner. In about thirty seconds, Brett was going to be facing what could possibly be the toughest challenge of his life. She completely understood that.

She also believed, now, that he was up for it. What she couldn't believe was him—when he told her he couldn't do it. He could. He just didn't know that yet. But he thought she didn't know because she wasn't listening to him.

And he was right. She wasn't listening to him. She was listening to his heart. Brett had taken up residence there. Waiting for her to listen to him. To really see him. So here she was, more than a decade late, but ready to do what he'd been begging her to do since she'd met him—to show him the way to love her back.

They'd arrived. She pulled into the nondescript parking lot and stopped the car.

"What is this place?" he asked, looking around at the small space. Over a hedge was a thrift shop. Farther down the block the computer center where Nora was working. And a street sign.

He was going to figure it out. He knew what businesses the Stand owned and operated. He knew the address.

So she didn't give him time. Getting out, she hurried around to meet him and approached the outer door to the shelter. She'd sent Lila a text before they'd left Brett's house.

Someone should be waiting for them inside.

He stopped just short of the door. "Wait. What is this place?" A look of horror crossed his face. "What are we doing here?"

He was too quick for her.

"Brett?" Her voice was calm. "You promised."

He looked at her. At the door. He knew.

"Please? Just come inside with me."

He stopped cold. But didn't run away. "No one knows who you are." She was giving him that. Taking his hand, she opened the door and pulled him in behind her.

The group that waited for them took even Ella's breath away. Everyone she'd ever met at the Stand was there. All crammed into the public vestibule. They wore welcoming smiles.

Not one of them, not even Lila, who she didn't immediately see in the crowd, knew what she and Brett knew.

They were there to give support to a victim. None of them knew they were meeting their founder.

SEARCHING FOR LILA, needing the other woman to smooth her way, Ella led Brett to the group of people. The managing director always hung back; she knew that.

"Hi. I'm Maddie Bishop." The slim, young blonde stepped forward, her speech slurred but still discernible. "I live here, and I'm married and have a baby, who I take very good care of."

"Good, Maddie." Lynn Bishop, still in her scrubs, stepped forward. "Welcome," she said. "Lila was unfortunately just called to an emergency, so I'm in charge. This is highly unusual, actually a first, but Ella asked to have some support out here for you, so here we are. I'm Lynn Bishop, and you just met Maddie, whose biggest challenge is to talk to men without fear."

Others followed suit. Introducing themselves. Telling Brett and Ella just a little bit about their reasons for being at the Stand. Lila had come through in a huge way. She'd understood what Ella had needed—for Brett to see that there was a world where victims lived and thrived and learned to do much more than merely survive.

Not just to know it, but to experience it. To feel it.

As Chloe had done. And Nora and so many women and children before them.

Nora introduced herself. She looked better, less vacant, but still far too thin. Ella told her so, asking about Henry as Nora gave her a hug. The baby was in the nursery being watched over by a grandmotherly resident who hadn't wanted to come out front.

One by one, people came up to them. Brett greeted each one of them with detached politeness. He was friendly. Charming. But gave no indication that he recognized any of the names he was hearing.

She knew he had to recognize them. Additionally, he knew far more about these people than they were telling him.

It was also clear that none of them had a clue as to who he was. There was no reason why they should. Ella had kept his secret. But he'd had to trust her on that one.

Her heart was in her throat, but Brett didn't appear to be feeling anything at all as he took in the scene around him as though from a distance.

Scared all over again, Ella wondered if she'd done too much too soon. Exposing him to an overload of emotion when he'd allowed none for so long. He was locking himself away again. She could feel him drifting...

But an overload of emotion was what it was going to take to show him he wasn't going to suddenly sprout horns because he allowed himself to feel.

And what better place than The Lemonade Stand to take his chance? She felt sick. Her knees were shaking, and she looked for a place to sit down.

And then Sara Havens was there. "This is Sara, Brett," Ella said, ready to split apart at the seams. "I've spent the past couple months getting to know her. Sara, this is my…ex-husband."

She'd brought him there to out him. To force him to face himself, for his sake, and hers, too, and for the sake of the child she carried.

But mostly because her heart wouldn't let her leave Brett—even during all of the years they'd spent apart.

"Welcome," Sara said. "I've enjoyed my time with Ella. And I'd like a chance to speak with you, as well. So—" she glanced at Ella "—does your ex-husband have a name?"

Brett looked at Ella. She held his gaze. She was in control—this was her show and the hour wasn't up—but she was going to leave it up to him how he played it from there.

His gaze bored into hers and she watched as the light dimmed, as moisture started to appear, and then something changed. Something entered Brett's gaze that she didn't recognize.

"He does," Brett said. His chin tightened. His jaw got stiff. "I'm Brett Ackerman."

Not one person reacted, other than out of the same polite interest he'd given them. They were strangers, there if he cared to join them. If not, they'd move on.

Ella held her breath. He could leave it at that. No one would ever know who'd visited them.

He could continue to hide away in the safe home he'd created for himself someplace deep inside. But it was a home he'd have to live in alone for the rest of his life.

If he turned away now, he was committing himself to a lifetime of solitary confinement.

And leaving her and their child out in the cold... Her panicked thoughts were interrupted when Brett spoke again.

"I'm pleased to meet you, Sara, Lynn, Maddie... everyone. What Ella needs...the reason she's called us all here together today, is because she needs me to tell you...that... I am the founder of The Lemonade Stand."

THE ENTIRE ROOM went silent. Brett could hear every breath he took. Could feel the beating of his heart in his chest.

Sara Havens, for all of the glowing reports he'd read about her ability to handle any situation with grace and calm, gaped at him. Lynn Bishop, a woman he'd pictured as much larger and sterner than the slender, graceful, strawberry blonde she was, was the first to speak.

"You're our mysterious founder?" She was

one of the Stand's senior employees. Next to Lila McDaniels and Sara.

"I am."

He could feel the stares all around him. The residents. He'd recognized every single one of them. By name. By story. Not by their faces.

"Ella?" Sara was looking between the two of them, the question tugging at every sinew of her body.

"Yes." Just the one word, but Brett had a feeling she'd told Sara far more than he was comfortable with.

He didn't like how the woman looked at him. As if she knew everything about him. And had expectations. As if she wanted to hug him and punch him all at once.

But perhaps that was just his take on the situation.

A low buzz started in the room full of people. His instinct was to leave. As quickly as possible.

For a moment he thought he might need a seat. Or an ambulance. He couldn't breathe all that well.

Fresh air was all he needed. Space.

To be left alone.

"You are *him*." Maddie stepped forward, sounding as though she had a couple tongues in her mouth.

She'd been deprived of oxygen at birth, was neurologically challenged, Brett knew. He also knew that the young woman had been married right out of high school to a man who'd kept her locked in a room and beaten her on and off over the next decade.

"I want to thank you for paying for The Lemonade Stand," she said, enunciating with obvious effort. "I am very happy here, and if you did not do this, I would not be happy. Or have a baby."

"I'm happy, too." A tall man, also obviously challenged, stepped forward, putting his arm around Maddie. "I am in love and have a wife and so my brother can be happy, too." Darin Bishop—Brett would have known even if the man hadn't introduced himself.

And so it went. One by one people came forward again, thanking Brett. Telling him how he'd saved their lives.

One by one, he listened. He smiled. He encouraged them.

And one by one, they pierced his heart.

"YOUR EX-HUSBAND, the one you came here to talk about two days ago, is our founder." Sara stood just off to Brett's right side with Ella, watching him.

"Yes."

"You knew he was the founder of this place?"

"I was married to him when he bought the land. So yes, I knew." She'd heard the dreams first. For a couple years. She'd helped with the plans. Had thought The Lemonade Stand was going to be their project. Together.

And then he'd cut her out of his life. And away from everything she'd invested her heart in for so many years.

She'd invested in Brett because she loved him.

And she was never going to be free of him for the same reason. It wasn't about control or manipulation, being a groupie or too dependent, or being a victim. Some of those things played a part, but ultimately, between her and Brett, it was the love that mattered.

That was the bond that was stronger than all the others.

Stronger than fear.

As the room eventually cleared, Sara looked at her. "So what now? Does Lila know?"

Shaking her head, Ella looked at Brett. "No," she said. "But she needs to meet him. Do you know when she'll be free?"

"Not for sure." Sara frowned. "I wasn't there when the call came in, but I know it had to do with the sexual abuse of a female police officer." At that point Sara couldn't say more if she wanted to. "She's probably going to be late. But I'm assuming…" she glanced at Brett as he turned to them, "you'd like a look at the place?" He looked to Ella. "It's her call."

Brett wanted to leave. Would probably sacrifice a limb or two to make it happen. She read that much in his expression. But he'd made it through the hardest part. She couldn't have been prouder of him.

"It's up to you," she said. "I'd like to show you the grounds. It's dark, but they're lovely at night. And we could get a look at the offices and therapy rooms now while they aren't in use. But... it's up to you."

His smile was slow in coming. But when it came, when he said, "Lead the way," Ella allowed hope to reenter her heart.

BRETT WAS GLAD when Sara Havens finally left them to themselves. The woman saw too much.

Ella showed him the hallways, the conversation areas, the cafeteria and state-of-the-art kitchen. She showed him offices, therapy rooms, a library that rivaled the public institution downtown and a multipurpose theater-style auditorium complete with stage and sound system.

He was impressed. Beyond impressed. His money hadn't paid for much of what he was seeing. Donors and volunteers made The Lemonade Stand what it was. But his dream had been realized far beyond his expectations.

Eventually they ended up outside in the Garden of Renewal—a natural masterpiece designed by Grant Bishop, Darin's brother and Lynn's husband. Ella sat down on a bench by a fountain, and he joined her. Happy to give his knees a rest.

"I know my hour's up, so you're no longer under obligation to do what I say, but I want you to marry me, Brett."

All of the breath that had just started flowing through his lungs again disappeared in a whoosh.

"I know you're worried about the possibility of a latent rage lurking within you. I know there's no guarantee that it isn't. There are no guarantees in life. There are only chances. I know the risks in loving you, Brett. It's a chance I choose to take."

Brett wanted to shoot a basket. In a really high hoop. To take a scalding hot shower and sit out by his pool. Instead, he had to sit on a bench and respond.

But before he got around to it, Ella started in again.

"The best we can do in life is face our challenges head-on. To look them in the eye and decide how best to deal with them. One by one. You taught me that."

It was his way. To not put off the unpleasant, but rather, deal with it as the quickest way of getting rid of it.

"Well, the challenge we have here is your fear of someday becoming abusive. You thought you were doing the right thing by distancing yourself, but all it did was make us both miserable. I think you had the answer all along, you just weren't seeing your own work. Look around you, Brett. You have provided any protection, any cure, any safety net we could ever need right here. When you offered to give me your house, when I saw myself willing to settle for what you said was the best you could give me, I knew that I was in over my head. I came here, Brett. To talk to Lila and Sara. And now I'm bringing you here.

"This is your shelter from the storms that might rage someday, Brett. This is your place where all of your secrets will always be safe."

Something rumbled inside him. Something huge. Uncontrollable. And before he could stop himself, Brett started to tremble. His chest hiccupped. And his eyes flooded.

He hadn't shed a tear since his first year of college. Had sworn he never would again. And as the aching pain of so many years alone, of regrets he could never appease, of lost loves he'd never recover, ripped out of him, she sat there with him. Holding him. Kissing his face. His neck. Saying words he'd never remember in a voice he'd never forget.

And when the pain was spent, at least for the moment, she told him how much she loved him.

He wanted to tell her he loved her, too. She kissed him fully on the mouth. Drawing out of him the things he didn't yet know how to put into words.

"Will you marry me, El?"

He'd asked once before and gotten it wrong. That had to be a mistake he could fix.

"Yes, Brett. As many times as it takes." He thought she might be smiling. He almost did, too. And then she said, "And if I ever feel you slipping back into your cave, I'm coming straight to Sara. I won't suffer quietly and alone again." And he understood.

She didn't completely trust him yet. He'd hurt her. Badly.

Issues didn't disappear overnight.

But she loved him. As he loved her.

"Give me time, love. I'll show you that I can do this."

"I know you can."

"I know it now, too."

"So this is your choice? To marry me?" In spite of her big words, he saw the doubt in her eyes as she asked the question.

"It is." His words came right on out. No hold up at all.

"Okay, then."

"Okay."

He sat there, arms itching to take what was his and get on with it. Take her home with him. To his bed. Their bed.

And spend the rest of his life showing her just how open his heart could be.

Except that he wasn't sure he knew how.

"I've got a lot to learn."

"Yeah, me, too."

And that's when he truly got it. He wasn't all

that different from everyone else. He had his challenges, but so did she. So did everyone.

The trick was to face them.

And to share them when you were lucky enough to have someone who was willing to sit in the fire with you.

Ella guided his palm to her stomach. And he knew what she was asking.

"I'm not panicked, El," he said. "I've been waiting for it to happen, but it hasn't."

"No nightmares?"

"No dreams, either." He had to be honest. "But no, no nightmares."

"You had a dream, Brett. A big one. And it came true. You're sitting in the midst of it. The Lemonade Stand."

She had no idea how true those words were. His dream, his biggest one, was to have a loving family of his own. And right there, that night, she'd made it come true.

He rubbed the mound of her belly, wondering if fate had created their child that night on the boat. Knowing that with a child ending their marriage, it would take a child to bring them together again.

"We really should find out if we're having a boy or a girl," he told her. "It's time she had a name."

"I did find out," she told him. "On my last visit."

And she hadn't told him. Most likely because she'd thought he didn't care. "So?" he asked.

"You're right," Ella said. "It was time she had a name. So I gave her one. It's Livia."

He choked up again. But didn't lose it a second time. He was too busy kissing the mother of his child. And drowning in the love gushing from a heart that had burst free.

THERE WAS A text waiting for Brett the next morning.

I'm proud of you, was all it said.

And, for now, it was enough.

* * * * *

Look for the next
WHERE SECRETS ARE SAFE *book*
by Tara Taylor Quinn!
Coming from Harlequin Superromance
later in 2015.

LARGER-PRINT BOOKS!
GET 2 FREE LARGER-PRINT NOVELS PLUS
2 FREE GIFTS!

❖ HARLEQUIN®

Romance

From the Heart, For the Heart

YES! Please send me 2 FREE LARGER-PRINT Harlequin® Romance novels and my 2 FREE gifts (gifts are worth about $10). After receiving them, if I don't wish to receive any more books, I can return the shipping statement marked "cancel." If I don't cancel, I will receive 4 brand-new novels every month and be billed just $5.09 per book in the U.S. or $5.49 per book in Canada. That's a savings of at least 15% off the cover price! It's quite a bargain! Shipping and handling is just 50¢ per book in the U.S. and 75¢ per book in Canada.* I understand that accepting the 2 free books and gifts places me under no obligation to buy anything. I can always return a shipment and cancel at any time. Even if I never buy another book, the two free books and gifts are mine to keep forever.

119/319 HDN GHWC

Name   (PLEASE PRINT)

Address   Apt. #

City   State/Prov.   Zip/Postal Code

Signature (if under 18, a parent or guardian must sign)

Mail to the **Reader Service:**
IN U.S.A.: P.O. Box 1867, Buffalo, NY 14240-1867
IN CANADA: P.O. Box 609, Fort Erie, Ontario L2A 5X3

Want to try two free books from another line?
Call 1-800-873-8635 or visit www.ReaderService.com.

* Terms and prices subject to change without notice. Prices do not include applicable taxes. Sales tax applicable in N.Y. Canadian residents will be charged applicable taxes. Offer not valid in Quebec. This offer is limited to one order per household. Not valid for current subscribers to Harlequin Romance Larger-Print books. All orders subject to credit approval. Credit or debit balances in a customer's account(s) may be offset by any other outstanding balance owed by or to the customer. Please allow 4 to 6 weeks for delivery. Offer available while quantities last.

HRLP15

LARGER-PRINT
BOOKS!

HARLEQUIN *Presents*®

GET 2 FREE LARGER-PRINT NOVELS PLUS 2 FREE GIFTS!

PASSION GUARANTEED SEDUCTION

YES! Please send me 2 FREE LARGER-PRINT Harlequin Presents® novels and my 2 FREE gifts (gifts are worth about $10). After receiving them, if I don't wish to receive any more books, I can return the shipping statement marked "cancel." If I don't cancel, I will receive 6 brand-new novels every month and be billed just $5.30 per book in the U.S. or $5.74 per book in Canada. That's a saving of at least 12% off the cover price! It's quite a bargain! Shipping and handling is just 50¢ per book in the U.S. and 75¢ per book in Canada.* I understand that accepting the 2 free books and gifts places me under no obligation to buy anything. I can always return a shipment and cancel at any time. Even if I never buy another book, the two free books and gifts are mine to keep forever.

176/376 HDN GHVY

Name	(PLEASE PRINT)	

Address		Apt. #

City	State/Prov.	Zip/Postal Code

Signature (if under 18, a parent or guardian must sign)

Mail to the **Reader Service:**
IN U.S.A.: P.O. Box 1867, Buffalo, NY 14240-1867
IN CANADA: P.O. Box 609, Fort Erie, Ontario L2A 5X3

**Are you a subscriber to Harlequin Presents® books
and want to receive the larger-print edition?
Call 1-800-873-8635 today or visit us at www.ReaderService.com.**

* Terms and prices subject to change without notice. Prices do not include applicable taxes. Sales tax applicable in N.Y. Canadian residents will be charged applicable taxes. Offer not valid in Quebec. This offer is limited to one order per household. Not valid for current subscribers to Harlequin Presents Larger-Print books. All orders subject to credit approval. Credit or debit balances in a customer's account(s) may be offset by any other outstanding balance owed by or to the customer. Please allow 4 to 6 weeks for delivery. Offer available while quantities last.

Your Privacy—The Reader Service is committed to protecting your privacy. Our Privacy Policy is available online at www.ReaderService.com or upon request from the Reader Service.

We make a portion of our mailing list available to reputable third parties that offer products we believe may interest you. If you prefer that we not exchange your name with third parties, or if you wish to clarify or modify your communication preferences, please visit us at www.ReaderService.com/consumerchoice or write to us at Reader Service Preference Service, P.O. Box 9062, Buffalo, NY 14240-9062. Include your complete name and address.

HPLP15